Creature of Air
and Still Water

CREATURE OF AIR AND STILL WATER

By Malaika Cheney-Coker

Flexible Press

Minneapolis, Minnesota, 2025

Print ISBN: 979-8-9914928-2-9
eBook ISBN: 979-8-9914928-3-6

Flexible Press LLC
Minneapolis, Minnesota
www.flexiblepub.com
Editors William E Burleson
Vicki Adang, Mark My Words Editorial Services, LLC
Original cover art by Anna Wardega-Czaja

To Mama, always

~ONE ~

AT THE METAL gate, he willed stillness into his body, wishing he were tired. Nearly thirty hours of travel and still his limbs trembled with energy. One heated breath gusted through him. Another. Then he picked up the metal knocker and struck the gate.

It answered back in tones of angered hornets and gongs. Intimacy could be forgotten. In another life, he had passed through this gate daily, his hands deft and sure upon the bolt and panel that swung back to let him in. But now the keen metal that once remembered his fingerprints was drowsing under three coats of paints.

The reverberation of metal on metal shattered the morning's peace and brought a battery of dogs charging toward the gate, where they began to bark lustily at the stranger.

He took a step back. No human emerged. He pulled his collar tighter around his neck to hide the upper reaches of the crusted scratches, rough as twine. The collar was already soaked with sweat and wilting in the morning's humidity. He slid his hand down to where he had ripped a scab while on the plane, the virulence of the bleeding shocking him.

With the barking of the dogs still at a high pitch, an old man staggered into view and peered at Seth through the grille in the gate with eyes blighted with sleep. His expression made it clear that it was a time of day troubled only by vendors and Jehovah's Witnesses and distant relatives claiming calamity. Clearly, Seth did not look like any of these.

The old man glanced at the suitcase beside Seth, then up at the straps of his backpack through which the young man had hooked his thumbs. He didn't notice his neck. With the dogs barking so loud, Seth could barely make out the old man's words. *Who are you?* he must have been asking.

"I am the Walkers' son," he shouted above the barking. "Can I come in?" The old man was clearly another in a succession of guards his parents must have had since he'd left Sierra Leone.

The man's face rippled with the liquid transparency of the old and contented. One eye continued staring at Seth with a cross look; the other, a rebellious eye with a milky cast, looked to a point just left of Seth. He took in this information, and the digestion of it undulated across his face. He blinked, slow as a gecko, and his brows rose with concentration.

"Their son? The one who lives in America?"

"Yes."

The old man pondered this, each eye staring off to a separate horizon of disbelief.

"Do they know you are coming?"

Seth pulled at his collar. During the first flight from Atlanta, en route to Freetown, when the tufts of cloud rolled away, he had gotten his first glimpses of the ocean and the way it heaved against its vast membrane. There had been many acceptable lies to offer them for his coming, some plausible enough to be dignified with the name reasons. Some had gotten so far as to have been made into drafts of emails: . . . *checking in on you, seeing how you are managing;* . . . *time for me to think about the future and maybe buying a plot of land in Freetown.* But he'd never pressed Send.

"Well, they . . ." He gulped. "Will you let me in, please?"

After staring at him for a few more seconds, the old man drew back the onerous bolt and opened the gate. Seth lifted his suitcase and crossed the threshold.

On the second flight from Brussels, his layover, he'd thought of those unsent emails again, languishing in his Drafts folder. Dutiful, his fingers had struck them onto the screen, knowing he must inform them he was coming. And yet those same fingers had refused to press Send.

There was a period after Sam's death when he had written them all the time. Vigorous emails, detailed letters, thrust like arrows over the ocean. Like a magician pulling out a never-ending handkerchief, he had drawn out great lengths of text from himself, descriptions of projects he was working on and places he had visited with his ex-girlfriend, Gaia, and where in the city he hoped to buy a home. Each time he sent one, he burned with embarrassment. Yet he kept writing, even though it was rare that they answered his missives and any responses were terse. He had remembered this period of frenetic writing and felt how he would be the last letter personified. A missive in flesh. But for *The Thing*.

The same stubborn image kept recurring in his mind, the very inverse of something forgotten, like an obnoxious guest laughing too loud, trying too hard to be the life of the party: Without warning, he would stand in the doorway, and the fierceness of day would dart about him like sparks from a crackling fire. They would see his face, behold in it not beauty, nor cleverness, but completeness perhaps, in a way they had never noticed—like a jigsaw puzzle, the final piece locked into place to reveal something not breathtaking, but rather whole and purposefully rendered. They would turn to him in surprise and motion for him to come in. Nothing more would need to be said.

But as he crossed the threshold, that shadow would enter behind him. They would feel it, like rot swarming under a log lying in the forest—and nothing would really be different.

His parents' compound did not look too different, but Seth only had eyes for the ring of coconut trees at its far reaches. New construction had blocked his view of the river as he walked toward the house. But now he was no more than a thousand meters away from the river, yet still unable to see it—or at least, not for the moment. And now a new fear—what if, after coming so far, it turned out that Gaia and Dr. Holland had been right and the signs treacherous?

The old man, who'd introduced himself as Pa Kamara, ushered Seth toward his tiny guard post and proffered a low stool.

Seth forced himself to sit, his knees resisting like bent springs.

"You must be tired, my boy. Such a long journey."

"I am," he lied, sagging his shoulders.

From his stool, Seth looked up at the old man now looming over him, illuminated from behind by the late-morning sun. He was not anybody he could remember his parents mentioning.

The dogs had gradually settled around Seth once they ascertained that he was there to stay. One of them rested its long snout on its front legs and opened a suspicious eye every now and then, seemingly to remind Seth that they continued to surveil him.

"Did you say they don't know you're coming?"

"No," replied Seth, forcing a bland tone.

The old man went back into his quarters and returned with a wooden chair that he sat at a diagonal from Seth. Seemingly from nowhere, he procured a chewing stick and worked it slowly between sparse yellowing teeth as he looked into the distance, his gaze absent.

Seth looked to his left at the makeshift side gate put together from corrugated sheets that led to the brush and ravined terrain winding toward the river. All he would have to do would be to let himself through that gate and fend off the brush, and there it would be, lying at his feet.

"Can I go through that gate?" he asked the old man.

The old man swept a palm over his chin dotted with white stubble.

"Ah, my boy, why? Must you not rest after such a long trip?" Seth noticed a wariness in the old man he hadn't detected before, a stiffening of the spine and a focusing of the eyes.

Unable to stay seated any longer, Seth got up, desperate to pace, run, climb a tree even, but not wanting to unsettle the old man. He decided to walk a lap around the yard on what he hoped would appear to be a sightseeing mission. When he returned to his previous spot, he found the old man engaged in a new activity. He was sweeping the concrete around his quarters with a broom made from the spines of palm fronds, though his mind seemed otherwise engaged.

"It's been a long time since I've seen the river," Seth said. "Let me go have a quick look." If nothing happened when he got to its banks, would he have to provoke something? If he submerged himself just enough to get the taste of drowning, would it reawaken the fullness of knowing he had once entered, when the confines of his mind flattened like cardboard houses?

When Dr. Holland had first given his diagnosis back in Atlanta, the words rasped around Seth like skeins of steel. How many times, he thought, had the man rattled off the same words, as if affixing labels to cans coming down a conveyor belt? What did he really know of Seth? But even if he had cared to know, if he had asked and Seth had mentioned his first experience at the river to the man, it would only have further confirmed the diagnosis.

Seth had sat back in his chair and felt his back harden against it. Dr. Holland looked at his nails. He must have been accustomed to resistance.

"Denial is common, Seth. But don't stay there too long, or it will only get worse. Much worse."

Now the old man was directing a brazen stare at Seth.

"What are those marks upon your neck?"

Seth's hand flew up to his collar.

"Heh . . . emm . . . a fight with my woman."

The old man appeared to start choking, and Seth leaned toward him before he realized it was laughter.

"Eh, that is some woman, my boy. No wonder you ran all the way to your parents' house." But as the old man resumed sweeping, his strokes were slower, and he seemed more pensive.

The first time Seth woke up with blood on his pillow, he knew something had been taken away while he slept. In the bathroom, he examined his neck. Porous welts, all swollen, some showing thin, bloody furrows. Dr. Holland had told him point-blank that he was doing it to himself and he needed to trim his nails down to the quick, told him he might even have to consider sleeping with restraints. It was then that he stopped his visits.

"Eh, my boy," said the old man, putting down the broom as suddenly as he had picked it up. "Let us eat. I will be warming up my food on the coal pot. You must join me."

Though food was not on his mind—in truth, it hadn't been for several weeks—Seth, touched by the old man's graciousness, agreed to join him. When the food was warm, the old man gave Seth a spoon, and they ate from a single plate, local style. Seth, bringing up spoonfuls of potato leaves on rice, forced himself to concentrate on chewing and swallowing.

No sooner had the old man taken the last bite than Seth got up and took their plate to the kitchen.

"I think I will go on now to the river."

"The way has not been brushed recently."

"It's okay. I will be careful."

The old man stared at him blankly. Then he put both hands on his head and began to wail. "Eeeeaa!"

"Pa Kamara—"

"Eeeeaaaa, God Father, my missus, she will sack me today—o!"

"What is wrong, Pa Kamara?"

"You will put me in *wahala*. What if a snake bites you? Who will she blame?"

Then Seth felt it—the first tendril of tiredness. And as much as he welcomed it, he remembered that there would be a bitter underside. He fell with a sudden thud upon his stool. The old man was clearly pretending. Seth certainly didn't want to get the old man in trouble, but he could easily explain to his parents that he had gone against the man's wishes. Another thought raised its head—perhaps the old man had ascertained Seth's mental state and was trying to protect him from himself.

"I will wait, Pa Kamara. No one will sack you today." He sighed.

The old man's face relaxed, and Seth thought he saw a tinge of smugness around his mouth.

"Which one of the brothers are you, the older or the younger?" Pa Kamara said.

"The younger one," Seth said, trying not to look at the old man, for the anger in his eyes would have seared him. "My older brother, Sam, is dead."

"Ah, yes, that's right," muttered the old man, seemingly to himself. "I always thought it was the younger one who had died."

When they were still in school, Seth would dutifully say his name—Seth Emmanuel Walker—when asked, but in his head, he introduced himself as Seth-not-Sam Walker. If Sam's name had been Peter, their parents would have named Seth Paul or Patrick or something of the like that did not disturb the harmony they wished to create, the way one must have matching salt and pepper shakers on one's table. One day he asked his mother who had picked his name, and she looked into the distance before bearing down on him with eyes like blackened coins.

"Why does it matter?" she queried.

They had hoped that Seth, coming four years after Samuel, their firstborn son, would be a girl, but he was not. They had relaxed then, comforted that the lessons learned from parenting a boy could be applied again. But he was nothing like Sam.

He did not think of himself as a Walker either, did not feel like he belonged to them. And he believed they felt that way too. Also, if there was any movement that defined him, it would be running. It wasn't that he ran as a sport, though he had grown tall and strong limbed, his face expressive and broad; rather, it was the only adequate expression he could think of for the molten, simmering discontent that had troubled him even at an early age. Now he knew it was the early symptom of *The Thing*, which, treacherous, had slept in his blood for all those years, like some cunning virus.

Seth moved from the stool and planted himself on the bare concrete, spent. He drew up his knees and rested his head on them. There was no explanation to give his parents. But regardless, tomorrow he would make his way to the river. There, perhaps, a deeper knowing would roll up its banks.

"You must be the son your mother talks about with the big job and the nice house."

"I don't have those things anymore."

"Does she know?"

"No."

The old man's eyes went off again on their divergent odysseys. "Ah well," he mumbled to himself, "with their own children, people can be softer."

The tiredness grew like a storm claiming the kingdom of air. Unable to keep his eyes open any longer, Seth asked Pa Kamara if he could sleep in his quarters; he fell like a brick onto the musty blanket covering the old man's bed. When his eyes jerked open again, the sky had darkened, and he could hear the beep-like squeaks of the bats coming to life in their roosts high in the coconut trees.

He heard the heavy drone of the diesel engine long before the old man did, which further confirmed his suspicion that his parents employed Pa Kamara purely as an act of charity and were under no illusion that he was of the slightest use in guarding their house. After the dogs had been barking for a while, the old man lumbered to his feet, ambled over to the metal gate, drew back the bolt, and let the panels swing back on their hinges. The car rolled into the driveway with Alfred and Evelyn, who nodded briefly to Pa Kamara. Seth stayed on the other side of the gate, almost close enough to touch the car, yet obscured by shadows. They looked straight ahead and did not see him.

~ TWO ~

"COME WITH ME," he said, and Evelyn stood, her heart quivering. She shook the crumbs from her skirt and quickly put down the piece of bread with its half-moon bite. It was only when they were out the door and well down the street that she realized she hadn't asked where they were going. But it didn't matter, really; she was alone with her father.

He seemed to have read her thoughts.

"We are going to the cobbler's to pick up my shoes."

"Why aren't you going with James or Yvette?"

"Because I need a bodyguard, and you are my best one." He shot her a sly grin as mischief darted about his wide lips, his handsome face

It was a typical lazy Sunday afternoon with cyclists threading through the people walking leisurely on the street. The neighbors congregated on their front verandahs curiously watching passersby while sipping English teas, nibbling on gossip, and fanning themselves with folded newspapers and Japanese fans that opened like peacock tails.

"Stay away from the gutter, Evelyn." He placed a hand on her shoulder, the fingers clamping and guiding with strength she didn't know fingers could possess. "And pick up your feet when you walk. No need to act like you're from Kroo Bay, or I'm going to have to pull you out of school and put you to work selling groundnuts like those other little girls you see passing by with the basins on their heads that weigh more than they do. Would you like that?"

"No, Papa."

They came to an intersection. Evelyn started to turn right toward where she thought the cobbler to be.

"No, the other way, Evelyn. We are going to another cobbler down this way."

And yet it seemed the moment gave him pause, for he stood there at the intersection looking down the street as people passed them.

"If you follow this road all the way down, you'll get to where the Temne live, the people who sold this land to the British so our ancestors would have a place to live."

"Where did they live before that?"

"They were slaves in America and in Jamaica, using their strength to dig the earth and plant and pick what grew out of it. Some of them were poor working people in England, and some of them were free black people tied up like chickens in ships that were on their way to places where they would be sold as slaves. Then the British caught the ships and brought the slaves to Freetown. And that is why we *Krios* are so different from everyone else in this country."

She realized that she should ask an intelligent question, something to impress him. But he spoke again, before she could think of one.

"Remember this always, *mi pikin*, forgetting is like lying. Forgetting is like turning your back on the truth without even knowing it, because when something is gone from the mind, it's as if it never happened, and any lie can take its place. Do you understand that? This is what makes civilized nations: people with a sense of history."

She pondered this. Several people passed them as they stood at the intersection, unconcerned with the man and the girl, thinking only of their own want and joy. A white cat with a spectacular black patch on one eye gave them a brief, piercing look before sliding past them on soundless feet.

"Do you see this road we are looking down?" he asked.

"Yes."

"I mean, do you see it?"

She wondered how it was possible for her not to see the road, as they had been standing there staring down it. Perhaps it was a trick question.

"If somebody asked you thirty years from now what you saw when you stood at this junction and looked down Granville Street with your father, what would you say?"

"I see wooden and cement houses and dusty trees and metal gates with curls and bars. I see a man pushing a wheelbarrow down the road and an old lady looking out the window of one of the houses."

"What else?"

"I see a boy and a girl walking down the street. She is wearing a dress the color of rust, and he is holding a gray shopping bag."

"What else?"

People moved along the street like bumblebees in erratic flight, uncooperative with her task. Even on this lazy Sunday afternoon, life proffered a full canvas.

"There is a lot." She looked at him with uncertainty, and then, "It depends on what is most important to remember."

"The smartest of my children," he murmured.

"One day you may be looking down this road, and I will not be standing here with you. I want you to remember the good I've done, no matter how old you are. Your memories will always be your own, and no one can take them from you."

He put a hand on her shoulder, and with those fingers that were at once strong and tender, he steered her in the other direction. At first Evelyn did not want to go; she needed just a little more time to study the street for a test of remembering she must pass in the future.

The old lady opened her wooden shutters all the way and poured a cup of water into her front yard. Evelyn wondered what pattern the water had made when it fell.

Will I remember the old woman one day?

~

THE COBBLER'S WORKSHOP smelled like glue and leather. He gave Evelyn a little stool to sit on.

"Your daughter, sir?"

"Yes, my middle child."

"Well, she looks very much like her father."

Evelyn's father smiled. "You wouldn't know it from her seriousness, but she's also the one most like me of all my children."

"Is that so? Well, many times it's the girls who turn out like their fathers."

"Let's hope she will be a better person than me." He looked at Evelyn and winked. "I like the job you've done with these shoes."

"I'm glad, sir."

He tapped the sole of one shoe with a finger. The motion made a satisfying *thwack*. His nails were the color of cola nuts and almost perfectly oval, just like hers.

"Very good. These shoes will have to last me for a while. How much?"

The cobbler told him.

"What! So much! I'm going to have to leave her behind as an apprentice to pay for these."

~

THE NEXT DAY Evelyn couldn't wait to see her father after school so she could tell him all the things she remembered. Like the good things he'd done (for she guessed that telling him this would make him happy). That she remembered how he had given them all a bigger allowance last year because he had gotten a raise and said so should they. That he had let young, fiery-eyed men come to his house and talk about the governor and the chiefs upcountry and why they couldn't trust the British or the chiefs, and she had heard one say to another of her father, "If only JB would get into politics." They admired him; she could tell.

When she and her younger sister got home from school, they found their mother in the outside kitchen sitting on a stool, vigorously plucking the last feathers off a chicken. She nodded at the girls.

"How was school?"

"Fine." Evelyn had little to say to her mother. Her sister ran off to get out of her uniform.

"Bring me the big enamel bowl from the kitchen."

Evelyn returned, holding it for her mother, who reached for it with water-shriveled hands.

"Your father is gone."

Even though she could feel her mother's tug, Evelyn held on to the bowl, curling her fingers around its thin, flared rim with a tenacious strength.

"Do you hear? Your father is gone. And I don't expect to hear a moment's sniveling about it. There is no time for that."

Her mother relinquished her hold on the bowl and lifted the plucked chicken by its legs. Water and blood streamed down from its pale, pimpled flesh, falling with a musical tinkle into the basin.

"I guess that woman is the only family he needs. Now give me the bowl, child, and stop standing there like a sack of rice. We have to fix dinner."

~

OVER THE YEARS, and as she moved deeper into adulthood, Evelyn learned about remembering. She could still feel in her fingers the exact weight of touch needed to ease the key through its arc in the lock of that rented house they had off Wilkinson Road; the house they'd lived in when Sam was very little and Seth was just a solemn-eyed baby. Even in middle age, she could still see, with startling clarity, the green shutters of the window of her childhood bedroom with its paint peeling like dried fish scales and how her sister's voice rose up from the verandah like a spire of smoke and entered through that same window as Evelyn lay in bed, the words clear as crystal shards even now: "I would say my sister is different when you get to know her, but no one ever gets to know her."

It didn't matter, she told herself; one day she would be known for remembering. She could now so easily be forgotten—her face broad and undecorated, her voice flat, her fingers thick and slow. One day she would be remarked upon for her ability to conjure up the past until it hovered like a genie, radiating power over the present.

Sometimes, if she lingered long enough on the memory of her sister's words rising up, she would remember too that she had been wearing a brown dress strewn with little white flowers so perfect she wished she could have shown it to her father.

Once, before they were married, she had told Alfred about the first time he came to her mother's store. He was a man of medium height with a slight stoop, skin the color of wet dust, which made it some shades lighter than hers, and a scraggly beard. Even so, what parts of his face were hairless were smooth as a mango; so dry too, despite the crush of humidity that day. And even while he was in the store, he took out his handkerchief, folded into exacting squares, to wipe it yet again. She remembered that he held a book, *The Emerging Economies of Post-Colonial East Africa*, and while waiting for her to measure out his cups of *gari*, he opened it to a marked page, the bookmark being a newspaper article that he had folded into a slender rectangle, some words underlined.

He looked at her in amazement when she told him this. A year later, when he asked her to marry him, she looked at him with sharp intent, unsurprised, memorizing his face in that moment for the rest of their lives.

When Sam was born, luminous and loud, she was overcome with fear that she would lose him, for surely he was too good to be hers. He was a happy, glistening creature, flawlessly cherubic and fine-featured. Every face in front of his made him smile. He laughed at the most mundane things: his reflection in the doorknob, the thump of the dog's tail on the floor. He reached up to people to have his round limbs encircled in their eager grasp, to grab their cheeks, their hair, in his pudgy fingers. He reached toward her year after year, even when she turned away, when she spanked him, when her eyes smoldered with an anger that took hold of her at its whim.

When he did wrong, which was often, she would scold him, her voice a stinging smoke, her eyes alive with a quest, for change him she must, though she could not explain why. It did not seem to matter because Sam remained unchanged. As a boy, and then a young man, he would come up behind her and hug her. She would break free or chide his foolishness, and hurt would briefly gather in his face until his inner sun dispelled it.

He grew up to be popular with all, heavy-handed and hearty with slaps on the backs among the boys, charming and gentle with the ladies, even the older, thick-waisted ones like his mother. To her he returned again and again to show his boundless affection. She marveled that love had found her.

She stored memories of him with great diligence, as though placing pictures in an album she expected to be shut too soon, so when he left her (for at the very least he would marry and lavish his love on another), the memories would bring her comfort.

As for Seth, it was as if from birth he already had things on his mind. He was moody, vaguely familiar in his mannerisms and behavior, yet utterly mysterious. She could not fathom the source of his emotions or see a coherent image in the weave of them. Because of Seth, she came to believe that things are never truly forgotten. A tree, though dying, carries in it the memory of the rain that fed it and the lightning that struck it. Eventually it will fall, not because of the lightning but because the memories of fire and water will war within it to be remembered. The tree will pass on the memory of both to the seed, or to the very air if there is none else to receive it.

She guessed that Seth carried memories from a time before him and could feel them without knowing what they were. But memories would be remembered, no matter what must be destroyed in the process. One day she watched him standing on the verandah, his hands straight and still by his sides, looking, with sorrow enough for three worlds, at the rain falling. He was barely old enough to use a fork and knife. She thought for a moment whether to bring him in or to join him, but then she thought of the wilderness she would see in his eyes and wanted no part of it.

"Why are you so tough with the boys, Evelyn?" Alfred would ask her. She would reply, "Because they are boys. If we are not tough now, they will grow up to be unruly men."

Actually, it was because she could not be other than she was or had become. So to compensate, she stored memories for all of them, becoming the scribe of their days, dispatching images of their elaborate games, their round-faced friends, their garlanded birthdays into her vast mental warehouse. She would remember for them one day (for men could not be trusted to remember what they had for dinner the night before, even if it had walked onto the table and served itself to them).

One day there would be a time for softening and remembering. The memories would come forth from the vault, and she would remind the boys, then grown, of the games they played as children, stun them with her precise recollection of the toys their little hands had clutched at, the birthday parties they had come back crying from, the friends they had made for only a season and then forgotten about. For each of the rare times Alfred recounted an event and laughed in the telling, she stored it away in the hopes that one day, when he was old, she would retell it and make him smile. Then they would understand that to remember was to love, to care enough to fold the touch and word of a person into the mind's bosom. They were bound, just as the love and remembrance of her father had grown and intertwined like some vine twirling around a stake.

When Sam died, she felt something that had bound her ribs begin to come undone. The fear of losing him departed, and she could not quite define what took its place, only that it felt like an acidic sludge that slopped back and forth in her chest.

Alfred's brother, Ade, had paid a rare visit to deliver the news. Seth had not wanted to deliver it over the phone and had told his uncle instead. From the verandah, she had watched his orange station wagon crawl through the gate. A mixture of curiosity and dread rose up and left her transfixed. He was not known for social calls, so why would he turn up unannounced if not to deliver bad news? Ade's car door opened, a tentative foot came out, and still she stood like a pillar, until she heard Alfred making his way to the front door.

"Who is it, Ade?" she said when he entered the house, interrupting his feeble pleasantries. "Which one of the boys is it?" But she knew already.

Seeing him off at the door, Alfred clutched his brother's hand, wordless. *Let him go*, Evelyn had wanted to say to him, *for Sam was never meant to be ours*. And she rose to her feet, unsteady, marveling at her foolish thinking that memories could clothe life in the way flesh clothes spirit, wondering whether it would be possible to undo her life's work to learn a new word: forget.

~ THREE ~

IN THE KITCHEN the darkness was whole, unbroken by manmade light, like a fine cloth made from a continuous weave. The night rushed in through the louver windows, its sails billowing not just with darkness but with spells and duplicitous dreams. Evelyn sat motionless at the kitchen table, her form dense and indistinct. As they waited for Alfred to turn on the generator, Seth turned to face her granite silhouette.

Evelyn and Alfred had both frozen upon seeing him and then hugged him without ceremony. She had barely changed since he had last seen her, remaining somewhat rectangular in form, her skin firm and dark; she wore a wig of short, straight hair, much like the ones she had always worn. Alfred, however, seemed slightly more stooped, his hairline receded, and with more gray scattered throughout his hair and beard.

Evelyn's gaze had bounced off Seth to fall on his suitcase, which she looked at pointedly for some moments. Alfred held Seth's arm with a tight grip as they took the three shallow steps up to the verandah, even though his step was strong. Then they settled into their old seating order around the kitchen table, and Alfred dutifully asked Seth how his flight had been.

Seth shrugged noncommittally. "Fine. I slept though most of it," he lied.

"Let me go and start up the generator with Pa Kamara," Alfred said. "Seth, you know you've come back to find us in the Dark Ages still—literally. We're lucky if we get electricity twice a week.

I hope you were not under any illusion that you would come back to find progress in this country."

"I'll go with you."

"No. Stay." Alfred gestured with his chin in Evelyn's direction. "You can continue chatting with your mother."

Evelyn had barely said a word since they came in, so there was no chat to continue, strictly speaking. Seth heard Alfred's footsteps on the tile floor echo and then fall away.

Sometimes in Seth's emails, he had used the red poker of Sam's loss; done the unthinkable in subtly pointing out the dead man's shortcomings—such as the way he had failed to leave his house in order, in the unexpected event of his demise. Seth had had to shoulder much of the load in assisting Sam's widow, Joanna, with sorting out his estate. The administrative burden of it aside, he felt as though he needed to serve as a cultural attaché of sorts to her; that as an American, even a first-generation one, even one who had been married to a Sierra Leonean for several years, she needed his assistance to navigate Sierra Leonean funerary customs and even the expected conduct of the bereaved. Propelled by something unspeakable and voluminous, Seth had pushed such pokers into the flesh of their grief, turning away from part of himself in doing so. But none of those barbs had been acknowledged in the few responses he had received.

Other times, consumed with remorse for this heedlessness and filled with a desire to please, he would send things rather than words, filling drums with household items like placemats and bath towels and several sets of the hair moisturizers and scalp treatments that his mother had once asked him to buy (did she still use them?) and shipping them to Sierra Leone.

"You know, it's not like in the old days when you could barely get matchsticks there," said Gaia. "You can buy most of this there now."

Still, he had to do something.

Now he waited; for what, he was unsure. But it felt like a bulging sack filled with writhing animals that could not be identified but whose willful limbs could be made out. If nature abhorred a vacuum, with Sam gone, how would the rest of them be poured into the space he had left behind?

"Still no light?" Seth ventured, using the term for electricity he had grown up using.

"What?"

"You get light—how many times a week did Daddy say?"

"Not often enough."

Waves of the cursed energy washed over him like a thousand mornings waiting in line to begin. He wanted to climb, to fall down and twist upon the floor like a spinning corkscrew, to throw down a bookshelf and scatter the books. Instead he pressed his hands down on his juddering knees and concentrated on sitting. But his hand crept up to his neck yet again. He felt the dry crustiness of the scabs underneath his fingers. What had he said to Pa Kamara about them? He couldn't remember. When the lights came on, they would see them.

The scratching had continued on and off for a month before he cut his nails as Dr. Holland had advised him to, with irreproachable confidence that this would resolve the problem. He had worn jackets into the pharmacies, even in the warming weather, to buy rolls of bandages, cotton, antibiotic ointment. At the checkout counter, he kept his eyes down, hurried to put forward his card and pay, certain that all eyes were on his swaddled neck. After a month, too desperate to fear the truth much more, he cut his nails down to their very stubs, so low they ached. Two nights later, he woke up, his neck bleeding from new unequivocal scratches.

The following night he refused to sleep. He sat on his deck surrounded by the shrill cries of the cicadas. He tried not to think of Dr. Holland's prophecy, those ill, obscured warnings he'd made as he wrote out Seth's prescription, followed by soothing declarations that all would be well if Seth took his medicine. Over and over, he looked at his blunt fingers. He fingered his ravaged neck. How would Dr. Holland explain the scratches now?

The sounds of the neighbors' generators reverberated in the distance. Seth jerked to his feet and walked to the fridge, opened the freezer. It let out a puff of stale air that was more wet than cold. Reaching his fingers into its shadows, he groped until he felt the wet, slender necks of the bottles.

"Do you want a beer?" he asked Evelyn.

"No."

He hesitated, then pulled one out for himself and groped his way toward the drawer where he hoped there would be an opener. He found one and pried open the cap. He returned to the table. He pulled in his first sip. She continued sitting still as a monk in meditation. It was a ploy. She knew how much her silences worked the rest of them into frenzies. They knew that she knew, and yet they couldn't help themselves.

They had sat in silence that time too, Evelyn drinking beer on the afternoon of the incident with the pineapple. He could see the lopsided label peeling off the sweating beer bottle, the Fanta he'd held, the slices of pineapple between them as they rested in each other's company. They had sat in silence back then too, but it was a kind silence, lathering forgiveness and promise like rose soap. She had taken the pineapple from him gently and peeled and cut it herself, inviting him to sit with her, to bite into its sweetness.

The waves of energy became serrated, grating, like a car without shock absorbers hurtling over a craggy road. His limbs began to jerk slightly, and more sweat gathered from the effort of trying to sit still.

Seth got up. "I'll be back, Mum." He hoisted his backpack and groped his way down the dark hallway toward the bathroom.

There was even less light in it than in the kitchen, given its sole tiny window ensconced high up in the wall. Squatting on the floor, he unzipped the backpack's various outer pockets and felt around for the round cylinder. He found it at last at the very bottom of an inner compartment beneath a tangle of cables. Ah, yes, he had wanted to make it difficult to get to, not wanting to take any, so his mind would be clear when he went to the river.

"These will slow you down, calm you," Dr. Holland had promised, and he had nodded, trying not to betray any indication that he wouldn't take them. But now with his mum . . . he could not be seen for what he was.

He straightened himself up at the sink and turned on the tap, preparing to take a scoop of water in his hands with which to take the medicine. But as the water ran and he put both hands under it, the waves of current ran their serrated edges over and through him, and he twitched and jerked with the sheer pain of it. He put his hands up to his neck and began to rip at the scabs, wanting more than anything to be free.

There was a vile pleasure in ripping the scabs, followed by pain. Wetness upon his neck now, blood. The wounds had not healed yet. Shit. In the dark it would be impossible to see how badly the blood had stained his collar. Reaching into the backpack again, he fished around for something else to wear and pulled out a T-shirt. But if he changed into it, his wounds would be exposed for all to see once the lights came back on.

He grabbed a hand towel from its rail and dabbed his neck feverishly. Then he washed the towel out to the best of his ability and hung it back on the rack. Screw it. There was no way to hide. He changed into the T–shirt, crumpling up the bloodied shirt and stuffing it in his backpack. Then he rolled up some toilet paper and dabbed his neck some more until the paper seemed to come back free of blood. He opened the door.

Back in the kitchen, the mound of Evelyn was exactly as he had left it. The darkness seemed even more complete upon his return. He resumed his place at the table and brought the beer bottle back to his lips to drain the last ounces.

From the depths of the garage, the generator bellowed its thunderous greeting as it was cranked to life, and shortly after, the lights came on. The clarity of everything was startling. Evelyn's face was before him, as crisp in detail as the lines of an open palm. And on it, he saw not the tenderness he hoped beyond prayer for or shock as she looked at his neck, but an expression he had never seen her wear—terror, like that of a feral animal cornered. She barely looked at him; she seemed not to register his neck. Instead, she rose from the table and left the room in haste.

~ FOUR ~

IN THE EARLY days, Evelyn felt the grief flowing out of her fractured heart like magma, searing everything it touched, hardening over her to bury, fossilize her. She could sense its urgent source, the vigor of its unending flow. When she turned to forgetting Sam (not that to forget him meant to lose thoughts of him from her mind; only fools thought that such a thing was possible), she expected it would bring with it release and restitution, like returning carefully hoarded stolen treasure. After all, her years with him had simply been borrowed time, someone else's lot that had fallen to her. He was a stolen angel child.

But a thought was different from a memory. A thought was a pale, uncooked thing, a presence of Sam but with his form cloaked, his face featureless. A memory planted a flag in your heart and unfurled it like the leaves of a tree, each leaf a piercing detail.

So she stopped inventorying the memories, stopped reviewing her mental stores of each month of life, from the orb of his infant head lolling against that purple blanket with sheep her cousin had given her when he was three months, to the month when he was fourteen and had played commando outside for hours, marking up his face every day with mud and charcoal. She released the memories, giving them permission to fall into the abyss of disremembrance.

Yet even without the nap and bristle of memories in her mind, she felt him. In fact, in the first year after Sam's death, Evelyn found him more present in the house he had moved out of years ago than he had ever been. She felt him in unusual places. Sam in the suds of the dishwashing basin in the kitchen. She would put her hands in the water, preparing to wash dishes, and feel that his hands were in there, waiting to touch hers.

She felt him in the rain flies lying dead on the verandah floor at dawn that stirred with the draft of the opening glass door, their wings bearing them where they no longer wished to go. Looking down on them, she felt a loss as great as though they had been bearing news from Sam and had died before they could deliver the message.

She cleared his things from his room and gave them to charity, poured libations to him outside the threshold, that his spirit might be appeased. The night after she gave away his things, she sat still, one leg out of her car, not bothering to swat away the mosquitoes that settled on her arm, listening to the bullfrogs and crickets claim the night.

As her mind clenched in fear, she told the memories they were not only released, they were banished. It took violence to banish them, like the ripping of one's fingernails, like cutting and splicing one's veins until they flowed somewhere else, yet spurted and bled in that time in between. But anger steeled her; perhaps she was destined to leave earth with nothing but the single clean blade of her power—to remember that which others could not, and also to *not* remember, to command her mind to do what her heart could not.

The memories defied her. They darted about in her mind like sprites, crowded around her like beggar children. She rejected them as they arose, saying, "He was a mistake, a miracle, a spirit child that fell into my arms for a spell. He is no longer mine." She forced herself to recall other memories; those of her brothers and sisters, her mother and father, and of the days before her father left when she had been happy. And gradually, the memories subsided, until after a year, there was quiet—a vast horizon of it with room for her to walk.

One day in those peaceful years, she stood at the sink making rice pap. She held the damp rice flour between her fingers and rolled it between her palms to form little pellets. Closing her eyes, she let her fingers do the work, for now in these months, with the memories of Sam finally sleeping, it was safe to let her mind wander.

Outside she heard a familiar refrain coming from the street. "Honey-honeeee, honey-honeeee!" Then the dogs were barking at the gate, and its metal bolt was drawn open with a clang. Voices. Lamin's, the houseboy's and the Honey Man's.

Evelyn was pleased. It had been months since the Honey Man, once a regular vendor, had come by. She and Alfred had missed the pungent wildness of his dark brown honey in their tea, the honeycomb bits suspended like fossils in its amber depths.

She washed the flour off her hands and stepped outside to look for her housemaid. The sun rained light as though trying to expend its storehouses of flame. But it was a fickle day, fickle time of year. It could just as easily shower within the hour. The air was thick as cotton, and clouds clustered in the sky like a herd of listless elephants. Rainy day, sunny day, who could tell which would claim the story by nightfall?

The girl was squinting over the smoking coals upon which they would lay a pan to toast the rice pellets. She looked up.

"Go and call the Honey Man into the kitchen."

"Honey Man, Ma?"

"He's at the gate.

The girl left, a look of confusion on her face.

Back in the kitchen, Evelyn surveyed the pan where she had been placing the finished rice pellets. The perfect size. Now she would add a bit of nutmeg to give the pap the extra edge. She looked up as a shadow appeared at the doorway. The girl's.

"There was no one at the gate, Ma." She looked at Evelyn, her face blank.

Evelyn frowned. How was it that the girl could not manage the most basic tasks? "How can that be? I heard him myself. Did he leave? Did you look down the street to see if he was still there?"

"No, Ma. Lamin said no one had come in the gate."

She thought to ask the girl to look again, but this would be foolish. Could she have been wrong in imagining that she had heard the honey man and the house boy's and Lamin's voices at the gate?

All of a sudden, the kitchen grew darker, and Evelyn and the girl turned to look out the window.

"Get those clothes off the line. It looks like it's going to rain." Sunny day, cloudy day, rainy day, who knew which?

The girl left, dragging her plastic-slippered feet on the floor. Evelyn felt a dull throbbing in her ankles, a reminder that she should sit down and put her feet up, as now in her middle age, they tended to swell. But there was about a cup full of rice flour left in the bowl and just about enough lemon-sugar water left to make the paste with.

Suddenly there was Sam, standing before her, seven or eight, maybe nine years old, holding out a bowl and asking for more rice pap. The pot fell from her hands, dropping to the floor with a shrieking clatter, and she felt the liquid splash cold against her feet and ankles. She blinked and Sam was gone, but her heartbeat remained, frenetic as a bird with a broken wing.

The girl came running into the kitchen. Evelyn turned away quickly so she would not have to look the girl in the eye. In the bathroom, she washed her feet in the tub and then went into the living room to lie down. Her heart was still hammering. On the couch, she pressed a cushion against her stomach and felt the blood pulsing at her temples. It was no ghost she had seen, she was sure. But why had he been there, so real she had believed in that second she could touch him? Sam had been dead three years, and nothing like this had happened before.

That evening Alfred ate the potato leaves stew she and the girl had prepared, and then he went rummaging in the cupboard for tea biscuits. She despised the man for his ignorance, his lack of prescience of how air itself had bent today. Unreasonable though it may have been to have such thoughts, they adhered stubbornly to this man who in all things lacked perception of what was around him. Instead, he clutched his transistor radio, lassoing the history-making of far countries into his mind.

After dinner Alfred turned on that very transistor to listen to the news, and she put on a kettle of water for their tea. She stepped outside while it boiled. The neighborhood was quiet. It was a night like all others. She took in a mighty breath and then let the air leave her lungs to rise into the void.

Rice pap was one of the foods of mourning and of celebration. Of course, they had had it at Sam's funeral, at his forty-day ceremony, and at every funeral she had ever attended. But the spirit world was a kingdom of cunning. How could she have forgotten that these foods in themselves evoked the dead? She felt enormous comfort at this revelation. There would be no more such foods. There would be peace in the house again.

And there had been for another year.

Then Seth came back. After the initial shock of seeing him standing in the yard, the purple evening shrouding his face, she had to fight back the anger so as to at least give him a civil greeting. The boy was contrary in every way, sticking out his stubbornness like a defiant nail from a smooth plank of wood.

Why couldn't he at least have called to announce his arrival? Because he was indifferent to the wishes of others. And because his visit could portend no good. With no small satisfaction, she watched Seth writhe under the mantle of silence between them. His form, as he got up to get a beer from the freezer, was larger than she was used to in their low-ceilinged kitchen. He cleared his throat with a sound like the gears of a car grinding; a sound just like Sam used to make.

Then the generator grumbled to life, and the lights came on. Suddenly she felt like she couldn't breathe, for her breath was taken away by a pain that flowed through her in a quiet stream like the letting of blood from torn flesh. She looked at Seth and saw a shadow of Sam, a silhouette that should have been Sam. She wanted to cry out for surprise at the treachery of the heart, which, without warning, could crack like a wafer.

~ FIVE ~

WHEN SETH VENTURED downstairs the next day, it was mid-morning, and Alfred and Evelyn had long since left for the day. At the kitchen table, he found a loaf of *Fullah* bread, a few scoops of margarine squatting in a small bowl, and two aging bananas.

But he was hollowed out by a hunger from another place. He walked past the table toward the door to the outside. Wrenching the handle, he pushed the door open, leaning into the blinding morning light that greeted him as if into the afterlife.

As a child he had known the words were being said, even if he did not hear them. Why must he rebel? Why must he be so stubborn, resisting what was expected of him for no other apparent reason than to thwart cooperation? Then, somehow, he had found his way into adulthood and respectability, into a world beyond his childhood one where there was room for a spiky differentiation of character. But then that last fight with Gaia and the months of dealing with *The Thing* had brought back the old shadow, the feeling of being banished to a corner.

"Go on to the river!" Gaia had seethed during that last terrible fight after the breakup. The time they had both reached out with a brittle hope that there was still something worth saving.

"Of course I will. I don't need your permission. We broke up, remember?" Seth had countered as he paced the living room, trying with all his might to restrain himself from overturning the coffee table or kicking the rest of the furniture.

"When someone asks, I'll say, 'He saw an ad for some business called Stony River and jumped on a plane.'"

"I told you, it wasn't just the ad. There was the magazine article in Dr. Holland's office about rivers giving livelihoods, and then right after there was my screensaver with the word *river*—"

"That's because it's an extremely common word!"

"Go to hell."

"Go back to Dr. Holland."

He looked at her, panting, his face hardening. He hadn't been able to tell her, had never told anyone about that day at the river when he and Sam struggled against the swollen current. He had felt his life slipping away like watery broth, and along with the terror came tremendous clarity. He saw the glistening white of the egg he'd had that morning. He felt the soft nub of their cat Theo's nose. He felt the sand clinging to his legs that day Alfred took them to the beach. Then he saw his Lego blocks, which he had played with countless times before, but they did something he had never seen. They rose and built themselves into structures—tall buildings and houses and even spires and trees—the outline of a city. And then, as suddenly as they built themselves up, they were shattered. But with a magnetism that seemed pre-ordained, they rose again and cleaved together, forming without effort another cityscape. The process repeated itself over and over during what seemed to be an age but was probably not more than two seconds. And he felt that if he were to die, he had grown old before doing so and filled out his years, stretched out his bones before the current carried it all away.

Sam pulled Seth with strength he was not aware his brother possessed, and by a miracle, they made it to the bank where they collapsed into the bent beams of each other's arms. And Seth shuddered, not only because his brother had nearly taken and yet saved his life in the same moment, but because he had seen something that he understood he would never forget.

The fight with Gaia had ended with him motioning his head in the direction of the front door. And she had looked at him calmly, giving him time to be sure of what he was asking. They both knew that from this point, there would be no return. He was terrified by the depths of his determination, for in that moment, he understood that he would sacrifice his relationship with her for the sake of being right about the river—that he would find an answer to what ailed him on its banks. Maybe it was because he couldn't face the prospect of what being wrong about it meant. Or maybe it was because he had been defective all along, as they had suspected, capable of turning callous and reptilian.

Seth hadn't even mentioned the signs about the river to Dr. Holland because he could just imagine the impassive look on his face, the professional austerity of expression concealing his mental cataloging of this as the greatest proof yet of Seth's psychosis. At the same time, he imagined that he would once have found it farfetched that he would fly home on the suggestion of mere signs.

~

WITH THE HARSH sun a river of light to ford, he walked toward the side gate that the old man had so valiantly kept him from. When he reached it, he marveled at how shoddy it was, really two corrugated steel sheets held together with a thin piece of scrap metal. Its posts leaned at precarious angles.

Then he put his hand on the gate and saw that it was trembling—not with fear, not with anticipation, but with some other accursed feeling. Then the trembling was in his legs and at the base of his spine, and once again, the serrated currents began to ride him. Like at that fateful party those years before, when the energy had shot up his back as though from a fire hose, bringing him to his feet, giving him no other option but to flee.

He cursed it. His heart began to throb, and his chest seemed like it was being squeezed, and he thought to go back into the kitchen for a sip of water, which he knew would do nothing to help. All of a sudden, he was seized by a desire to pace—even better, run—anything to dispel the frightful energy that would overtake and violate him. Wresting himself away from the ramshackle gate, he made his way toward the main gate and let himself out.

It was *The Thing* that caused the wanton energy, the rage that had made him lie to the police, the scratches on his neck, the devastation that was now his life. It lived in his mind, a creature both of air and still water. In the air, it was surrounded by cloud and mist, parted not by *The Thing* itself but by its hot breath—the exhaust of a brooding beast. At night, it was an aquatic being waiting for him in the depths of a swamp, cloaked by sediment and darkness. It possessed him with a raw intimacy, knew his every thought, yet as it stirred, all he could feel of it were its movements, its powerful body stirring the water, causing sinewy currents to pull him toward it.

When its breath filled him, Seth felt as helpless as a balloon expanding in the heat of a despotic noon sun, stretching and stretching until it seemed the only way out was to give in to rage. And even after he gave in to rage, he was still not spared the shattering of self and soul. Afterward, he felt scattered, merely scraps of skin that once held together a being now lying about like old orange peels curling in the sun.

He tried to name it—Torment, Restlessness, Depression, Confusion, Possession, even—thus giving him a way to fight it. But it refused every name. Restlessness would bait him, snapping at his ankles like a rabid dog. No sooner would he turn, summon the courage to fight, than he would find his foe different—a tired sadness hardening as inexorably as cement.

Dr. Holland had given it a different name. "You said you've never had these symptoms before?"

"No."

The man looked at his notes and rubbed his chin. "Curious," he murmured. "Your symptoms seem like a classic case of bipolar II, but the onset is usually before the mid-twenties."

Seth listened to the words, let the sound "bipolar II" roll around his mind, but it gained no purchase.

"What about *The Thing?*"

"*The Thing* is you, Seth. It is a state created by your mind."

Seth smiled politely. He had been raised not to question authority. *It is an invader*, he countered in silence.

Dr. Holland swept his hand down his open ledger as though dusting off any crumbs of doubt. "It is almost certainly a late-onset case of bipolar II."

Seth nodded because there was nothing else to do.

Now on the road, trying to restrain himself from running, he walked with brisk steps and no destination in mind. But in what seemed like no time at all, he found himself turning onto the long beach road, and then, what must have been about twenty minutes later, he was at Langston Beach. Now at last he could run. And so he did, until he saw the black rocks on the other side of the peninsula approaching and knew that he had been running for at least a couple of miles.

To his left and right, those he passed gave him strange looks, dressed as he was in his flip-flops, jeans, and soaked undershirt, his neck carved with welts. At last the force of the puppeteer waned, and his legs began to soften and ache. He collapsed on the sand and faced the glistening sea. It shimmered before him just like that day he had spent with Sam and their father on this same beach.

Alfred had decided to take the boys on an outing to the beach. They played in the water just beyond where the waves broke on the smooth plane of caramel sand. Later, sitting at the beach bar, which was no more than a wide-girthed straw hut higher up on the shore, Alfred struck up a conversation with a man to his left who seemed to be about the same age.

"We danced like fools when the British gave us our independence," said Alfred. "Not just one day but the next and the next."

The man hummed noises of agreement.

"Go take a walk, boys," said Alfred.

Sam was convinced they could walk to the end of the beach where the bay jutted out, studded with black rocks. Seth didn't think they could get there and back without Alfred wondering where they were, but he didn't say so.

When they got back, Alfred and his friend were still at the bar, somewhat slumped on their stools, drunk perhaps. Seth wondered if Alfred would be angry at them for taking so long. But when Alfred turned to Seth and Sam, there was no anger; his eyes were a bit red, as though a sudden tiredness had overtaken him.

He got up and stretched and shook the man's hand and pushed the boys forward to say goodbye to him.

Then he walked them to the water's edge and put his arms around them. Seth leaned into his side.

"You boys may never be able to come back. The country is going down the toilet."

The wind whisked away his words, so it would have been easy to believe they had never been spoken. The setting sun had changed the water to something of shifting color. It rolled and dipped, forever changing as each of its legion parts negotiated their place in time and space. Seth tried to imagine what lay beyond their ocean, their known world.

Seth wouldn't become a lawyer or a doctor, even though they, like all *Krio* parents, had hoped with fervor that their sons would gravitate to those most noble of professions. But he did sail across that ocean with a cargo full of their dreams. Tired of languishing in the corner, he had wanted to please, to be praised, to be seen. He had pursued a profession that he knew they would approve of, giving in to the wisdom of them and everyone else, that this would render him whole. And perhaps it had. He had enjoyed the fruits of that decision. What was a human being if not malleable? The rightness, the certainty of being that had kept him sequestered in shadow as a child, seemed to him in part rebellion against what was, rather than sculpting of what he could instead be.

But in the case of the river, the certitude, hubris—whatever it was—righted itself like a ship besting the storm, impudent, thrusting its bow upright. He keened toward the river as toward a siren song. If he was wrong, then he was damned—there was no other way around it.

If God had meant to speak to him once through the river and vision of the Lego blocks, then the message had not been delivered. Seth had seen but not understood, witnessed but not known whether he was an eavesdropper to mystery or an invited one. But now, perhaps, the river would complete the sentence. Wiping his face on his sleeve, he arose and slowly walked toward the main road to hail a taxi home.

~

AT HOME, HE drank three glasses of water, changed his clothes, then sat quietly at the kitchen table trying to steady himself. After making his way outside again, he undid the wire barely holding together the ramshackle gate and let himself through. There was a path, overhung with elephant grasses but not to the degree Pa Kamara had seemed to indicate. His footsteps quickened.

The path widened, the clayish stones under his feet became larger and lumpier, and the grass and thickets gave way. He came onto the bank, squatted on his haunches, looked at it.

The river lay shriveled within its bed, impotent as a trickle of wastewater, a milky eye in its socket. Perhaps it was the prolonged dry seasons he had heard of, or extraction of the water farther upstream. On that day of the red plastic slippers, it had roared with a reverberation he could hear in his ears still.

He wanted to cry out but couldn't. He had come to seek the river's counsel, but it had none to give, its lucidity dimmed, its strength not merely ebbed but strangled out of it. It had once threatened to take everything from him, but he could no more be angry at it than he could at a senile old man withering on his deathbed.

It is not at all unlikely with this disorder that your mind will play tricks on you, Dr. Holland had said.

He threw a handful of pebbles into the river. A bird cried somewhere in a tree. From the top of the steep bank on the other side, he heard a woman scolding in loud tones. It could not have been a more ordinary afternoon.

When he had stood with his father and Sam at the water's edge that day, looking out over the limitless Atlantic Ocean, he had imagined the world beyond, and it had seemed conceivable that he would sally forth as their prayer and return to them as the fulfillment of the request; that he would be able to fashion him-self in some far land into the thing they desired. Now at this water's edge, just a stone's throw from the bank on the other side, he keenly felt the limits of self, the shame of his return. There was no more pliability, only a flattening against the walls of his shell as *The Thing* expanded and took over more of him.

What happens when bipolar disorder is left untreated? he had typed into Google. The words leered back at him from the page: psychosis: a complete break from reality that may include delusions and auditory or visual hallucinations. There was a warning too that those in a psychotic state should be hospitalized as they were capable of inflicting violence upon themselves or others.

Then there was another word so terrible he had looked away from it and scrolled up the page. He put his fingers up to his neck. The scratches were real; others had seen them. There was no break from reality. He looked down at his blunt nails, nails that could not have caused those scratches.

A guttural sound clambered up his throat, and he strangled it so swiftly within his mouth that he nearly choked. He reached into his back pocket for the orange canister of pills. The first time he had taken them he had promised himself that it was more out of curiosity. And when he did, it was as though the gravity of the earth rose up like a tide, pulling roots of trees even deeper into itself, drawing thoughts toward sleep and the silent rot within the soil. Just last night he had thought about taking them—at least long enough to steady his mind so he could put forward a coherent explanation to Alfred and Evelyn, even if it was a lie.

Delusions. That final word had sneered at him from the screen. Dr. Holland had used the same word. It mocked him, telling him he was not to trust his mind. But neither the words on the page nor Dr. Holland had accounted for something far stronger, more primal than his mind——the desire to fight until life was spent. He shook the container vigorously, listened to the airy clinking of the pink pills. Then he hurled the canister into the river. It barely made a splash as the water received it.

~ SIX ~

THE PAIN DID not recede. During Seth's first night back in the house, Evelyn lay awake until the wee hours, infused with its poison, which grew in potency until it seemed that the croaking frogs sensed it and gradually tapered off into silence.

Seth had ruined it all. She had not known it would happen this way. How could she have anticipated that his voice would carry some of the same underwater tones as Sam's, that while looking at the back of his head, she would be flooded by the sudden memory of the scratchy feel of Sam's hair under her hand? Seth wiped his sweating face with his sleeve, and she saw Sam bending down to carefully brush the scuff marks off the boots that his aunt in America had sent him. Seth picked up the newspaper, and the half-moons in his nails were Sam's, the sight passing through her eyes and searing the back of her head.

She had tried to focus on something else: the just-from-America smell of Seth's clothes. The twitching of his leg beneath the table. But he had pried open some window in her mind. As she lay in bed, the memories assaulted her, rising like angry spirits from a cleft rock.

She had always resented Seth's need for her, and yet it was he who had to be sought. Whereas Sam had always come to her, his love finding her no matter where she might be hidden, with Seth, she knew she would have to go to him, and she did not know how or want to.

She had tried to love him before, but love could not be forced. It slept on tree branches as it pleased or smoldered alone in caves.

It leapt from clotted ash at the mere thought of fire or else interred itself deep in rock. She could not love him, or at least not in the way he wanted. And now, as though he hadn't understood, he was back, wanting, always wanting.

But she had even less to give than before. She could barely breathe or think. She must be rid of the weight of him, his wanting. The right thing to do would be to turn him away in such a way that there could be no doubt; to free him from hope. This she would do for him, even though he might not know it until the end of her life. She would hold his memories, stroke them like fine cloth, never turn them away. In truth, it was Sam who was meant to remind her of Seth—at least that was the way she had planned it. Long ago she had joined the boys together, all because of Seth. He was the first sign of disruption in the order, the first lesson that memories were unruly things and that the brain tends toward forgetting, even for those schooled in remembering.

Memories of Seth's life were shapeless things. As hard as she tried to hold onto them, they resisted and seeped away. It is the second child syndrome, she told herself, when upon testing her memory, she failed to remember his first words, his favorite games.

So she bundled Seth into Sam, the boy so vibrant, so amply dimensioned, that he could anchor all else. She tied their fates, their lives, their stories together so in this way, she would not neglect Seth. When Sam wanted to learn how to play tennis, she made Seth take lessons too, even though he seemed to have no interest in the game, and the instructor complained that he would wander off to tie and retie his shoelaces or chisel the bark of nearby trees.

Even though they were four years apart, they were assigned the same tasks. She bought them the same clothes in different sizes. She even made them account for the same deeds. Alimamy, one of their first servants, loved Sam. But then there were the bitter complaints. Sam would sneak into the devout Muslim's room and get behind him as he bent himself over and over upon his prayer mat, head toward the city of pilgrimage. He would hear Sam's giggle puncturing the sanctum of his prayers and turn to find the boy behind him, grinning like a drunk, imitating his every move.

She called Sam down from his room to give him a tongue-lashing for his irreverence.

"Call your brother down as well," she added.

"But Mummy, *he* did it," Seth protested when he too had been tongue-lashed. It didn't matter; in all things, she tried to join Seth and Sam so it would be easier not to forget Seth. She had been so successful that, in time, it seemed that Seth too could not separate himself from Sam. Like that one time. She had been watering the plants upstairs when she heard Alimamy calling to her from downstairs.

"Missus, Missus, I am leaving!"

She had never heard Alimamy sound so agitated. "What has happened, Alimamy?" she said when she got downstairs. "Why are you shouting loud enough for the neighbors to hear?"

"Your son, that wicked boy."

It suddenly seemed plausible that Alimamy would want to leave.

"Yes? What has he done?"

"I'm finally on to his tricks. All this time I have been chiding myself for being slow when it seems he has been following me, undoing my work. He even made me think I was losing my mind."

The latest misdemeanor, it seemed, was that Sam would spy on Alimamy picking pellets and unhusked grains out of the rice that was to be cooked for the day. Alimamy used a large flat basket for this very purpose so he could spread the rice out. Then he heard a noise of some sort, went to investigate, and when he resumed his task, found that there seemed to be twice as many pellets in the rice as when he left off. No doubt Sam had made Seth, his puppet, complicit in this too. And there had been more. Sam returning damp clothes to the washbasin after Alimamy had hung them.

That Saturday, Sam was sentenced to helping Alimamy with his chores. Alimamy had reluctantly agreed to stay on if due punishment was meted out. Evelyn decided, for once, that it would not be fair for Seth to suffer along with Sam. So she took Seth to the club in the bay area where the boys usually spent their Saturday afternoons splashing in the pool with other noisy privileged children.

When they got back that evening, she went to look for Sam. Alimamy would surely have left for the day by now. But there they both were outside, Sam in the crook of Alimamy's arm, Alimamy under Sam's spell, both leaning against the wall, both chuckling in low voices over something known only to them. Who was he to command her son's affection in this way? She determined to fire Alimamy the next day. Alfred would wonder, but she would give him a good reason.

"Why didn't you let me stay home with Sam and Alimamy, Mummy?"

Seth was behind her. He had crept up like a shadow, the boy without a presence of his own.

"Staying home was meant to be Sam's punishment, not yours."

He looked at her uncomprehending, as though he too had forgotten that he was not a part of Sam.

~

She would continue to chronicle his memories in the way she always had. Unlike the memories of Sam, which she would turn away, scatter into the wind, Seth's would be counted like pieces of silver. One day, perhaps when she was nearing the end of her life, she would make a gift of them to him. In the same way the *griots* of the old empires of West Africa had accompanied the kings and emperors, recounting the oral traditions, he would be chronicled.

~ SEVEN ~

ALFRED RETURNED HOME that evening without Evelyn. He had brought three newspapers and a malt drink for Seth. "They're all equally bad," he said of the newspapers as he sank into his favorite chair on the verandah. "But for however long you're staying, I thought you might want to get a sense of what's going on around here." As for the malt, he endorsed it as one of the few good things that the city still produced.

Seth unscrewed the malt and leaned forward in his chair. "What did you say, Dad?"

In truth, he had heard everything Alfred had said, but the words simply jangled around without meaning as though he were listening to a foreign tongue. It had been that way ever since he came back from the riverbank. Just like that, the fight was gone from him, though he knew it would return. He'd had a sensation of falling, of losing control, of being unable to organize his thoughts or present himself in a clear way. He had at least remembered to wear a dress shirt and button it all the way to the top. The stiff fabric brushed against the welts, but at least Alfred didn't seem to have noticed anything awry.

"How long will you be here?" asked Alfred.

"Eh, a few weeks, perhaps."

"Ah, we'll have time then. Time to go around together so you can see Freetown for what it really is." His shoulders loosened. "The deterioration is horrifying," he said, his pleased look contradicting his words.

Seth was so used to waiting for his father that if you had asked him, he would not have realized he was doing so. Not waiting for him to come home or start the car, but simply waiting in some flaccid way for Alfred to be someone different. Then, more quickly than anyone could have imagined, Sam had left for the States, and a few rainy seasons later, Seth himself left, forgetting that he had been waiting all along.

He took a sip of the malt. The malt was better than he expected, even after Alfred's endorsement. It sent forth bitterness and sweetness and a creamy something else that was perhaps the mood of the grain on the day it was harvested, a brooding fullness.

"What did you think of the city as you came from the airport? It's barely changed in all these years, has it? We are stuck in a rut is the issue, no progress. The only thing that flourishes here is corruption."

Seth looked at him, helpless. A witty retort or chiseled question was needed in response, one worthy of his adult status, his Western education. But he simply could not put the thoughts, less the words, together.

A surge of something viscous and angry began to bubble up within him. Excusing himself, Seth went to his room and took off his shirt, passed his hand over the welts. They felt reassuringly real, new ridges on the landscape that was his body. They were terrible and marked as some artist's relief creation, wretchedness written upon him. He put his shirt back on but left it unbuttoned near his neck.

Walking back to the verandah, he observed that the light was still strong, bright enough that little could be hidden. A flash of shock lit Alfred's face as he laid eyes on Seth, and Seth could almost see the intake of breath. He sat in front of Alfred but looked away, feeling the small sivers of pain under the welts as he turned his head. Alfred made wheezing noises but said nothing.

"How do you like the malt?"

"It's good."

"Your mother drove her own car today. She went to have her dress for some wedding fitted, and now she's probably stuck in traffic. It gets worse the later you leave."

Just then the dogs erupted into a cacophony of barking as the sound of a car laboring over the craggy road intensified.

"Your mother is coming," Alfred exhaled.

Some minutes later, Evelyn joined them on the verandah, sweating despite the relative cool of the evening, her eyes small raisins in her puffy face. After grunting a greeting at them, she gave Alfred a few terse updates of her day. Shortly after, they sat down to eat dinner at the kitchen table where they had always had their family meals—except for holidays or when they had guests over.

Though her mien was calm, displaying none of the inexplicable terror he had seen on her face the other night, he thought he saw her chest heave with the fullness of something to tell, in the same way his strained and creaked.

The sensation of falling sharpened into something like that of not having something firm to grasp, to break the fall. The old certitude that had ruled his life like a metronome was broken. The river had betrayed him, yet to trust his instincts was all he knew how to do. Like a mechanical doll that could only be wound one way, he found himself helpless, against reason, believing in his sense of rightness, grasping at twigs as the waters swept him away.

Evelyn busied herself with pulling bones out of her dried fish. Then she wiped her sweating face with a washcloth that had been lying next to her place setting. She put it down and pushed the remaining fish bones to a pile on the side of her plate. Then she put her fork down and looked at Seth. It was the first time she had looked at him—a look that was direct and pointed—since she came home, indeed, since he had arrived. When she spoke, she dealt out her words like cards, even-paced and measured.

"Seth, how was your trip?"

It was an opening, and he took it, chest heaving with all that must be said, even though Alfred cast his eyes downward and Evelyn stared at him with eyes that seemed to be looking through him.

The beast swiveled and swam deep within, raring for trouble. This too he knew—he would tell the truth, although it would destroy, rather than illuminate.

~ EIGHT ~

IT HAD STARTED the night of the party, in the manner in which a disease "starts" after weeks of silent incubation. The day had rolled along dutifully on its rails; at work, in the financial district of Atlanta to the north of the city, there was the usual tethering to his desk with bouts of wandering here and there. At home, he surrendered himself to the couch as per his routine and halfheartedly watched a cop show while thinking how he'd rather stay home that night than go to the party and feign a gaiety he did not feel. Only Gaia's presence there would help make it more bearable. They had been strangely disconnected of late, and it would be good to put that behind them, starting tonight.

If the party hadn't been for Olayinka, he would have stayed home. But he had known her since childhood. Olayinka with the caterpillar-fuzzy cornrows had sat on the same loose-jointed benches in Anglican confirmation class as Seth and read out of the same dusty prayer books. Her grimaces and droll jokes had raised them to the surface for air time and time again when boredom and the drone of their dour teacher threatened to smother them.

He heaved himself off the couch at last and went upstairs to get dressed. In the car, Seth's sour mood coalesced into a corporeal permanence and settled in next to him like an unwanted passenger. The driver to his left suddenly cut in front of him without signaling. "Idiot," Seth sputtered as he braked and then hit the gas, his foot savage.

He looked at the time and sighed. Only 9:30 p.m. The night was still young. Most Sierra Leonean parties were just nosing awake at this time. He was in a nondescript part of southwest Atlanta, and he passed laundromats, decaying motels, gas stations, and fast-food joints. Finally, just after the Lucky 7 Chinese mart, he found the hall and pulled into its parking lot. He cut the engine and unlatched his seat belt, then sat there, dreading the chitchat that awaited him. Even though he knew Gaia had not called, he picked up his phone yet again to check.

For a moment he considered turning back, but he was sure some of the guys hanging around outside the hall had already spotted him, for they doted over Seth's Infiniti in the way a mother inhales her newborn's face. Sure enough, someone was looking in his direction. It was Jah. Jah was short, with the dimensions of a potato, and was knowledgeable about all things Sierra Leonean in the city. For his extraordinary compendium of knowledge, he had earned the moniker "The Mayor." He was standing at the entrance like a night watchdog, fully inhabiting his body's obsidian density. Three other men were hanging out by the entrance, deep in animated conversation.

With a sense of doom, Seth closed the car door behind him and approached the men.

Jah held out his hand, and Seth grasped it. They clasped hands, then clicked thumbs. They thumped each other briefly on the shoulders. He went around the circle greeting the other men thus.

"Seth, I must kill the fattened calf to celebrate your appearance; it's been a while. Where is that lovely Gaia of yours?"

Jah, ever the bloodhound for trouble, would no doubt be piqued to know why Seth was appearing without Gaia. But there was really nothing to hide about their relationship, nothing that couldn't be worked out between the two of them, away from the rumor-gobbling Mayor and his ilk.

Seth pulled his cheeks taut to maintain his smile. "She had a few things to take care of. She'll be here later."

"Hmm."

There were few realms of Sierra Leonean life in the city in which The Mayor did not exercise his omnipotence. When Sam died, Jah spread the word, and nearly two hundred mourners showed up at the memorial service. And if he got a whiff of a failing relationship, well, even Seth's mathematical mind did not want to contemplate the permutations and calculations that would fire up Jah's head.

Leaving the men to continue their surveillance at the front door, Seth wandered into the hall, which was throbbing with dance hall reggae. He spotted Olayinka encased in a fuchsia top, frilly as a carnation, and tottering on three-inch heels that failed to bring her up to eye level with the people she was talking to.

"Seth! Is that really you?"

He bent down to hug her.

"You make it seem like you haven't seen me in ages."

"Well, it has been ages. And look at you, getting those love rolls. Ooh! Gaia must be really taking care of you. Speaking of Gaia—"

"You look good too." He rushed on with a great show of enthusiasm. "Although I can barely see you from up here."

She sucked her teeth with a great show of being perturbed and made as though to smack him, but he dodged the blow with a laugh. Then she pulled down on her tight skirt and turned to the thin, sleepy-eyed woman who she had been talking to.

"You know Seth Walker?"

Seth and the girl shook hands.

"He and I have known each other for ages, before he became a big shot," said Olayinka.

Seth rolled his eyes. "Big shot? I sit at my desk all day and add up numbers until they tell me I can go home. Not so glamorous, let me tell you. She's only saying that because nobody ever expected much out of me."

"What do you do?" inquired the girl.

"I'm an actuary."

"Translation: He's very, very brainy," said Olayinka. "Don't believe what he says about no one expecting him to amount to anything."

Distracted, he assured them that his brains were quite mediocre and then, sensing his moment for a getaway, said, "If you ladies will excuse me, I should continue making my rounds."

Gaia. She was the envy of many. Perhaps it was the Mandingo blood along with the Irish that had been thrown in there somewhere, but with large downward slanting eyes and perfectly chiseled features, she was arresting. In person she was both charming and quick witted, occasionally cutting, though only when provoked.

If she were there, men and women alike would have started eying Seth with even more appreciation. He would have walked in the cloud of her perfume and allure, something knit of champagne and white flowers and an intricately tooled femininity.

His interest in Gaia had prompted Seth to seek The Mayor's help, feeling vaguely uneasy in doing so. For even then, he could never quite shake the feeling that despite The Mayor's jovial personality, receiving his assistance, like doing business with the devil, would one day come at an unbearable price. They had both been attending a Sierra Leonean soccer match at Brockledge Park.

"I like her. What can you tell me about her?"

The Mayor leaned back on the bleachers with a toothy smile and landed a friendly punch on Seth's arm. Being sought out for information was his nectar.

"Hot stuff, yet smart and serious and a straight shooter," he purred. "She is not for the weak. I hear she has a thing for older men, and she did have her obligatory stint with a bad boy—you know women, hee hee—but overall, this one is at a different level."

"So you're saying I don't have a chance with her."

"Are you seriously asking me that question? I tell you, there are some guys who would ask me that, and I would say to them, 'Would you buy a brand-new Benz and drive it to your job as a janitor?' But you now, you have that beautiful house, a good job. What are you waiting for? You want Angel Gabriel to come down and speak to her on your behalf? I know she's not seeing anybody right now."

"How can you be so sure?"

The Mayor folded back his lips in a broad smile.

"Well, I can't share all my secrets, can I?"

~

COURTING GAIA WAS one of those times when he appreciated his career path—the one he had chosen because *they* would approve of it. It had been easy enough to become an actuary with his mathematical gifts. And when he landed a job right after graduation, he had felt as though his life was shaping up in a way that quite surprised him, not the least of which because he quickly found himself earning even more than Sam.

A few years into the job, he began to entertain the first doubts of whether he could do the same thing for five or ten years more. It wasn't that he was bored with the work and its daily hacking away at forests of risk; indeed, in some ways he liked its quantitative, reliable nature. But there was a vague sense of missing something, like memories that had been blotted out by amnesia.

He toyed with the idea of traveling. Perhaps seeing the world would let the stale air out, fan his mind a bit. On a lunch break, he surfed the web for far-flung locations, places he knew little about, where the unfamiliar might slap him out of his torpor. He wrote Bolivia, Romania, Greece, and Iceland on a Post-it, intending to research them more over the next few days. One night he received the call from Joanna, his sister-in-law, about Sam. After returning from Sam's funeral in Freetown, he went back to work a few weeks later an only child and saw the Post-it winking brashly at him from the side of his keyboard. He threw it in the trash.

~

IN ADDITION TO a healthy salary, Gaia was another good thing that had come to him rather than Sam; Gaia, in whose hair his fingers had twined and entwined until it seemed hand and hair would not let each other go, and thus he and she would be bound forever. Gaia, who had called his mother without fail on Mother's Day each year and reminded him to do the same. Gaia, who had held his hand while he steered with the other as they drove down the highway that cleaved the city in two, the sunroof open, the glittering towers seeming to swirl past them, the lights becoming a blur as he thought of his brother. She understood his silence and allowed it to rest in the car like a sleeping child.

It was true that he had been busy and so had she. She had been studying for her CPA exams. But there was more to it; he had simply, without intending to, failed to make the effort to see her.

When they were together, she complained that he was distant and irritable. "What is going through your head?"

"Well, for one, how much my job is so different from what I thought I'd be doing."

She shook her head.

"Look around you, Seth. Most people don't like their jobs. Do you really think I enjoy accounting? But you do what you have to do and get on with your life."

"What if I decided to change jobs, Gaia?"

"And do what?"

He had not the slightest idea.

He had withdrawn even more, grown lax about returning her calls. When she came tonight, he would put both arms around her and interlace his fingers over the small of her back. He would let his fingers dive into the thicket of her hair, graze her cheek with his. He would ask her to be patient with him. And she would forgive him. Or would she, yet again?

~

HE CONTINUED TO make his rounds, as was the custom with these parties, churning out pleasantries, hugging those his age, decorously shaking the hands of the buttress-bosomed middle-aged ladies planted on folding chairs.

For the most part, everyone knew of Sam's sudden death. So Seth felt safe among these people—people who remembered Sam and would be careful to ask him only how his parents were doing and not where his family was and if he had any siblings. Many others had lost loved ones in Sierra Leone in the war or through random deaths that could have been avoided with good medical care. It was a felt kinship.

His greetings over with for now, he wandered over to the food table and fixed himself a plate. He then went and stood in front of a large plastic drum full of drinks presided over by a wide-shouldered man with an orange shirt. He had fished out a bottle for a young woman to his left and handed it to her, water dripping from a hand bedecked with rings.

"Okay, sweetheart, here you go."

The man turned to Seth, trained his eyes on him for a few seconds, and then started.

"My God! I can't believe it's you. What's up, man?" he said, extending an icy but firm hand to Seth after wiping it on his jeans. His tone was mellow with intimacy. Seth shook the proffered hand, quick and firm, while racking his brain for recollection of who the man was. He had found a confident and vigorous greeting could often mask such unfortunate lapses in memory. In fact, he had carried out entire conversations with people at the end of which they were none the wiser that Seth had not a whiff of an idea who they were.

The man did not seem to be in a hurry to relinquish his grip.

"Well, well, well. I never thought I would see you here of all places. A friend told me you lived around here, but I wasn't quite expecting to bump into you like this. And now look at you, all tall and mighty."

"Well, it has been a while," Seth said with a studied confidence. This much must surely be true. He would await enlightenment as to just how long it had been. Adolescence? Childhood? The man stepped back to look at him full length, intent as a bride studying wedding gowns.

"It's good to see you looking so well," he said.

"Thanks, you look good too," said Seth, his voice catching on a note of uncertainty despite himself. He studied the man a little closer. He had the protuberant eyes of a night animal. Yet his manner was relaxed and easygoing.

"I'm sorry to hear about what happened to your brother. But it's good to see you doing so well."

Seth nodded. "Yeah, man. Thanks."

"How are your parents?"

"As well as you can expect, thanks."

The man assumed a faraway look.

"They were good to me, your parents."

Seth began to wonder, even more intent to know how this man knew him and his family, and considered whether he might at this point confess that he had no recollection of him.

The man turned to greet a couple who had just showed up, chatting and then bending to fish out drinks for them from the drum. He turned to give Seth a brief smile as if to say, it was good catching up. Seth moved on, somewhat troubled.

Where was Gaia? She had said she would be there soon after him. He floated to the outskirts of a cluster of guys in a corner listening to Stuart, a kindly drunk who was a fixture at these parties. They chuckled and welcomed Seth into their midst with another round of hand clasping, back thumping, and ribbing.

"Do any of you know who that dude serving drinks is?" he asked.

They peered in the direction of the man, then expressed surprise that they could not name him.

"Have you asked The Mayor?" said Stuart. "He should know."

Seth nodded. Of course. The Mayor.

"So where is Gaia?" asked another of the guys. "And when are you guys announcing your engagement? It seems as though that's the only thing missing."

"What's that? Gaia, you said?" He pretended as though he had still been distracted by the mystery man. "Oh, she should be here any minute."

He pulled his phone from his pocket and was dismayed to see that he had missed a call from Gaia. He called her back, but she didn't pick up. It was time for another drink. On his way to get one, he passed a speaker almost the size of his body, a black, rectangular organ of sound, the bass pulsing out of it so strongly that he could feel it pounding in his core, propelling him with a force other than his own heartbeat. He walked past quickly, unnerved.

Another man was now serving drinks. After getting one, Seth decided to go off in search of his bulbous-eyed new acquaintance. He found him returning from the dance floor, looking for somewhere to sit.

"Over here," called Seth. "There are some free seats here." He tried to look casual, engaging, as the man walked over. "I have to 'fess up. I thought I knew who you were, but now I'm not so sure," Seth said, easing out his half-truth as best he could. Better this hopefully momentary embarrassment, he had reasoned, than a drawn-out, entangling conversation with The Mayor.

"Really? I used to come to your house when you boys were kids. I did cabinet work for your mother, her kitchen cabinets. Remember how when I would take breaks, your mother would give us soft drinks, and you would sit outside the kitchen with me on those big tiled steps, and you and I would talk about football?"

"I have a really bad memory, so I may have forgotten. How old was I then?"

"Oh, maybe twelve, thirteen."

Seth furrowed his brow. How could this recollection have escaped him so totally? He peered into the man's face.

The man leaned toward Seth like a conspirator, his bulbous eyes like peeled onions as they moved glossily in their sockets.

"And I remember how you were always thinking up tricks to play on your brother, may his soul rest in perfect peace."

It all became clear to Seth, and the familiar bitterness arose.

"Oh, you are confusing me with my brother. I am Seth, the younger."

The man cocked his head like an eagle and looked pop-eyed at Seth.

"Ooohhhh! But they told me it was Seth who died . . . or perhaps they told me Sam, but I had in mind you. I'm so sorry."

"That's okay."

He could see confusion flooding the man's features and almost felt sorry for him.

"So Sam is really dead. . . . But you seem so much like him now. You even look identical. Not that you didn't look alike when you were younger . . . but your personalities were so different."

"In what way am I like him?" Seth asked, trying not to betray his irritation.

"I really can't say . . . maybe it's the way I've seen people inter-act with you here, kind of like you're the center of attention. Not that that's a bad thing. Your brother was a jovial sort."

The man stood up abruptly.

"I'm going to get another drink. Shall I get you anything?"

"No, thanks." He understood the man's need to let his embar-rassment dissipate away from Seth.

"I'll be right back then."

He watched the man's retreating back without really seeing him. Inside he felt a stinging energy course through him until it brought him to his feet. It was not an inclination to dance or yell or hit a wall. It was a pure force that, like water, was so elemental it had no counterfeit. He could not wrestle with it or release it in this public place; conversation was too finely calibrated, and even dancing too measured. He needed to get away.

Without saying a word to anybody, he walked toward the door, trying to keep a steady pace when all he wanted to do was run. Some people were looking his way. Hopefully they would assume he was just going to get something from his car.

From outside, the hall throbbed with the bass heartbeat. Seth jogged to his car and got in. The car was cold; he exhaled, his breathing shaky. He started the car and hit the gas hard as he reversed. Pulling away on one side of the parking lot, he saw Gaia pulling up on the other. She was looking for a parking spot but didn't notice Seth's car.

The elemental force seemed to push his foot down deeper on the gas, against his will, as though to rule out any possibility of him turning around to see Gaia. What would he say to her to explain yet another transgression?

He pulled onto the road, racing toward the red light, knowing he would have to make a dangerously hard break or run it. But it changed to green, as though an angel had pardoned his madness. The road was open.

~ NINE ~

GAIA TWIRLED THE stem of her spotless wineglass between her fingers. She had refused wine, declined to smile at him. A territory of white tablecloth lay between them.

"Is this about Sam?" she said.

He thought about it. Could Sam's death be affecting him in ways he wasn't aware of? "No. I don't think so."

It had been a week since he'd fled the party. He'd promised he'd explain everything when they met, thought taking her out to a nice restaurant would help smooth the way.

"Is this about Joanna?"

"Why would it be about Joanna?"

"Don't think I don't know you have feelings for her."

"Gaia, she's my brother's wife."

"Widow. Seth, don't play games with me. Look me in the eye and tell me what's going on."

"I don't know."

"That's a cop-out answer. Tell me again. What happened the night of the party?"

"I told you. I just got tired of the whole party scene and a little dissatisfied with my life."

"What's wrong with your life, Seth? Many people would cut off a hand to have your life."

"I know, I know. But it's just that when I was little, I would never have predicted being the kind of person I am today, doing the type of work I do, being so concerned about being admired, having cool gadgets and nice clothes."

"Is that it? We all go through that, except that usually people are beating themselves up about things they don't have."

"Well, you asked for an explanation."

"And what about the car? Tell me what happened again?"

He gritted his teeth, forced himself not to blink too much. *Remember the lie, each detail.*

The night of the party he had gotten to the interstate and kept driving, farther and farther away from the city limits, going deeper south, past the dealership where he'd bought his car, past the outlet mall where he and Gaia sometimes went shopping when driving back from Florida. He was in the country now, in rural Georgia, and yet he kept driving, past cotton and peanut farms and the billboards advertising pecans for sale and adult entertainment for truck drivers. The roads were empty, illumined now and then by a pair of approaching headlights.

After almost two hours of driving with only the night as his companion, he felt his shoulders sag, and he pulled off onto an access road. Higher up, he saw a small shopping plaza, its parking lot empty, its storefronts dark.

He pulled into the parking lot. The side of the lot closest to the access road was fringed by streetlights. The rest of the lot was dark. He stopped the car diagonally across the parking lines and cut off his headlights. After he turned off the engine, he could hear the whoosh of the occasional car passing on the freeway.

He looked around at the sides of the car and felt they were the only thing protecting him from a vortex of night that would suck him in if it could. For a moment he thought back with longing to the warm throng of people he had left behind in the hall. With the stream of energy gone that had kept his foot on the pedal, he was unsure what to do next. Sweat crawled down his face. He opened his window to let in a gust of air, but feeling exposed, he rolled it back up.

The ordinariness of the night taunted him. There was no epiphany, no sign, no stranger in hat and trench coat crossing the lot toward him, no mysterious light turning on overhead. Bracing himself against a fear he still did not understand, he got out of the car and looked up at the stars. They hinted at nothing. He looked at the thicket of bushes in the distance, beyond the shops, but nothing stirred within them. He wished desperately for something to rail against, to fight, but his foe remained faceless. It had possessed him without his consent, then jumped out to mock him from the safety of some secret pocket of night.

Heat from his churning blood whipped in cycles from end to end with increasing centrifugal force. Gulleys and caverns within him whistled and gurgled, straining with the forceful flow of blood, his heart working like a giant bellows. He walked back to the car and kicked the passenger door viciously, denting it, marring its gloss-kissed perfection. His beautiful Infiniti. Not knowing what else to do, he wrested the driver door open and he sat down, running his hand over the fine leather stitching of the steering wheel, the egg-smooth finish of the seats, the lacquered wood grain of the console.

He clicked the switch in the ignition. The car yawned awake, its engine purring like the whirring of insect wings. After belting himself in, he oriented the car toward the parking lot exit and cruised toward it, hesitation rising up like the grinding of gears. He stopped. Then he pushed the gas, gentle but firm, down all the way, until he had smashed the car into the concrete base of the lamp pole.

Gaia was still giving him a cold look. He began slowly. "Like I said, I was tired. I drove out pretty far, and then there were those drinks I'd had."

"So you were drinking and driving."

"No. Well, I'd had just a couple, you know, nothing to get soused over, but I think they helped make me tired. And you know how dark it is on those country roads. So I pulled over."

"You got off the freeway?"

"Well, yes, at a point."

"You didn't tell me that part before."

"Oh, sorry, I thought I had. Before you know it, there was this pole I hadn't seen, and I was waking up, not even realizing I'd dozed off." He felt something fray and tear between them as he uttered the lie.

The impact of hitting the pole had coursed through him with a voltage that left him trembling for moments afterward. And yet, even more searing was the knowledge that he had crossed some threshold—something had been done that could not be undone.

She looked at him squint-eyed. Gaia was no fool. She would know his story didn't quite add up. Finally, she sighed. "If you were middle-aged, I would say you're having a midlife crisis. But let's look at you. Have you lost your looks and hair? No. Have you been fighting corruption or feeding hungry children or selling toll bridge tickets for decades or doing anything for that matter long enough to be tired of it? Hardly. So what is going on?"

He looked at her, struggling to voice his confusion and ultimately failing to come up with the words. A waiter approached and then, noting the sobriety of the scene, retreated. Seth began to butter one of the rolls on the table. Buttering bread was something he loved watching Gaia do. She was slow, thorough, yet efficient in her movements, drawing the flat of the knife across the bread in a sensuous way until the knife gleamed clean. Now Seth merely slapped on the butter and watched it melt. He broke the buttered side of the roll in half and gave her one piece. They always did that for each other. She took a small bite. They ate the rest of their dinner in near silence.

Driving away from the restaurant, he felt a tailwind, perhaps of a storm of grief behind him, perhaps the gust of a door slamming shut forever in some metaphysical place. She was wrong about Joanna this time, even though on balance she was right. He had harbored a secret longing for her, and his unfaithfulness in doing so troubled him less than the thought that it might be motivated by spite. Sam had stolen Joanna too from him; she had been Seth's study mate, and he had wanted time to discover her like an ear of corn wrapped within its husk. But Sam, upon meeting her at Seth's college residence, had inserted himself into the scene right away, taking that opportunity away from Seth. Then Seth, much to his dismay, began to desire her, and that feeling seemed to only get stronger after Sam's death, strengthened perhaps by the fact that being with her was now a possibility.

That night he had his first encounter with *The Thing* in the swamp. Then, beyond all explanation, Gaia forgave him again. But then the scratching began, and he had no choice but to seek help. Then the signs pointing him to the river began to appear, and it was clear after what he said to Gaia that the last slender filament holding them together had been severed.

Back when he and Sam were children, they would cut through the brush on the side of their house to go to the Matenge River. The water surged forward like a stampeding crowd, angry brown currents making muscular shapes in the riverbed as they swept by rocks braced like elephantine market women. Seth and Sam would throw things into the water to watch the merciless current carry them away. They threw in bits of branches, plastic containers—they had a game where each brother would throw in an object, and the first object to pass the toad-like rock close to the riverbank downstream would win. They did this over and over again, mainly because Seth usually lost and insisted that they try again, and Sam, eyes gleaming, would be only too happy to oblige.

This is what they had been doing on the day of the red plastic slippers, the day that started it all. Sam had been going through slippers like crazy because they were all the boys wore after school to roam and play. Evelyn, having bought him three pairs in as many weeks, said with exasperation as she gave him a pair of red ones, "You'd better not cut these anytime soon, or I swear, you will walk around barefoot. And if you get something stuck in your foot, you'd better cut it off."

Sam had pretended to look penitent and said, "Yes, Mummy," but the moment Evelyn's back was turned, he began to grin.

They were forbidden to go to the river after heavy rains, and this time the downpours had been heavier than usual. But the river beckoned to them, its voice sibilant. And Evelyn and Alfred were out of the house, or so they thought. After Sam's five consecutive wins at the toss game, Seth was grouchy and secretly felt like crying, though he would rather have thrown himself into the river than let Sam see his tears. The fact that Sam had clearly let him win the sixth round did little to improve his mood. And while he walked on the bank, his slipper, already making wet suction sounds in the mud, cut.

"*Pelempelem*, you are going to get in trouble with Mummy. She's going to give you a whipping."

Seth thought about this for a second, fearful.

"Why? She didn't give you a whipping when you cut yours."

"That's different. She likes me more," said Sam, grinning.

Seth felt hot all over, possessed by a rage so vile it threatened to stop his heart. He ran over to where Sam had left his slippers, so as not to lose them this time, grabbed one, and flung it in the river so hard his arm hurt. It was his best shot of the day. The slipper rotated several times, cutting a red arc against the gray sky before falling, followed by their disbelieving eyes (for even Seth could not believe he had done that), until it returned to earth at last and got trapped within the fingers of a tree branch stuck in the river.

Sam turned to look at him, unperturbed, a smile playing around his lips, his eyes gleaming with the knowledge of the awful thing he had said. It was the first day Seth could remember loathing Sam with more venom than his body could bear, for though both boys had known that their mother loved Sam more, neither had said it until now.

But as formidable as the hate was, it was usurped by the awe that infused him when he saw the Lego blocks building and rebuilding themselves in the illuminated screen of his mind after he and Sam had shivered in each others' arms on the bank after nearly drowning. Years later, he would see with new eyes Sam's role in his near drowning, and yet even that did not eviscerate the way Sam's taunt about Evelyn had.

Nothing was ever the same after the Matenge River. And now he understood—this rage was not new. Even as a boy, it had claimed him. He thought he had left it behind, but it had found him. Indeed, he had always carried it within him, just as he had carried *The Thing,* which fed the rage.

And one morning, after he awoke drenched in sweat yet again, he realized that the Matenge River had been in his mind all along, like a mossy forgotten stone in a riverbed waiting for him to reach his hand down and feel it.

~ TEN ~

EVELYN AND ALFRED had sat listening to Seth's story without moving, so in the dark, it seemed as though their forms had hardened and become one with the chairs and his words merely broke over them like surf dashing against rocks.

It had been a mistake to tell them; that he could see even before he was done. Even though he had held back much—the stranger who had mistaken him for Sam, his nighttime plunge into the barren countryside, the wrecking of his car—perhaps it had still been too much.

Alfred humphed, uneasy, and darted a glance at Seth, then back at Evelyn. Seth looked away. When she spoke, her voice was not angry, but tired and unceremonious as she threw out words like water cast from a cup.

"Why are you telling us all this? What is it supposed to mean?"

His obedient mind groped for an answer. He parted his lips; they stared back at him. Then he felt his face flush with anger. "Excuse me," he said, rising. And he left them sitting in the dark.

~

THERE WAS NOTHING to put in his suitcase other than what he had come with. He hurriedly threw his possessions into his backpack and suitcase. As he drew back the bolt of the gate, he saw Pa Kamara peep through the window of the guardhouse, eyes puckered with sleep.

"Where are you going?"

"I don't know."

The old man looked at him for a while. It was too dark for Seth to see his expression well.

"But you just came."

"I know." Seth nodded at Pa Kamara as he carried his suitcase through the gate. The old man came shuffling out after him to close it. His white T-shirt was ghostly in the moonlight.

"God go with you, my boy," Pa Kamara called after him.

He dragged his suitcase over the bumpy road, barely able to see where he was putting his feet. It would be almost a mile to the taxi stop. The road was so bad in places that Seth was forced to pick up his suitcase by the handle and carry it.

He could not create a dictionary for himself, a map to the country of his being. But should he expect less of his mother? Even if he wanted to, the restless surge, the beast in him would not allow it. It had already shown itself capable of destruction. If he continued along this path, would even he be spared?

The slender novice moon barely lit his path, but in his mind, there arose a map of the road as it used to be, for he had walked it thousands of times as a boy. He knew where it curved out like an elbow to the side of the river, at what point it was tarred for a spell, at what point it was flanked by a gathering of twisted bushes. His feet had kicked up clouds of red dust on it in the dry season. In the rainy season, all that dust had turned to a lagoon of mud that would suction his and Sam's plastic shoes. When the rains had been particularly heavy, entire streams would flood the road, while the sky, having birthed its rain, brooded overhead, a raw gray pulp.

Yet for all his knowledge of this road, his feet floundered on the stones, on the holes and dips and new curves and angles sculpted by many more seasons of rain and journey and road re-construction projects. Perhaps this too was grief—bearing knowledge of a thing that has changed. New people walked the road without knowing that his father had accidentally hit a dog right around where Seth was walking now. Seth had seen its blood soak into the dust.

He wished he could speak to his brother of the divorce from his parents that was being sealed by each step he took.

"Sam?" He said his brother's name in a whisper, hoarse, as though his mouth were forgetting how to make the sound.

"I'm leaving," he continued, thinking it foolish to look heavenward but finding his eyes drawn there, hoping his brother could hear him.

The Matenge River was silent, but he knew it was there, just behind the bushes. If only he and Sam had known then that the raging river would one day become as harmless as an old dog dozing in the afternoon sun, perhaps the two of them might not have been hewn apart in that way.

He stumbled along the road, feeling heavier with each step. After half an hour, he reached the taxi stop.

"Where did you say you were going again?" the taxi driver asked when Seth got in.

The man turned to look at Seth when he did not answer right away, not because he could not think of any hotels to which to be taken but because for a moment the heaviness lifted, and he was dizzied by possibility: the next town, the mountains above Freetown, the sea. His life was his own. And yet he knew *The Thing* had gotten into the taxi with him.

~ ELEVEN ~

THE MEMORIES OF Sam grew even stronger after Seth left, and his departure did nothing to ease the heaviness Evelyn felt. At night she stayed awake until long after Alfred's snoring had crested and abated, and when she did finally sink into sleep, she would awaken during the night, unsure of the hour. On nights when there was no moon, she stared into darkness so dense that whether she closed her eyes or kept them open made no difference. And whether she was awake or asleep, the memories passed in procession before her—new ones, early ones, bright as fresh paint, sharp as lemon on the tongue. In passing, they lashed her with barbed tails and warped her sense of time and consciousness.

When she had asked Seth to tell her of his trip, she had not wanted to hear all he had to say, for she could bear the burden of him no longer, the haunted grove in the forest that was Seth. She had invited him to speak to answers she could bear. Simple things she could commit to her memory as a final act.

She and Alfred did not speak of Seth. She had told Alfred that she did not wish to and threw his goodbye note in the trash right in front of Alfred's very eyes. In fact, they had not spoken much at all since Seth left.

"Did you notice his neck?" Alfred had asked.

"Why do you ask?"

He said nothing in response. She had seen Seth's scars and wanted not to see them, knowing that whatever the reason for them, she did not have the space within her to reckon with their meaning.

She took some time off from work, claiming illness. At home, when Alfred left in the morning, she didn't stir from the bed.

"I'll see you later," he said to her silent mound, knowing full well she was awake.

I hope I'm still here when you get back, she thought. But where would she go where the memories could not follow?

Even when they were not passing in procession through her mind, she could feel the threat of them, her vulnerability to something beyond her control. The air passing through the house mocked her, made her feel it could pick her up and take her away on its way out. The doors were too wide, the windows too large, and the sun poured in and swelled, becoming a dense substance of heat and dust particles swirling furiously in their own galaxies. She felt this congealed mass would flatten her against the wall until it crushed her.

To distract her mind, she decided to clean the house.

While dusting the living room she found the video, removing its rectangular form to find it left behind a clean, sharp edge of dust on the shelf.

"The girl is not dusting properly," she muttered.

When Seth had first sent the video to her, she had put it away without much thought, for somehow the mourning of others had never seemed credible. In fact, at the time, the thought of a memorial service in the United States had annoyed rather than comforted her. Who were these strangers to feign such love for her son? The real funeral had been in Freetown, where Sam was born, among those who could remember his skinny child legs, his gap teeth.

Now as she fingered the video, she was shocked to realize she was already thinking of how to play it. The recording started in a blaze of fuzzy white lines, and then there was a church full of somber people. Strange faces, all of them.

A woman crowned with a black-feathered hat got up to sing. The camera panned the front rows where members of the family sat. She saw Seth sitting up very straight, his face impassive, hands on his thighs. There was Joanna, returning the camera's gaze clear eyed and unflinching. Evelyn looked closely at her daughter-in-law—that skin the color of French bread, the perfectly groomed eyebrows, the usual mane of hair now twisted and pulled into an updo. Then there was her fashion sense, which never failed her, least of all in times of distress; her navy blue dress was of impeccable fit with latticed sleeves, and silver finery glinted on her neck and hands. Joanna was poised, she would give her that, too poised for a young widow at her husband's funeral. There was something unsettling about the girl.

She wondered what it would have been like to live near them. That was an experience that had been denied so many people like herself, whose children studied, worked, and bore children in a faraway land.

They were now giving eulogies. There were coughs and rustlings, then a young man about Sam's age took the podium. Evelyn could tell from his accent that he was from the Caribbean. His voice drenched in melancholy, he began to speak of college days with Sam, how Sam was one of those people who could get by without seeming to open a book, who looked buff in spite of never bothering with the gym. And how he loved mischief. One of his favorite pranks was to entertain ignorant Americans with farfetched tales of growing up in Africa—how he had grown up a goatherd, slept huddled next to the goats at night, and covered himself with giant banana leaves when it rained.

Having laughed along with the audience at the more light-hearted recollections, the young man turned somber again, training his eyes on his notes. He recalled how two years ago,

Sam had flown out to Minnesota to help him through a personal crisis, forfeiting his Fourth of July holiday plans. The young man looked up from his notes at the audience with a look of bewilderment, as though only now understanding the loss.

Other people came up to speak: co-workers, a neighbor, even Seth. But Seth revealed little in his eulogy. He talked of how Sam had played the role of big brother so effortlessly, succeeding in whatever he did and thus being a role model for Seth. If Seth's words revealed little, his face revealed even less. That boy had always been a mystery.

It was over so quickly. Evelyn wondered at how services in the States could be so short. Was this all there was to mark the ending of a life: clippings of songs, speeches, and prayers that lasted no longer than standing in line at the bank?

Evelyn went to the kitchen, thinking to make herself some tea. It was growing dark outside, but she didn't bother to turn the light on, preferring instead to see the awakening evening through the window, the murky clouds tinged with pink.

Quick as a gunshot in the night, it hit her. Two years ago, the young man giving the eulogy had said, Sam came out to help him. That was the year she had turned sixty, the year before Sam died, and the Fourth of July holiday had fallen just a week before her sixtieth birthday. Ah, how well memory served her.

Sam had not come back home for her birthday because he had broken his leg and was on crutches, his leg in a cast, he said. Yet how had he been able to fly out to this man? And even if he had managed to install himself on a plane, how would he have been able to help the man move in that condition?

Forgetting all thoughts of tea, she went back to the living room retrieved the tape, and pushed it into the player, her hands stumbling through the task. She fast-forwarded. The man said Sam flew to Minnesota. She pondered where Minnesota might be. It didn't matter; Sam had flown there. Why? All those times they had talked on the phone leading up to her birthday, he had seemed excited. She had passed on a list of things she needed for the party: paperware and plastic cutlery, silk flowers, aluminum pans, napkins. He had sent them in a shipment, including things that he intended to use when he arrived in Freetown. He had told her about the ticket options he was looking at, told her, his voice tender, that he couldn't wait to see her. Then he broke his leg when he fell from a deck.

Although she had imprisoned it, shackled and banished it, the memory came roaring back now—of standing there, knife in hand, a lit cake under it, all around people she barely cared for, and her firstborn son far away. Oh, how it had shredded her heart then. Now it literally knocked her to the floor, and she curled up in a fetal position on the cold tiles. On her sixtieth birthday, where was Sam?

~ TWELVE ~

Seth waited until the sounds of laughter in the courtyard died down and the periodic clatter of heels on the hallway tiles disappeared altogether. Outside the louvered window, even the street was quiet with only the engine of the occasional car moaning as it clambered over the cratered road. The dark girded its loins, gaining strength in the silence, and the shadows congealed like pudding. It was time to sleep, time to do battle.

"Please remove everything from the room," he had said quietly, pressing some folded bills into the perplexed hotel manager's palm when he checked into a small hotel in a hilly part of the city. But they had obliged. Now he looked around the bare room, every piece of the furniture but the bed removed as per his request. One thing that could not be removed, which would come, was the night and what it brought.

When sleep came for him, he stiffened, but it took his body anyway. The swamp was still, a green sheet with milky wrinkled skin that stretched into the distance, and so quiet that he thought he could almost hear the insects whirring over its surface. Even the trees at the farther edges were still, their leaves stiff in the spiritless air. Yet the mangrove roots that reached into the water would move every now and then, as though troubled from below.

The water was warm too. It closed around him like his own skin. It pulled him down into its plush folds, and there it got even thicker and warmer, as though boiled by a subterranean sun. He looked down and saw that the bottom of the swamp was pregnant with sediment—towers of it—like forgotten cities emulating the cloud world of the heavens. Here and there they billowed as though determined to form ever grander citadels. All of a sudden, there was a streak of silver like a flash of lightning piercing thunderclouds. Just as suddenly, it was gone, and the sediment churned with even more fury below until Seth could hardly see the outline of his own hand before him.

But then something grabbed his ankle, and it felt like a hand wrought from wire and covered with moss. The binding grasp felt both alien and animal. He clenched his arm like a vise upon a thing that had the bend and flex of human limb yet at the same time writhed, snakelike. Two snake-arms encircled his waist, pulling him farther down into a watery lair. He gritted his teeth and found that he was biting his lip hard enough to feel something give. In the next move, he bent down toward the limb in the crook of his arm and bit what felt like sinews cloaked in fur, girded with steel.

Blood eddied in the water and sealed every last crack through which light could penetrate. Water gurgled around them as they thrashed. A rhythmic pounding began from up above, and he wondered if it was the sound of children hitting laundry with the wooden *patas* on the large, flat rocks of the river.

The pounding became faster and more urgent, and then his eyes were forced open, and he was in his hotel room in Freetown. The pounding was coming from his door. Men's voices gathered outside and seeped in through the big crack under the door. "Let's just open it." There was a metallic tinkle-crunch of a key being inserted in the lock and the gasp of the door leaving its frame. Two timid heads rounded the door, the bodies following to plant themselves with caution near the door. They slowly edged toward the foot of Seth's bed.

"Sir, we were concerned," said a baby-faced young man with polished diction. "There was shouting coming from your room." He must have been the night concierge or manager. Next to him was another thin man—a night staffer, no doubt lowly and underpaid, as his gaunt frame bore witness. The manager was in a rumpled T-shirt and shorts. He too must have been woken from sleep.

"I . . . I was . . . I'm fine," Seth managed to utter.

The two men looked at each other.

"And also, the pounding of the wall," continued the manager. "A bad dream perhaps? Shall we move the bed away from the wall?"

"Yes," Seth croaked. "You can do that tomorrow morning. I shall be up the rest of the night now."

"Okay, sir," said the manager. The smaller man took a few steps backward, as though afraid to turn his back to Seth, and the two men exited.

Seth reached his fingertips to his lips, and even before they touched them, he dreaded what he would feel. When he took his fingertips away, they were wet, but thankfully, his lip was not severed. He got up and went to the bathroom to wash the blood away and tried to ignore the throbbing pain.

The next day, the manager he had first met thanked him for his patronage and, citing concerns by other guests, kindly requested that Seth find alternate accommodation.

~ THIRTEEN ~

ISAAC WANTED TO know everything that Seth could remember—skipping Mr. Cole's physics class on Wednesdays? Cutting through the bush road with the bowed grasses until they got to Evan's house to smoke smuggled cigarettes?

"I remember us trying to stone fruit down from the trees, and once we hit that poor boy," Seth said.

"His forehead was bleeding a bit, poor thing," said Isaac. "But the crazy thing was, he seemed almost happy, because when he demanded payment, with the blood, you know, we had to fork over everything we had."

Lunch hadn't arrived yet, so they merely chugged soft drinks out of thick glass bottles.

Pink bougainvillea blossoms overhung the outside walls of the popular downtown jaunt where Isaac had suggested they meet and where they now sat surrounded by other diners. Seth had arrived early and asked the restaurant staff to stash his luggage in a secure place. They cast several darting glances at him—the swelled welted lip, the tendrils of scars still visible on the sides of his neck, the expensive luggage—but they had acquiesced when he slipped some more paper discreetly into palms. Ah, Sierra Leone. It was impossible to take a piss without greasing someone's palm.

Isaac was the only friend he still had Freetown; board-thin Isaac of the stork-like movements and deep percussive laugh. One day at secondary school, when Seth had been standing in line to buy bread stuffed with *akara*, he felt a tap on his shoulder. It was Isaac handing him money.

"You dropped this."

His eyes were open, like a tunnel you could see through all the way to the end. They became friends. They had played soccer together, loaning each other spare shirts, walking to and from the field together, watching each other's backpacks. Seth had brought Isaac home with him a few times. Sam prowled outside their periphery, ignoring Seth's glares, and once Sam and Isaac began to talk, they hit it off really well.

Once Seth came home to find them engaged in a heated debate over whether Bruce Lee or Jackie Chan was the better kung fu artist. Sitting back comfortably on Sam's bed, both looked up startled to see Seth standing in the doorway. And although they began to hang out as a threesome when Isaac came around, Isaac spent most of his time with Seth. He never seemed interested in developing a closer friendship with Sam, despite the ease with which they joked. Seth loved him even more for it.

Isaac was the only one he could think of calling when the hotel asked him to leave. After all, there was no point in calling a relative—to do so would keep him tethered to his family—and all his other friends had left the country.

When they met, Isaac couldn't get enough of him, it seemed, punching him on the arm, thumping him on the back, fist-bumping him. Not for a long time had anybody been so happy to see him, Seth mused. *How is it that all this time I have not kept in touch with Isaac?*

Isaac was still animated as he reminisced about old times. Seth waited for him to wind down and broach the inevitable topic of why Seth was there. Seth found himself drifting drowsily, deflated and sad, as he often felt after the soaring anger. What would have happened last night if those men hadn't knocked on his door? Would he be here today? Would he be conqueror or vanquished?

"Come stay with me," Isaac was saying now.

"Excuse me?" Seth felt his concentration land at their table with a thud.

"I don't know where you're staying, but why not stay with me for however long you're here?"

Seth rubbed the side of his face. "I'm not exactly sure how long I'm staying."

"And your parents?"

Seth didn't answer. His thoughts clanged in his head like pots and pans.

"You're not staying with them?"

"No."

Seth looked at the broken concrete beneath their feet. Ants scurried within one of its dusty fissures carrying crumbs above their heads like trophies.

"Stay with us for bit. Me and Aunty Sia and Ettie. It will be like old times."

So there were other people. Women. He thought of the two men pounding on his door last night. The screaming and thumping they must have heard. He thought of the word "violence" leering at him from that Google search. But where would he stay now? Another hotel with another set of men inevitably pounding on his door in the middle of the night? Would he return to the States to no job, no place to stay, and rancor hanging in the air like smoke from burnt tires? Joanna would take him in, but his pride could not bear it.

He lifted his eyes to meet Isaac's, but Isaac was looking toward the inside of the restaurant. Seth half expected the restaurant staff to emerge bearing his luggage and for Isaac to stand up and receive it as if he had been expecting it all along.

"Do you know Hassan left also?" Isaac asked Seth, his voice faint and faraway.

"Hassan?"

"Hassan. Our Hassan. First, after you and then Amin left, Hassan and Peter-Paul and I got even closer. We got through those war years together, and we didn't take each other for granted. Dominic would join us every now and then, and we'd go to Stadium and just hang out, you know, waiting for the St. Anne's girls to go walking down Bedford Lane to their lessons and offer to walk with them. Peter-Paul got two girlfriends with that strategy," Isaac said with a chuckle.

"Then Hassan's mother, who had been living somewhere in America for ten years, sent for him. I was with him when they got the news, and his grandmother cried and slapped his face, then hugged his neck—because she was so happy, she said. Peter-Paul and I took the ferry with him to Lungi. We were so happy for him, but none of us would speak because we knew even if we saw each other again, these times were gone.

"It was me and Peter-Paul for a while, but of course, we were grown up by then, and I was teaching, and he got a job at IPAM. But every now and then, we would get together and shoot the breeze because he didn't live too far away. Then one day, he told me they were sending him to Ghana for a conference, and he asked me to keep his Bose speaker for him—you know, the one he worshipped like Jesus. He didn't trust his drunk nephew not to find it in the house and sell it, even if he hid it under a mountain of dirty underwear.

"So he handed it to me wrapped in a towel like it was a newborn, and I hid it under my bed and locked my room every day it was there. He was supposed to be back in two weeks, but I never heard from him. Then it was one month, then two. I went to IPAM to ask for him because I was so worried. He wouldn't abandon his speaker like that. And they told me he was now living in Ghana. He didn't even call.

"You're the first one to come back," Isaac said, looking straight into Seth's eyes.

Their food arrived, and although Seth, as usual, did not have much of an appetite, he was grateful to have something to busy himself with.

Isaac had seen the lip, must have noticed the scars. And, like Alfred, he had chosen not to ask. He must tell Isaac. Let him decide carefully. At least for the sake of the people he lived with.

The first bite of rice tasted like crumbled Styrofoam, yet he spoke through it. "I've been having some bad dreams at night," he said, gesturing to his lip.

Isaac raised his brows for second and then broke into a weak smile.

"We all have those. We have been through a war."

The next bites of food tasted better, and when the bill came, Isaac asked Seth where his luggage was. Seth pointed to the interior of the restaurant, his eyes so lit by the electric sunlight that he could not see much past the darkened doorway.

~ FOURTEEN ~

WHEN SETH WOKE the next day in his new surroundings, it was 9:14 a.m., and Isaac had gone to work. After coming home with Isaac, exhausted, he had tumbled onto the couch in Isaac's room in late afternoon and slept through the entire night. Isaac had reluctantly agreed to a reasonable amount of rent, and with that settled and the bill for their food paid, he had bundled Seth into a rust-encrusted taxi.

The house, when he stepped out of Isaac's bedroom, was dark inside and smelled like porridge. After he had washed up, Seth walked toward the portal of light that led to the cemented back-yard. A short, sturdily built woman who appeared to be in her mid-sixties looked up when he appeared. She sat on a low stool shelling black-eyed peas into a large basin.

"Aunty Sia?" Isaac had told him the aunt scratched out a living through a small catering business. Cooking must be a daylong endeavor for her then. Isaac, it turned out, made a living giving lessons on the side to supplement his meager teacher's salary.

She nodded and flashed him a quick smile. There were streaks of gray in her hair and an assortment of moles scattered like breadcrumbs on her temples. Her face was like canvas, washed and beaten, yet stretched smooth. Her hands, though small, were those of a working woman with coarse skin and thick, dull nails.

He put out a hand to shake hers and then dropped it, feeling foolish, realizing hers were wet with the translucent membranes of the shelled beans sticking to them. Her eyes lingered briefly on his neck and lip, but her expression did not change.

"How did you sleep?" she asked after their awkward self-introductions.

"Very well, thanks."

She dipped her hands into the basin again and kept them underwater until the bean skins floated off. She flashed him a quick smile, which did not reach her eyes.

"Have some breakfast," she said looking down at her hands. "We are poor, and I know what we have is not what you are used to in America, but you can make do with it, I hope."

Suddenly Aunty Sia's serious face erupted into a grin as she looked past Seth to the inside of the house.

"Ettie's home," Aunty Sia said. "Come here, child."

Seth was startled by this sudden change in the woman's demeanor and peered into the house to see what could have caused it. In the dark interior, he could just about make out a teenage girl of slightly heavy build and long braided hair looking at Aunty Sia.

"Come meet our guest."

But the figure took a few steps back, hesitant. Seth wondered if his appearance was alarming, if even from a distance the girl could detect a crazed look in his eyes. She turned away, and Aunty Sia's smile vanished. "The poor child. She's as shy as a gecko."

"Does Aunty Sia have any children?" Seth had asked Isaac.

"A son in England who she never speaks to. I am like her son, and Ettie is like her daughter. Ettie is a girl she's taking care of," Isaac had said in an offhand way, but Seth noted a shuttering of his friend's normally open face. He waited, but Isaac uncharacteristically offered nothing further. In any case, such ward-guardian relationships were common practice in the country.

~

OVER THE NEXT few days, a sludge-like stupor overcame Seth. Each afternoon he would struggle to tear himself away from it like a fly from tar paper. Upon emerging, he did his best to avoid the wary eye of his hostess. But despite everything, in his first week in Isaac's house, their friendship regained its beat. They stayed up late at night to talk, mostly working the past through their minds like prayer beads—school days (so monotonous at the time but in retrospect a patchwork of life), the times before the war (who knew living in a poor country could be so idyllic), and the people they knew (who was where these days and what were they doing).

Seth sensed that even in his addled state, his mind thin like weak tea, his presence watered Isaac. Their rekindled friendship buoyed Isaac's laugh, ushered his mind into happier times. Knowing his own unstable state, this terrified Seth. He wondered how long it would be before Isaac pulled back when he heard Seth screaming or thrashing and scratching himself in his sleep.

As Seth fell asleep, he would find himself, against his will, drawn into the swamp, his clothing billowing until the air from it bubbled up to the surface like cries for help, his mouth helpless, gulping the brackish, gutter-smelling water that pulled him farther into its depths. He pummeled himself upward with all his might, thrashing without thinking, his whole being lunging toward life. He would wake up in the middle of the night gasping for breath, his mind wrung out like a tea towel, his body trembling, whether with rage, relief, or exertion, he could not distinguish. Thankfully, Isaac snored on, oblivious.

In the morning, flattened by these exertions, he pretended to be asleep so as not to have to speak to Isaac. And yet they stayed up night after night talking, Seth on the bony couch, Isaac on the bed. Seth would protest that it was unfair to keep Isaac up late, but in the dark, Isaac's eyes shone all the more, and his lips were pulled back into a smile. In the morning, his face turned toward the back of the couch, Seth could feel Isaac's expectancy, the somewhat longer-than-usual way he paused around Seth, as though hoping he would turn around, give him a wink, a wave, a good morning yawn before leaving for work.

Seth began to leave the house every day, the lethargy now replaced by the familiar anger. On the streets, he would jump into taxis with destinations he decided on at a whim. The chatter of the other passengers—on the politics of the day, the price of fuel, or the antics of a celebrity—comforted him, even though he never joined the discussion. Sometimes he forgot where he was going and had to be reminded by the taxi driver. The drivers cast him suspicious looks as he got out of their cars. Upon disembarking, he would stand in a daze, looking at the people swirling around him, their lives brimming with a purpose that propelled them like soldier ants. He had to step out of the way many times.

He ate street food drenched in cooking oil, hot from charcoal fires. As he received the food into his depths, he thought of the quiet knowing of the earth beneath him and became seized with a longing to be subsumed by its mysteries. He lurked in the shadows of trees and buildings and roadside umbrellas, praying that what was hidden would be uncovered, either by the sun and its pure light, or by the shade in whose light alone certain things could be seen. And yet no answers came.

One night, as he fought against the sinews of the water that pulled him in, a new longing took hold of him—to descend and fight, to enter the kingdom of billows below and meet his fate. He sensed that an ancient darkness would be waiting for him down there.

But it was not for this, not to be subsumed within another, to be lost beyond return, that he had left the United States, torn himself away from his parents. Gathering all his strength, he clawed and lunged upward like a cat on a leash, choking and thrashing. Jerking awake, he saw his friend moving about in the dawn, preparing to leave.

If Isaac had noticed Seth doing anything unusual in his sleep, he did not let on. He was dressed in a crisp white shirt with gray lines, his worn black shoes holding the best shine they could.

The effort required to get up halfway and swing his legs to the side of the couch was staggering. "Have a great day, bro," Seth said to his friend.

Isaac grinned as though it were a holiday.

"It's a great day already."

~ FIFTEEN ~

"GO BRING THE Mentholatum and rub my feet, *mi pikin*," Aunty Sia said to Ettie.

The slow-moving girl got to her feet, stumbling around a little to find her slippers, and then shuffled down the dark hallway, still bumping into things.

"Turn on the lights if you can't see where you're going, child," Aunty Sia called after her.

When Seth finally did meet the shy Ettie, he wondered about her relationship to Aunty Sia, for she was nothing like the sharp, observant woman. He had found her in the backyard, humming to herself in a voice that reached nearly mosquito-high pitches and arranging bright soda bottle caps in shapes. She seemed to be thirteen or so, but Isaac later confirmed that she was fifteen. Seth would find her there on several more occasions playing games like these or, even once, staring at the wall, still as a sheet of glass. Each time Seth came upon her outside the kitchen, she started and said very little. He could feel her curling into herself like a startled millipede, so he would mumble some excuse about having forgotten something and walk away.

If Ettie's movements were slow and bungling as she navigated the house, her hands were practiced and deft upon her aunt's swollen calves and feet. The smell of menthol filled the air, and Aunty Sia sighed slowly, exhaling her tiredness. "Thank you, thank you," she murmured. Ettie bent lower, her thumbs now moving in circular motions. Seth averted his eyes.

Later that night, Seth wrestled with how to ask Isaac the question. He shifted uneasily on his bumpy couch and trained his senses toward Isaac, who was lying soundless in the bed just a few feet away from Seth.

"What is wrong with Ettie?" he said at last.

Isaac laughed in a short exclamation. Then he lay still and quiet for a few moments. At last, he got up from the bed and came to sit on the floor, his back resting against the couch where Seth lay, his face turned away. When he spoke, it was in a whisper.

"It would be too much for you to know."

"If it's not too much for you, why should it be too much for me?"

Isaac made as though to turn to look at Seth and then thought better of it. "I . . . I know how much you are struggling."

Seth wondered how much he knew. "What do you mean?"

Isaac did turn to look at him this time, his eyes pleading. "Don't make me say it. I've heard you . . . at night."

"Why didn't you say anything?" Seth said, his voice hoarse.

"Would you have wanted me to?"

Seth did not answer. Silence filled the room..

~ SIXTEEN ~

EVELYN OPENED THE chest before sinking with a thud to her knees before it. It was an ancient-looking contraption made out of salvaged metal, and it creaked its complaint of neglect when she opened it. Out of it she pulled a bundle of letters. The rubber bands that held them had aged, and they snapped when she tried to wrest them off. There in her hands was the totality of written communication from the boys in the days before e-mail, before she and Alfred had bought a computer and acquired internet access for the house.

After watching the video, she had tried to put thoughts of Sam not attending her birthday party out of her head. It was futile. So she asked Alfred.

"Do you remember why Sam didn't come to my sixtieth birthday?"

"Me? No. You're the one with the good memory."

But finding the answer didn't require opening the memory vault; the more she thought about it, the more it became clear to her why he wasn't there—she just needed more proof of her hunch. Anticipation electrified her hands as she took the pile of letters to her desk and spread them. There were birthday cards from the boys, never early or on time, always a few weeks or even a month or more late. Then there were the first letters that they had ever written while away. She unfolded Sam's first letter.

Dear Mum and Dad,

How are you? America is cold. Everyone is friendly, but then they forget your name the next day. I think you would like the campus. I liked the food at first, but then I got tired of it after a month.

I have a job working for the Campus Security department. My supervisor likes to collect stamps. He even has some from Sierra Leone, the very old ones that stick themselves. To be honest, he is a little crazy—I have never seen anyone who loves stamps like him. Please write me soon so I can share some new stamps with him.

Your son,

Sam

She wondered what they had written in return and whether the stamps had been pretty. The next one in the pile was a letter from Seth. She skipped that in search of the next one from Sam, her eyes scanning for the sight of his lumpy hand.

The next few letters revealed a Sam who seemed better adjusted, who was doing well at soccer, had decided to study computer science, and made no further mention of cold weather.

The last letter Sam wrote was in 1998, the year before that most terrible year of the war.

Dear Mum and Dad,

You should think about leaving the country. The news is terrible. I am fine. . . .

Aside from the odd birthday card, the next significant written communication came from Joanna, along with the first picture of Stella.

Joanna had written as if she were Stella:

Dear Granny,

This was taken when I was dozing after a crying marathon. Being a baby is hard work.

In the picture, Stella's mouth was an ornament of flesh in her small face, and one mottled reddish hand with its pinkie extended rested on her stomach.

For the two years after Stella was born, Sam had only mentioned her in conversations in the most perfunctory way, even after Evelyn's first visit to see them. Stella was doing fine, or she had come down with a fever the other day, or she had been talking for two months now.

And yet, people at the memorial service had spoken of Sam's raging love for his daughter. How he talked of her all the time and kept pictures of her everywhere—on his phone, computer wallpaper, desk.

She re-ordered the letters, bound them with a fresh rubber band, and replaced them in the chest, closing the lid carefully. Nothing she saw had given her any indication of a Sam any different from her own Sam or shed light on why he might have lied to her about her birthday bash.

Her hunch must be true then: It was because of Joanna. Joanna of the French father and Haitian mother who, for some reason unbeknownst to Evelyn, always radiated an air of superiority. What was there for Joanna to feel superior about when she was from such a sorry country, no better than Sierra Leone, really? Joanna who said to Evelyn, without a trace of apology or discomfort, "I want Stella to be at least four when she visits Freetown. That way she'll have had some time to build up her immunity." Did Joanna think that she, Evelyn, lived in a mud hut? Did she think Evelyn would not notice that Stella was scarcely a year when she took her to Haiti?

Evelyn should have suspected something like this from the very beginning, when she and Alfred had visited the United States for Sam and Joanna's wedding. When they returned from their honeymoon, not once had Joanna volunteered to take Evelyn shopping. And once, when Sam had promised to spend the whole day with them, he had called back, apologetic, saying something had come up and he would only be able to spend a few hours. She was as certain as she was of her own name that the "something" was Joanna. There was only one course of action that could be taken now; the trick would be to deflect Joanna's suspicion until she got what she needed.

~ SEVENTEEN ~

SOMETHING ABOUT ISAAC'S look as he came into their room told Seth he was ready to speak. There was the way he cast his eyes a bit to the side and his lips flared a touch, like some hesitant bud on the threshold of bloom. He almost expected Isaac to whisper his words, but when he began speaking, his voice was steady and hard.

"Ettie didn't always live with Aunty Sia. For a while it was just me and Aunty Sia; Ettie lived next door with her family in that green house you pass every day. She had a sister with thick curling lashes and a gap between her teeth—Sarah. Ettie was a little younger than Sarah, but she looked after Sarah as though she were her mother. Sarah was dreamy and forgetful, much like Ettie is now. Ettie was so little back then, a small, pretty girl, but she would hold Sarah's hand when they crossed the street, turn Sarah's collars right side out, look around to make sure Sarah hadn't left anything before they went from the house.

"I saw this so many times when they came over. Aunty Sia used to say, 'What would Sarah ever do without Ettie?' And sometimes she would say naughtily, 'Maybe when they are grown, they will marry two brothers and live in two houses side by side.' Aunty Sia was a different person back then too."

Isaac continued, as if in a dream:

They came over a lot for Aunty Sia to braid their hair. She would chide them and sometimes even pinch them when they wouldn't sit still—you know how she is—but she loved them.

Especially Ettie. I used to watch Ettie sitting on the floor, head between Aunty Sia's knees and sometimes resting her head on one knee, eyes closed, peace on her face.

Aunty Sia would make small huffing noises, rub Vaseline on the tracks in her hair, and then eventually say in a creaky voice, "Well, how was school?" She would always slip the girls treats—toffee, bars of soap, and sometimes even money—before they left. And sometimes they hung out in the kitchen with her, and she would slip them *akara* or plantains, hot from the pan, which they would toss back and forth between their hands.

After the girls left, Aunty Sia was usually in a good mood, humming to herself, perhaps thinking a little less about her late husband and her lowered status in life.

That was before the rebels came to town.

We had all heard reports on the radio and from frightened civilians fleeing the provinces that the rebels were approaching Freetown. For the very first time in all the long years of the war, the capital, the one place we thought would always be safe, was vulnerable to be taken like everywhere else. In the weeks leading up to the rebels coming, you could sense the fear poisoning everyone. I thought, if the rebels don't kill us, the fear will, but since then, I've learned human beings don't die easy.

Some of the reports you could dismiss as rumors, and others were true. First we heard that they were at Mile 91, and then we heard that they were unlikely to come to Freetown because ECOMOG—the West African Union—soldiers were protecting it.

I heard food supplies were running low everywhere. Pa Hedjazi's son was ambushed outside his store as he locked up. Later they found him lying dazed and bloody in his BMW, the tires pulled off, the car gutted. He wept, incoherently, in Krio and Arabic. The store had been completely looted.

An old classmate of mine told me of someone he knew on a little road off of Francis Street that was selling rice. It was five times the usual price, but that's war.

I knew Aunty Sia would be home, thinking of how to prepare for the rebels—of what to hide and where we would hide in the event that they did come to Freetown. From all reports, it seemed as though they were no more than four days away. So little time. I imagined her thinking of where to hide her gold jewelry that I had only seen her wear two times. The television set, the DVD player, where could these be hidden? And yet, having our possessions stolen was the least of our worries. We all knew the awful things the rebels had already done in the provinces. You know them too—hacking off hands at the wrists or at the elbow at their whim, making bets about the gender of an unborn baby and ripping open the mother's stomach to find out. For these gun-carrying children and young men, killing, raping, and maiming was like swatting flies.

I thought, what would they want with an old lady and a skinny young man without money or possessions. I was such a fool in those days.

That day I went out looking for food. People walked by me in a hurry. It was a Freetown you could not imagine. The few taxis that were running were charging three times the price. I only had money for food, so I had to walk. I saw two men on the other side of the road carrying a fifty-pound bag of rice between them as if it were a sick person. They kept their eyes down.

'Are you crazy?' somebody yelled to them. 'If you don't watch out, you'll be lying dead in the gutter for a bag of rice. This is not the same country as before.'

They hurried all the more and then disappeared down an alley. I passed several amputees and beggars sitting by the side of the road, their legs crossed, holding up stumps. No one even looked at them. I even saw a little boy of no more than three or four screaming, alone on the street. After casting a hurried glance, people simply kept walking.

I headed down Waters Street thinking from there to branch off to McCauley Street and then two other smaller roads before getting to Francis Street.

'Turn back!' I heard somebody shouting, and people were coming toward me on Waters Street shaking their heads, too scared to even speak. In a city of free talk, there had come a time when we had nothing to say. It seemed the ECOMOG soldiers were barricading that street; why, I didn't know, but perhaps they were trying to fence off certain parts of the city. I turned around, trying to map in my head another way to get to Francis Street. The only other way I could think of was around Tengbe Road. But there was a six o'clock curfew. The ECOMOG soldiers had warned that they would fire at anyone who disobeyed curfew, even civilians. It was that brutal.

I weighed the risk. We had been living hand-to-mouth for a while. With food already so scarce and expensive, we had not been able to buy even a few extra pounds of rice, let alone a bag. We had a liter of palm oil left and one powdered milk tin filled with *gari*. If the city were to fall under 24-hour curfew, even with just me and Aunty Sia, we could make it no more than two days before running out of food. In the provinces, those who flee into the bush can find something to eat. Not so in the city. I could have tried to make it out for food the next day, but by then, that source might have dried up. If I began to jog, perhaps I would be able to make it along the Loop Road route. Yes, I could be shot for breaking curfew, but that was a chance I would have to take. And so I did that, picking up the pace, noting that other people were walking so fast that at times they broke into a jog.

I had been doing this for an hour or so, becoming so tired I thought I would faint. After a while, I just wanted to lie down on the ground and give up. But through some strange strength, I kept going. I passed an old friend of mine. We were going in opposite directions, and we stopped for the briefest of moments to talk to one another. He said the government report that the rebels were some four days away was erroneous and that even the BBC seemed to have no clear idea, but his guess was that it was more like two days. Only two days to prepare ourselves. I grew cold at the thought. He was off to check on his older sister, who had just had a baby, and spend the night there before heading off to his family's house in the morning. We shook hands before we resumed our frantic journeys, and I wondered if I would ever see him again or, if God did bless us with such an encounter, if both of us would be whole.

I heard gunfire in the distance in rapid succession, and women around me began to shriek. It wasn't the first time we had heard gunshots with the ECOMOG soldiers around, but usually they were not in rapid succession like that. By this time, I was maybe a mile away from Francis Street. I was beginning to doubt whether, even if I got my goods quickly, I would be able to return home on time. I kept thinking about those at home, not only Aunty Sia, who I lived with, but my little sister and my other brother, who I supposed were at home with their father and his new woman. I hadn't spoken to them in over a week, and when I tried to over the past few days, all the lines had been down.

I saw a man throwing possessions from the window of one house, as though he had gone mad. People walking on the street below ducked and cursed.

'What do you think you're doing?'

Maybe he didn't want to have anything of value when the rebels came.

I finally got to Francis Street, only to find the house I had been told about locked. It was a bitter disappointment. One frightened and confused woman outside told me that the owners had run out of food and then locked the shop, fearful that whatever remaining supplies they had would be looted. In any case, she told me, there had been a line, and I probably would not have been able to get anything before curfew anyway.

It was bitter news, but I had no time to waste contemplating it. I turned around, orienting myself toward home as fast as I could. It was growing dark. I heard wails in the distance and wondered what they were about. At this point, had there been any taxis on the road, I would have been sorely tempted to use the food money on a ride. Private cars were stopping for no one, for it was an atmosphere of distrust. No one could blame them, for who knew? Some people may be rebel sympathizers.

I looked at my watch. It was only an hour to curfew, and I wasn't sure I'd be able to make it on time, but I was too tired to jog. I just kept walking and thought, whatever happens, happens. Then I noticed people looking off in the distance. I turned too and saw a large crowd coming down the street. It was not a wide street. I quickly went down a side street to avoid them but then saw that there were already tons of people milling, running, pushing on the main street I had just been on. 'The rebels are here! Run! They are already in the east and are pushing into the city,' people were shouting.

I ran faster than I knew I could run. I stepped on something soft that cried out—a person lying there, no doubt—but I never turned to look.

It was dark already. There was no power in the city; not a single streetlight was on. The few cars that were on the road had been abandoned. Their drivers must have been forced to halt and had to flee on foot like everybody else. There were so many of us that we were almost touching each other, even though we could barely see one another. Then I saw headlights switched on from a side street, shining on us as we passed by, and then I noted, in this light that now seemed too bright, that some of the men and boys had long objects bulging beneath their shirts. A chill went down my spine as I realized that these were rebels. They were already with us, trying to hide among us.

Later we learned that the rebels had been successful in capturing Freetown in part because they had used humans as shields. Frightened civilians fleeing the east into the center of the city had no idea that they were being joined by rebels in civilian clothing until it was too late.

Somehow I managed to make it home. Aunty Sia was waiting in total darkness. I told her what I had seen. We spoke in the dark, afraid even to light a candle. Sleep would be impossible.

At daybreak we went to our neighbors, the Karews, Ettie and Sarah's family. The Karews were like family. We had all lived together, sharing news of loved ones overseas, of deaths and accomplishments, and, of late, the war. We had heard gunshots throughout the night. When they opened the door for us, after peering through the side window to make sure we were unaccompanied, they simply embraced us for they knew why we were there. We were in this together. There was Mr. Karew, his wife, and Sarah and Ettie. Their son Junior, who was close to my age, had died three years prior in a tragic accident.

We were with them the whole day and together we stayed up all night beginning to doze before dawn. They came in the morning. We heard loud pounding on the door, shouts of 'Open this door!' and then a battering. By that time, we had already hidden the two girls, Ettie within a hamper under a pile of dirty clothes, Sarah under a bed with boxes obscuring her. We adults stayed to face our fate.

There were three of them: a thick-muscled and very dark dude who appeared to be in his late twenties, a shaved-head one with warts on his scalp who appeared to be about eighteen, and a boy of about twelve with a long scar on his cheek. The oldest wore heavily tinted sunglasses, so we could not see his eyes, but he grinned benevolently at us like a godfather. He wore combat khakis and a tight University of Michigan T-shirt.

The kid glared at us as he swiveled his AK-47 to aim at each of us in turn. He was fully dressed in a combat uniform much too large for him. The teen was out of it and seemed to be sick because he kept coughing a loose, gargly cough.

We said not a word and watched them, too stiff with fear to do anything. The oldest one was chewing gum like a goat. He settled himself into one of the Karews' armchairs and looked up at the kid.

'Well, here's your chance to make up for your previous mistakes,' he said.

The kid blinked furiously and gripped his AK-47 even tighter. 'Idiots. Don't you know what to do when you see a gun pointed at you?' he barked. 'Drop to your knees and put your hands up, or I'll hit you so hard I'll make your mothers' stomachs tremble.' We obeyed at once without a word.

The teen disappeared into the house, and we heard drawers being opened, thuds, and other rummaging noises. The man with the shades had spotted a cabinet with a few bottles of alcohol in it. He went to inspect it and came back with a bottle of whiskey in one hand and a glass in the other and then resettled himself in his armchair to pour his drink.

We heard a scream from the interior of the house, and the teen returned dragging a screaming, crying Sarah. He slapped her on the back, making her cry out even more.

'If you don't stop squealing, I'll really give you something to squeal about,' he said, pushing her to the floor. She stopped the noise right away but trembled like a tin house as she knelt beside us and put her hands up.

'We hear you bastards are peacekeeping with the so-called sympathizing forces,' said the kid, and then realizing he had jumbled his words, corrected his sentence in a more aggressive voice, as if to compensate for his embarrassment.

The teen kept bringing things to the living room. It was an odd assortment: a school backpack that belonged to one of the girls, an iron, an electric fan, a CD player.

It wasn't long before he found Ettie. We knew only when he appeared pulling her by the arm. Ettie was always quiet and self-contained. She didn't make a sound, but of course you could see from her eyes that she was terrified. He pushed her to the floor and instructed her to do as the rest of us were doing.

I looked over at Aunty Sia and saw her struggling to keep her hands up.

'This junk is of no use to us,' continued the kid, motioning with his chin to the growing pile being created by his fellow rebel. 'We need money. We eat money. We have a war to fight. You.' He pointed the gun at Mr. Karew. 'Go get us some, and if you are lucky, we will not kill too many of you.'

Mr. Karew began babbling something like 'yes, whatever you say,' and went into their bedroom. He returned in a few minutes.

'This is all we have in cash, but whatever else you see in the house, take—'

'How much is that?' The teen grabbed the money from Mr. Karew's hand and counted it with movements as practiced as a bank teller. 'Four hundred thousand leones,' he announced without looking up.

'Is that how much you want to insult us with? Four hundred thousand worthless leones?' screamed the kid.

The oldest rebel had filled his glass again. His legs were stretched out in front of him, but in the first sign of restlessness I had seen from him, he looked at his watch.

'Lt. Cold Blood, we cannot stay here all day,' he said. 'We have more duties to attend to. And isn't there something you are forgetting?'

The boy's face went blank for a moment, then a jolt of recognition passed across it, and he opened his mouth to scream the next insult. But he was interrupted by the man.

'Never mind.' The man took off his glasses so we could see him better. He had the eyes of a corpse—bloody and dull. It was truly frightful.

'Worse than being supporters of these so-called peacekeepers, our sources tell us that you were somehow involved in our shit-hole of a government.' Here he got up, walked over to Mr. Karew, and in a quick movement kicked him in the groin. The man keeled over, clutching himself.

'But it's not true. I have never been involved with this government,' said Mr. Karew, breathless.

'That's what they all say,' sneered the man. 'However, we cannot take that chance.'

He snapped his fingers in the direction of the kid. 'It seems they are all of one family, though I am not sure about those two.' He pointed at me and Aunty Sia.

'Who are you?' he shouted at us and came toward me, turning his gun as if to hit me with the butt of it.

I can't explain to you my emotions in that moment, Seth. All I remember now is that in that moment, I couldn't even remember my name. The kid waved his gun in an arc, his face contorted into a sneer, but even that couldn't hide his uncertainty. The man turned to look at him with scorn.

'What have I taught you, Lt. Cold Blood? It's always more interesting when done another way.' The room was quiet. The man put his sunglasses back on. I have no idea how he was able to see a thing in the room. Unfortunately for us, the effect was even more frightening than when he had first taken them off because now we could not see who he was looking at or guess what he might be thinking.

'Both of your daughters will have to come with us,' he pronounced. At this, both parents cried out. The man broke into a smile.

'Would you rather we kill them both before your eyes?' The parents began pleading that they kill them instead. They called the name of their son who was already dead and begged for mercy that their two remaining children be allowed to live.

'Well, perhaps we will only take the older one then. The other one is still too young to be of use.'

From out of nowhere, the teen produced a large nylon shopping bag, and he began to load the goods into it.

'Well then,' continued the man. 'People say that we rebels are unreasonable, unmerciful, but that is not the case. We do not kill when it is unnecessary. But understand that there has to be a due penalty for your acts of treachery. We will start with the eldest first, with granny over here, and work our way down.'

He looked at us to see what effect this announcement would have on us. It began to dawn on me that this was all about the thrill of the chase for him, that the act of killing had become so routine that he had to draw it out in twisted ways to get any pleasure out of it.

'What is this granny worth to you?' he said, raising his voice as he looked around.

The kid aimed his gun at her. There was a small gasp from Ettie. Aunty Sia moved not a muscle in her face, but she did speak.

'I have lived my life,' said Aunty Sia. 'Kill me and let these good people live. They have not been involved in—'

'Shut up, old hag. Did I ask you to speak?' hissed the man. 'So she is not worth—' He turned to Ettie, who had gasped, now weeping, tears streaming down her face.

'Aha, somebody's beloved grandmother, I see.'

He took a step closer to Aunty Sia, smiling. Ettie was closer to Aunty Sia than anyone in the family, even more so than Sarah.

The kid, seeing his chance to assert himself, aimed his gun at Aunty Sia and curled his finger around the trigger. I felt I should do something, jump up and push the gun away, distract the man; after all, it was my duty to protect Aunty Sia. But, Seth, I'm ashamed to say I couldn't move. It was as if my blood had leaked out of me, and even my voice was gone.

Then to our shock, we all heard Ettie say, 'I am crying not for her but because you want to take my sister away from me.' She was only eight at the time; a little girl. We were all stunned at her boldness in speaking.

'The granny is just our neighbor, not family, so it doesn't matter if you kill her.'

I knew her ploy was to front the pretense that Aunty Sia meant nothing to us, thus taking away the rebels' pleasure in making us suffer by killing her. But I was stunned that at eight, she had the presence of mind to do that.

The kid lowered his gun and looked at the man, confused. It seemed he was not used to such occurrences. From outside we heard a burst of gunfire and the blaring of vehicle horns. The teen who had been busy packing up the goods sighed. He had squeezed as much as he could into the plastic bag and then bundled up the rest in a bed sheet from one of the rooms.

'How long will you continue this love fest with this family? And can't you see the girl is trying to play you?' he asked. The man and the kid turned to look at him. The teen came closer to us. I realized he must be older than I had judged him to be.

He turned to look at Ettie. I couldn't breathe; none of us could.

"Little girl, you think you're smart, eh? Well, we don't like people who think they're smarter than us."

He pointed the rifle at Ettie.

"Eeeeee!" cried Mrs. Karew, bleating like a sheep.

Ettie closed her eyes, trembling and crying.

Then he lowered the rifle and walked toward Ettie. He grabbed her hand and forced her to hold the rifle. She screamed like there was blood gushing out of her. We all began to scream and wail.

Lt. Cold Blood came to help hold her steady. They held up her arm, kept her finger curled around the trigger, pointed it first at Mrs. Karew. I closed my eyes. I couldn't bear to watch. All I heard was the noise. And then another. And the screaming was less for fewer of us remained to scream.

Isaac stopped talking and began to weep, and Seth tried to regain awareness of his thoughts, feeling as though he too had been shot. Even though he had not lived the experience and had only just heard it, he could not hold it in him, could not take in any more pain, anymore than the drinking glasses he had hurled against the wall could now hold water. In this way, he understood the measure to which he had shattered and wondered if he could be of any use to anyone ever again. Feeling helpless, he nonetheless put a hand on Isaac's shoulder.

"I'm sorry I made you remember all this again."

"I need to," Isaac said in a raspy voice.

"What happened to Sarah?"

"They took her with them. We never saw or heard anything about Sarah again, but we heard of many other girls and women who were abducted when the rebels were chased out of Freetown a week later."

"Oh, Isaac," Seth said.

Isaac turned toward him, his cheeks wet.

"For years after, I was an old man inside, Seth. And then one day, I couldn't tell if I felt old or young. I just was."

~ EIGHTEEN ~

IN THIS ONE thing, his mind, which otherwise worked against him like wind taunting loose hair on a stormy day, cooperated. He could not think of the story Isaac had told him about Ettie and Aunty Sia. He did not have the reserves to stomach the sadness it brought, so he cast it from his mind. But he could not rid himself of the image of Ettie rubbing the old woman's legs, her hands shining with Mentholatum, her head bending lower as the old woman groaned in relief, the ritual like a sacred cup passed between them.

To rid himself of this image, he thought to take to the streets again, though he knew they were devoid of revelation for him. He heard himself ask the taxi driver to take him to the restaurant where he and Isaac had eaten together when they first reconnected. The food appeared before him, and he looked at it, not quite hungry and not sure what he was supposed to do next. He waved away the boys hawking newspapers and plastic-bodied made-in-China goods. The young waitress came by and gave him a sweet smile, cocking her head like a keen-eyed bird.

"You're not eating, sir. Do you not like the food?"

He looked at her hopeful face, her neat cornrows, evenly spaced like rows of grain that would yield their fruit in season again and again.

"Thank you," he said to the waitress. "It's very good, but I'm not as hungry as I thought. You can take it away."

She frowned briefly, then nodded and lifted his plate.

As he left, he saw three young men clustered against the wall of the restaurant, lounging in the shade of a mango tree. A fourth was directing a Land Rover into a parking spot.

With no idea of where else he might go, Seth stopped and turned toward the men.

"May I join you for a minute?"

They looked at him with surprise for a moment and then eased into smiles.

"Join us, *bra*," said the one who had been directing the woman in the Land Rover. Seth could tell that he was the alpha male. He nodded, and one of the other men, a thin man with a broad, puckered face, slipped away and returned with a chair for Seth.

Seth regretted not being a smoker, not having a packet of cigarettes to pull out and share with them, so he contented himself with sharing his name and asking for theirs while cracking a joke about needing the secret to the men's cool and collected vibe.

The young men laughed, gracious, and ribbed back that by the time Seth was done visiting with them, he would have the secret. Seth mistrusted the yearning that threatened to spill out of his eyes or ride up and out through his voice, so he tried to keep the conversation light—weather, sports, the big evangelist holding a crusade in town. And yet as they watched people coming and going from the restaurant and as the leaves whispered softly above them, the conversation turned to other things.

The young men told him a bit of their stories, of how the civil war fanned out like an oil spill, so they fled the provinces for Freetown. They told him of fleeing Freetown, traveling across the border to neighboring Guinea, and bitterly realizing Guinea would never be home. They whispered of all they had lost, even their families, and of what they tried to regain that slipped like water through cupped hands. And then they murmured darkly of things without naming the things; things that happened to one, perhaps two of them, when they were forced to join the rebels, were made to turn on their relatives; of communities, homes, where they were no longer welcome.

Seth considered the unspoken words, remembered the common stories of war, so many, so different, yet so similar in their hallmark of terror—the severing of hands, the turning of children into killing machines, the baptizing of peaceful farmers into henchmen of death.

"How do you survive?" he asked them.

"We are *dreg-man dem*," replied the alpha, speaking for his companions. "We hustle, we beg where we have to. And you," he said, peering at Seth, "what brings you back to Freetown?"

"I came to get my head straight," he said, wishing he could say more and relieve such a great load, but *The Thing* could not be spoken of. But because they kept looking at him with such sympathy, he told them of his brother's death, his separation from his parents and from Gaia, and the loss of his worldly goods, somehow managing to keep from them the salient point that it was he who had divested himself of his possessions.

He looked at them furtively; they nodded with understanding, not making light of his plight, even though he, relative to them, had lost little. "*Alman ge den yone*. Everyone is dealing with their own sorrow," said one of the men who had rarely spoken thus far. He absently massaged his wrist with a large-veined hand.

His companions murmured in agreement.

"Everyone thinks they are suffering alone, but when you talk to other people, you find out that we are all wretched together," lamented the man with the puckered face, emotion raising his voice to a slight moan.

"Like children abandoned by their mother to the street," cried the alpha with poetry in his voice, carried away, it seemed, by the pathos of the moment. "Oh, Sierra Leone. It's like we've been cursed. But even suffering has to end one day. God will feel sorry for us."

Seth groped for words and had nothing to say, so he merely moaned in solidarity. A cool breeze from the sea with a faint odor of rot rippled down the street, and the men leaned back to enjoy its caress, once again as peaceful as lizards in the sun. He leaned back with them, and together they watched the people passing by: women with African print dresses beautiful as butterfly wings; young boys holding tin trays of wares, eyes darting about for customers; men in striped shirts laughing into phones or hailing taxis. An ordinary day in the city.

Yet now he could feel what he hadn't felt before—the ghosts groaning in the ground beneath them, the dark moltenness upon which this city floated, like an island upon a sea of magma.

The men were laughing now, joking about the latest episode of a radio soap opera featuring a con artist and the unsuspecting family he worked for. Seth got up to leave. He shook their hands, slipping a few bills into the hand of the alpha and asking him to divide it up. The men nodded at him with appreciation. The thinnest one of the lot looked up at Seth with haunted eyes and a gap-tooth smile and said, "At least the war is over now."

"Yes," Seth said as he nodded in agreement, but the statement somehow felt like a lie.

He had barely gone two hundred paces down the road when he decided to return and ask the men if they hung out outside that restaurant often. Perhaps he could sit with them again during one of his wanderings in the city. They were sitting in exactly the same tableau he had left them in. He looked toward the alpha who regarded him with a somewhat flat expression and then a slight raising of the eyebrows.

"We should do this again," he began. "How often do you guys hang out here?"

The alpha furrowed his brow. "Excuse me, have we met?"

Seth laughed. "That was convincing. What, you an actor or something?"

The man turned to look at his companions, puzzled. "I'm sorry. What are you talking about? I've never met you before."

Seth felt a surge of irritation at this extended role play but as he looked at the other men's faces, he saw that they too were genuinely quizzical. There was no trace of recognition in their faces for Seth.

Seth turned and fled down the street.

~ NINETEEN ~

IN THE DARK room, the TV cast shape-shifting waves of color on their faces like impetuous disco lights. Isaac sat in an armchair, spindly legs splayed, cawing with laughter at the show every now and then. Aunty Sia lay on the sofa, legs elevated on one armrest. And Ettie sat on the floor in front of the sofa, short braids sticking out of her head like antennae, covering her mouth when the funniest parts of the show brought up little giggles.

Telling his hosts he was stepping out for fresh air, Seth went to the front porch. Since the event with the men, he had spent much of the time Isaac was gone during the day sitting on his couch-bed holding his shoulders, listening to his breath whistle through the cavities of his being. Psychosis. The word had seemed both terrifying and reassuring on his computer screen. It was like a handle on a door that could be opened and then shut again to conceal the terror that lay behind it. And yet at the time, his eyes had darted away from the word as he felt the familiar heave of defiance within him. This "illness" was an alien creature within him; it was not of him.

When he was little, his parents had had a friend who was building a house in the neighborhood. Uncle Elliot, he and Sam called him. And every time he stopped by, he politely asked the boys how school was and sometimes slipped them small bills, which they ran off with gleefully. To the boys' parents, he spoke of the rising cost of cement and the idiocy of slow-fingered workers and long trips to far beaches for the harvesting of sand.

Over the years, Uncle Elliot had begun to sound increasingly erratic, his voice rising to a shout as he repeated the same stories of the workers, telling their parents that when his house was finished, his troubles would be over, for he would be able to rent it for a small fortune—enough to retire, enough to prove to that thieving brother of his that despite cheating him out of the family inheritance, he had done well.

Seth had overheard Evelyn and Alfred speaking in whispers about how the house was driving Elliot mad, and no wonder his wife had left him, and perhaps his sister would take him in as he continued his downward spiral. But how would she deal with the incoherence, his uncontrollable outbursts, his depression?

If madness had descended upon someone he knew, someone who had once looked at Seth with the sharp, keen eyes of a bird, then was it so farfetched that it could happen to Seth? Was the beast in the swamp, the creature of air and still water, no more than the vaporous exhale of a rotted mind? And if so, would he get worse like Uncle Elliot had?

He could always go back and submit like a tamed cat to Dr. Holland's regimes. Take medication. Learn what he was supposed to do to be perceived normal enough to work. And would it be the kind of work that he did before, or would he have to work at a grocery checkout line?

Isaac stepped out onto the porch to join him.

"I need to ask you a favor."

"Yes?"

"Can you stand in for me with my economics tutorial in a couple weeks?"

"What?"

"You know, the class I teach at the house. I have an event at school I need to stay late for."

Seth looked at his friend—the scratchy hair, the gaunt face, the eyes sparkling as ever with an abundant amity.

How could he refuse Isaac? How could he leave him to return to the States? Yet, how could he not?

"Sure, man." And whether it was a lie or the truth, he did not know.

~ TWENTY ~

"THE BLOOD OF Jesus is against you." Seth felt the palm pressing down on his head, the fingers constricting around his scalp. Pastor Promise had lowered his voice to a hiss, his tone even and hard. With his other hand, he grabbed Seth's forehead and began to push him back, all the while repeating, "You, Water Spirit, the blood of Jesus is against you."

Seth had seen the ubiquitous signs of "deliverance ministries," promising freedom from satanic oppression, poverty, and illness. Such ministries existed in Atlanta too, usually run by impassioned West African evangelists peddling tales of *juju* and the omnipresence of Satan and his minions in every fiber of life. He remembered that The Mayor was rumored to have overcome a drinking problem through the ministrations of such a preacher.

For a while he had thought that the way forward was to go back—to accept the Dr. Holland's verdict and thus his prescribed treatment. He had even gone so far as to call Joanna, asking her if she would mail his prescription to him if he called it in.

"Are you sure you need it?"

"Looks like I need it," he said. But the hesitancy in her voice had been enough to send his original defiance roaring back. He would not be able to bring himself to take the medicine.

Just behind Seth were two ushers, uttering impassioned "amens" to the pastor's pronouncement, covering cloths draped over their arms. Seth resisted the pastor's force, stiffening as he felt the hot breath from the seething mouth of the man of God.

He somehow didn't feel "taken" by the Spirit in any way that made him want to fall.

He wondered now, as he had when debating whether to come, how such a process could work on him. He hadn't even told Isaac of his plans. Not that he had ever doubted God's existence or the sovereignty of Jesus; it was a more a matter of suspecting that more was required of him. It was not enough to merely accept God's existence but to desire and yield to him. But how could he love one whom he had never experienced and trust one whom he did not know?

What if I don't know if I believe in Jesus in the way I'm supposed to? Seth had asked the man of God earlier.

You must.

But what if I can't?

The demons will still answer him.

But how do you know it's a demon.

What you've described—the creature in the swamp—it is a water spirit. Classic case.

The fingers kept clenching like pincers around Seth's head, and he felt the palms steadily pushing him backward. He did not want to fall. He did not want to lose control nor entrust himself to the arms of the waif-like ushers. But what if this was what Pastor Promise was expecting?

Then, for some reason, he thought of a bridge over water and under its curvature a concrete wall lined with cracks and drips of moisture. The ground was paved with cardboard boxes and boxes, and here and there were carts filled with reusable shopping bags. He could hear the rush of cars overhead and feel the slight shudder of the ground beneath him. And then he felt leaded and soaked with weight, as though gravity had folded in upon itself and become condensed, pulling him into its heart. He found himself wanting to fold like a multi-flapped box that by some trick, some origami wizardry, could halve its volume again and again until it was gone. His heart lifted at the thought of disappearing, of dying.

"Spirit of death," said the man of God, his voice low and gritty like the sound of gears grinding. "I rebuke you in the name of Jesus." His head was bowed over Seth's, palms over Seth's ears so he heard a roar like the cry of the ocean. And then there was silence as though someone had simply hit the mute button on life.

~

WHEN HE CAME to, he felt warm hands on his body—Pastor Promise pushing down ever so gently on his belly. Seth heard a gurgling within it as though he had just drunk water and it was swirling through his innards. Over him was spread a green cloth upon which the man's hands rested. He turned to his side and retched into a wide-mouthed plastic cup that seemed to appear out of nowhere.

Pastor Promise saw that he was awake. "Be free, in the name of Jesus, my brother." His voice was kinder now, the grittiness gone.

Seth looked at him blankly, uncomprehending.

"Buy my book on water spirits. Ask one of the ushers for it on the way out."

The ushers were standing to the side looking bored. Seth wondered how often they witnessed such an occurrence and how dramatic it was. Did people froth at the mouth and convulse? Spit out profanity in bestial voices? He tried to take a measure of his feelings and noted above all that he felt disoriented, as though he were a machine that had been taken apart and reassembled with a slight difference.

But Pastor Promise was offering him a hand up now. A young man came to the side door of the sanctuary, which was empty but for Seth and the trio presiding over him. The man nodded, and Pastor Promise looked at his watch.

"Be vigilant," he said to Seth. "Call on Jesus. Come back and see us."

"Am I free to go?"

"You are truly free."

And Seth got to his feet uncertainly, realizing he didn't remember what freedom felt like.

Each of the next few nights, he grew rigid upon his couch-bed, too afraid to hope, too afraid to sleep. He thought of the favor that Isaac had asked him, and it seemed impossible to execute. Yet he saw again the bridge of wet concrete and the cardboard slabs, but he no longer felt drawn to them.

Isaac sensed his concern. "You'll do fine," he said to Seth one day in their room.

One night, on its own accord, his body fell into a deep, sodden sleep. He awoke the next morning with no memories of the night. He checked his body, which was unmarred by recent scratches.

It was like that the next night and the next few ones as well. Silence and dreamless sleep. In the mornings he breathed heavily and sat up dazed, afraid to believe that he was free. He took the economics book with him outside and tried to read a few pages.

~ TWENTY-ONE ~

"Is it true that you live in America?" said the girl with the spiral plaits.

"Used to," responded Seth. "Now if you can turn to page seventy-three of your economics book."

The kids made no such move to open their books, indeed, gave no indication that they had even heard him. They had arrived within a ten-minute span of each other and, after giving him a perfunctory greeting, took seats around the dining table and busied themselves with their phones. Until the spiral-plaited girl asked the question, unabashed, and they all looked up.

Isaac must have mentioned to them that Seth lived in America. There was a term for Sierra Leonean returnees—*juscam*. Jokes about them abounded, including that you could literally smell their aura, like the human equivalent of a new car smell—the grime, the plague-like dust, the malarial fevers having been purged from them by houses with cotton-soft conditioned air, industrious machines, and fabric softeners scented like candy.

"Is it true that America is dangerous, you know, with all the gangs and the gunfights?" Joseph pressed.

"Well—"

"Is it hard to get rich in America?" asked another boy. Seth realized he had already forgotten his name. "Mr. Sesay said you're rich."

"Eh? Rich?"

The kids were looking at him in admiration. It had not always been this way. Once he was a boy who had wondered what it would be like to be admired.

"Seth has not done well," the instructor told Evelyn one day when she came to pick the boys up from summer school. Seth had been idle, distracted, the teacher said. He had dawdled in the book corner, playing with Victor, who was notoriously slow. Evelyn would have to encourage him to try harder, the woman said. "He is not too young to be taking his education seriously."

Evelyn narrowed her eyes; Seth knew harsh words would follow.

"My uncle says the best thing to do if you're in America is study nursing. They need nurses," the spiral-plaited girl said solemnly to the other boy, donning the mantle of authority on the matter. Now she turned to Seth for confirmation. "Is it true?"

Seth thought of the nurses he knew. Friends of Gaia. Friends of his. Friends of the friends of theirs. Many more than would have a natural aptitude for nursing. "Ah, nursing," he had heard people say when someone mentioned that was what they did. "Great job security and good pay," they would say, while heads bobbed upon necks in approval.

Sometimes he heard the nurses he knew complain of the dirty work of stemming the tide of death and decay, the sadness of watching patients neglected by close relatives as they succumbed to the entropy of their bodies. But mostly, they endured the work. He had never asked any of them whether they liked it.

"With all due respect to your uncle, that is bad advice," he said, his words riding a surge of emotion that surprised him.

"Mr. Kargbo says you are good at maths," said another girl after a long pause.

"I guess so. Why?"

"Can you look over my homework for me?"

"And mine too."

"And mine too."

Seth was only too relieved for a diversion from the struggling economics lesson. Surely Isaac wouldn't mind. The kids too grew excited, happy for a break in their routine. As he looked over the first book, he thought back to bending over that other book so many years ago, the numbers scurrying like ants on the page. Victor's book. How long had it been?

He could still remember the dejection that hung around those days like the smell of pee lingering in dank stairways. The days when no one thought much of him.

"Come to the board, Seth," Mrs. Nichols had said. "Show us that you can learn while talking in class."

But he had been whispering, not talking, to Victor. Victor didn't seem to put any effort into his work for it was generally accepted that he was a slow child with a placid face and disquietingly big forehead, thoughts thick as gruel. He didn't even seem to mind the beatings anymore, tearing up briefly, and then returning to his usual monochromatic placidity moments afterward. And as for Seth, it was accepted that he was mediocre, if not stupid.

But Seth had been making himself do badly—not quite as badly as Victor, but not well—in solidarity with the boy. He and Victor were among the ones who were caned for being the worst performers.

Thinking back on this, Seth grew angry as he remembered their frequent punishment with no attempt to help them learn or find out why they were doing so poorly. Once Mrs. Nichols had stood by Victor, berating him for his abysmal scores on his homework assignment, while he had looked up at her half-grinning, half-penitent in a confused and goofy way.

From that point on, because Seth sat next to Victor, he tried to whisper answers to him and thought maybe some time he could explain to Victor how to do the sums. But Mrs. Nichols had called him out before then. He could still remember the walk to the blackboard, the comfortless, cratered concrete floor beneath his feet. He broke the chalk upon his first stroke, he was so nervous. They laughed. But as he wrote, his stub of chalk clattering on the blackboard, they all stopped laughing.

Reviewing the children's work, he did not notice Isaac's sudden appearance but looked up at the sound of the deep voice. He was there, smiling and easygoing, explaining how he got done sooner than expected with his meeting.

That night, they discussed how the lesson had gone, Seth perched on the front porch railing and Isaac on a seat strung with nylon. After Seth explained how the session had digressed into a math tutorial, Isaac lifted his head, electrified by a thought.

"You know, Seth, maybe this is your mission. Maybe you could start giving maths lessons. There's great demand for it. There's only three good maths teachers in the city. You could help a lot of children, you know. Even Ettie. Especially Ettie. You could do a lot of good."

Once he had desperately wanted to do good. To pull himself and others out of the slow, smoldering fire of mediocrity, or what was deemed stupidity. Then math had opened a secret passage made only for him, and he had walked through and emerged into another life. But he had not done good. He could no longer remember what had happened to Victor for he had simply stopped noticing him.

Now the memory of that day came roaring back—the towering expanse of that blackboard overlaid with its milky wash of chalk, the eyes burning into his back, the chalk breaking.

As he lay awake on his couch-bed that night, he understood what he must do, though whether he would be able to do it remained a mystery. He had not dreamed of the swamp since his visit with Pastor Promise. He tried the new name for *The Thing* on his lips—Water Spirit. A memory stirred of swiveling and turning in dense water.

"Be gone," he said and closed his eyes.

~ TWENTY-TWO ~

EVELYN TOLD HERSELF she didn't like American TV, but she watched it for hours on end anyway—talk show hosts peddling in the shame of people's lives like greed-tainted merchants, garrulous lawyers braying about the money to be made from injuries, and on and on. But she liked the commercials best. Who would have thought that you could sell devices for washing your feet in the bathtub without bending down? Or a contraption for hanging strips of bacon in the microwave?

Mercifully, the memories had not followed her. It was as though when she spurned them again, they retreated into the walls of the house that had swallowed Sam's essence into itself. Perhaps it was only in that place that gave them being that they could defy her.

At first, she was appalled that Joanna didn't make breakfast for her in the morning as Evelyn would have done had the tables been turned. Some things simply could not be excused by the fact that the girl was American; after all, wasn't hospitality—and some measure of deference to one's in-laws—a universal custom? When she first arrived at the house after a lackluster reception from Joanna at the airport, Joanna had simply pointed out where everything was, raising her voice above Stella's whimpers, for something had gotten into her, it seemed. No doubt it was the presence of the strange woman that she was being told was her grandmother. She had looked at Evelyn warily at the airport and held her hands firmly at her side when Evelyn tried to give her an awkward hug.

Evelyn's early fears—that living in this house with Sam's wife and child would embolden memories that would arise to haunt her—did not materialize. In fact, it was the opposite. Removed from her own house and family, where the memories thickened like cobwebs in every corner, there was the stillness of a wilderness. Her mind could focus on the task at hand—prying the secret to the change in Sam out of Joanna.

"Why are you going, Evelyn?" Alfred had asked.

"Stella needs us," she replied.

"Why are you going now?"

She countered that she could go later—if he would go with her, if he needed more time to prepare.

He hesitated, then gave her a pointed look. "Joanna is, well, she's been through a lot."

She met his gaze, told him it was all the more reason why he should come—to shore up the support to Joanna. It was as she expected; he did not contradict or clarify. As usual, she had judged him perfectly. He raised a hand and let it fall. She inquired about his headache in soft tones. In the distance a motorbike blared. From within the house, dust drifted inexorably to the ground.

Joanna left home at about 7:30 each morning and dropped Stella off at kindergarten on her way to work. Evelyn had suggested that since she was here, perhaps Stella could stay with her during the day sometimes. Joanna had said, "Sure, as soon as Stella gets used to you a little bit more." Evelyn stiffened when she heard this. She had never heard such a ridiculous or more insulting thing, but this was America, where children got treated like adults and adults insulted their elders.

The truth of the matter was that they both knew the only reason for them to maintain contact was Stella. Evelyn felt that she was on solid footing representing her son's stake in the girl. What did it matter, then, if in the process she decided to find out what Joanna had done to Sam?

But Joanna spoke little of Sam. When she did, she was matter-of-fact and unsentimental. She mentioned once that Sam had set them up with a telephone service whose charges kept going up, and she was going to have to switch carriers. While driving into the city one day, she pointed out flatly where he used to work.

Joanna was a graphic designer, an artistic type. After Sam died, she had moved to a smaller house. Still, the house was big and comfortable enough, with three large bedrooms and a great room with a vaulted ceiling.

When Joanna and Stella were not home, Evelyn devoured their surroundings. She would go into Joanna's bedroom looking for traces of Sam. But, of course, Joanna had already gotten rid of all his things, as Evelyn knew she would, except for some framed photos here and there. Evelyn had already gone through their photo albums. There were few pictures in them. Most of what they had must be those electronic pictures, she reckoned, that people took, and afterwards you had no idea what happened to them after all that pointing and clicking.

In the morning after they had gone, Evelyn would walk out to the back deck, which faced the woods. She did like the fresh air and being able to look out, though she did not like the woods with their trees closely thatched together. So much could be hidden under the canopy of such silence and shade.

The house was full of art: long canvases with wispy, blurred people given form by a few careless strokes. In the living areas, the canvasses were bursting with riotous colors: oranges and rusts with the vibrancy of clay soil, explosive greens and opulent purples. One of the paintings appeared to be of a bus, a public transportation vehicle that could have been from any number of places in the developing world. It was painted red with beetle green trim. Its base and top were garlanded by curls of yellow and orange flame, and on its sides were painted headshots of people—local celebrities perhaps. On the front, a slogan—Man Eat Man Society—and inside the bus, people crammed together on their colorful ride. The road the bus traveled was brown and streaked heavily with gold paint that intensified farther in the distance until it seemed to merge with the horizon. The horizon was itself golden with the light of what looked like either a distant fire or a bursting sun, brash with epiphany.

Evelyn did not like the painting. It was too much movement and raging color, and besides, the people on the bus seemed idiotic. She wondered how much of the art had been acquired during Sam's time (most, if not all of it, she surmised) and how costly it all was.

There was something else that disturbed Evelyn—Joanna's raising of Stella. Joanna in many ways treated her like an adult. The two of them ate on solid plates with large chunky silverware that the child could barely wield. Stella could answer the phone and say, "Who is this, please?" and "We're not interested." She could say grace and operate the microwave, standing on a beautiful little wooden stool with hearts cut into it.

Evelyn would be patient. The truth was somewhere, waiting for her, breathing quietly in the corners of the house, lurking in the cool way Joanna looked at her sometimes; in the way she turned the child against her grandmother (for no doubt Joanna whispered words of disregard for Evelyn into her daughter's ears). Had Joanna even really respected Sam?

She was sure it was Joanna who had dissuaded Sam from coming to her birthday bash. The woman had never liked Evelyn and had never cared for Sam to maintain ties to his past, his family, his country. And she must have had Sam wrapped around her little finger—what with the art, the BMW. It was obvious that Sam had been financing her expensive taste.

One night when all was dark and still in the house, Evelyn wandered out onto the deck and looked into the woods and felt them drawing her into their damp, webbed heart.

Evelyn knew the taste of bitterness. She could remember watching thieving Leticia write with her fountain pen—the one Evelyn's father had given her, with the metallic blue lacquered finish pretty as sunlight on water and the gold tip. She thought of her father leaving without ceremony. For a long time, she blamed her mother for lying to her, for keeping the truth from her, or for at least failing to pass on a message she was sure her father had left. And the bitterness lapped up against the steep rocks in her.

When she had felt alone on the day of her sixtieth birthday party, she sensed the tide of bile rising again as she thought of Sam and his broken leg—but she was stronger than the tide.

"Where is Sam?" they had asked. How crisp, how assured she had been in her response about his injury, his deep regret at not being there.

Now, with her granddaughter and daughter-in-law asleep upstairs, she came in from the deck and turned off the lights in the house. As she headed up to bed, she promised herself that the truth would be made known.

~ TWENTY-THREE ~

WHEN THE IDEA seized him, it was as intolerant, petulant, and intoxicating as new love. It was a vein of lighting in his brooding sky, and he reached for it as a dying man will grasp at a cure that could kill him. Because why else would he keep thinking of Victor as though, while still living, the boy-now-man's spirit should walk with Seth, haunting him with his heartbreaking grin? Why else would he keep seeing him, his stubby pencils lying helpless in his unkempt hands?

Now as Isaac led the way through the supermarket aisles, Seth trailing like a bored child, he felt himself Victor, watching Seth walk away that fateful day, toward the blackboard and then across a gulf that Victor would never be able to cross.

Isaac's gaze lingered over the contents of the shelves, as though he were taking an inventory. Seth knew he was window shopping, a chance for his eyes to linger over foreign imported products that were far out of his reach. Isaac, like most people of his social status, bought their knock-off goods and cheap Chinese fabrications from street vendors and local markets and the ubiquitous *Fullah* shops.

But Danish butter cookies—those could only be bought in supermarkets, and it was those that Isaac had decided he and Seth would bring to the beach outing, along with *akara*, prepared courtesy of Aunty Sia.

After the exorcism, Seth had awakened each morning from sleep that was undisturbed, yet barren, his neck unscathed. He was thankful to be spared the swamp and its horrors and the physical ravaging of his body. Yet every day now, there was an emptiness of sorts, as if the night had held back from him some critical yeast that was to bring him both levity and completion in the morning.

Isaac had noticed only the cessation of the nighttime travails and Seth's seeming calm in the morning.

"Sleep well?" he even said half-rhetorically to Seth one morning, playfully throwing a pillow at him.

And Seth began to notice changes in his friend's behavior. He sparred with him more, going as far as to say Seth should open a hotel for people who suffered from nightmares. One day Seth understood Isaac's behavior for what it was—relief.

Then the idea came, and suddenly it was all Seth could think about. It scattered itself around his mind as though sprouting from spores, as though drawing from the air a hidden plenitude of water. He told Isaac about the idea, feeling a tinge of something he hadn't felt in a long time—excitement.

"It will be a summer camp for secondary school kids. We'll help them find their talents. It's not like teaching math, but it will still help them in school." The words were a mixture of true and possibly not true. He knew it as he said them, but sometimes all one could do was take a chance.

Isaac's face had become still with concentration, but eventually he grinned at his friend—an implicit offer of support. Seth felt a nearly unbearable debt of gratitude mounting. Yet it had been a week, and Isaac had showed no sign of action. They were actions he, in particular, would need to make right away, namely, working his contacts in the school system. Seth knew that without Isaac's support, his plans would go nowhere. And yet here was Isaac, showing far more enthusiasm over the upcoming beach outing than he had shown for Seth's idea.

The beach outing was the following weekend, but it was only yesterday that Isaac had received the text. And he had read it several times, with Seth wondering what the point was, given that the brief message could not have been different upon the third or fourth read.

"Mami Wata beach," he mused with a distracted flick of his earlobe. "Let's hope it doesn't rain, but even if it does, they've made some improvements to the place. There are some nice grass huts. We won't be in the posh touristy part where they've built a resort, but the beach is just as beautiful wherever you are. That's one thing you must have missed in America, eh?"

"The resorts?"

Isaac's chest heaved—no doubt with a sigh he'd tried to stifle but could be detected nonetheless.

"No, the beaches."

"Yes, the beaches," Seth said, his tone flat. He tried to pull another set of thoughts together other than the ones that were clogging his mind. What had Isaac said about Hakim and the beach party? The chair Seth had been sitting in—a multicolor wire frame number strung with plastic ropes—did not lend itself to upright sitting. Still, even in his slouch, Seth tried to look alert.

"And this is the Hakim who went to academy with you?"

"No, he went to grammar school with you. He was probably a class behind you . . . anyway, he remembers you. And his cousin is visiting from England, so you should have a lot to talk about," Isaac said, shooting Seth a sideways glance. "Like I said, maybe his cousin will be fun to hang with. You know, he gets the work stress and whatnot you guys deal with over there in those countries."

They were at last in the snack aisle, and Isaac's eyes alighted on the familiar round blue tins. Thank God, they would be out of there soon, Seth thought, though from here it was on to buy towels at Elizabeth Park. It was understood, but left unsaid, that the threadbare towels they had at the house would be too much of an embarrassment to take to the beach.

Isaac's excitement at the prospect of the beach day was matched only by Seth's dread. It would be filled with effervescent, gregarious people who were young like him. People not without problems but, unlike him, whose lives exhibited a natural buoyancy—a desire to float, to have fun. They did not sink to the bottom of swamps or deal with an ill-defined sense of aridity. Even with the excitement of the camp bringing some levity, they would sense that he harbored shadows. And then there would be talk—there always was. Freetown was still small. Though he had managed to stay under the radar, it only took contact with the right set of loose lips to—

"You will like Hakim," Isaac said now. "His father is a doctor, you know. A funny but paranoid man. Once, when Peter-Paul was still here, we were going to another beach outing, along with Hakim. This was not too long after the war. And one of the *bras* had a guy out there at the beach. His man, he said, could pull something fresh like lobster out of the ocean and put it, claws still snapping, on the grill. All he needed was a heads-up of when we'd be there so he could make sure he caught it that day." Isaac's face relaxed into a smile with the recollection.

"Would you believe *di Pa* talked us out of calling our guy on account of having treated someone who got such bad seafood poisoning he still walks with a limp? We laughed at the time, though I can still taste that grilled lobster we never had."

Sometimes the truth, despite widespread exhortations of its virtues, was a substance simply too pungent, too unrefined, to be used in everyday life. So Seth could not speak to Isaac of forgotten children, such as he once was, as Victor had no doubt continued to be. Because how could he possibly tell Isaac that in a world where so much needed to be done at all times, this idea of the camp had become his singular obsession?

The success of his later years should have erased the shame, and for a while it had. It was not just the shame of being the son that was not Sam, but the shame he and Victor had shared for being stupid. For not only having the wrong answers to questions in class but being thought incapable of finding the right answers. Along with his shame, Seth came to despise the smart kids, including Sam, for the adulation that came their way. Then he felt even more wretched because of the depth of his animosity.

Seth and Victor didn't much play together outside of class, never visited each other's homes. And yet Seth felt a closeness to him that he had never felt with his own brother. Until that fateful day when Mrs. Nichols had called him to the blackboard. Then he had risen like a new planet, forgetting Victor.

Isaac did ask him again, later, why he wanted to do the camp. Seth replied, "You asked about me giving maths lessons, Isaac, and I can't do that. But we can teach these kids something, right? Expose them to some different subjects over the summer. You're a teacher, and you're always talking about how poor the educational system is."

Isaac had seemed satisfied. It was in the early morning, feeling like he was waking up in an empty, echoing place, that Seth heard a voice say with a tone of mockery, "Is this about doing good or about doing it your way?"

Isaac had picked up a tin of cookies but seemed to be in no hurry to leave the store.

Seth sighed. "Isaac, you said you would talk to a few teachers and principals."

A momentary confusion crossed Isaac's face, and then he chirped, "I didn't forget. I thought I might do it the week after the beach outing because there's this upcoming conference in Ghana that many of them have been distracted about," he said, nodding for emphasis. "And who knows? You might get some ideas talking to Hakim and his cousin. For the camp, you know."

Suddenly it was clear to Seth that Isaac was hoping, clutching at this last straw, that Seth's obsession with the camp was a passing fancy and that perhaps speaking to sane mortals would set things right—mortals who understood some of this strange ennui that afflicted those who had been overseas.

The thought flickered across Seth's mind that *The Thing* was not gone, had never disappeared, only shape-shifted. It had seemed to disappear, only to be replaced by parching aridity. And that had been displaced by an idea that *The Thing* was possessive and consuming and would have him, regardless of what was lost in the process.

"Seth?"

There was a moment's hesitation before he turned. It seemed improbable that anyone here would recognize him. He turned to find a woman of about his age in skinny jeans and a blouse with a diagonal cut. Something about her style of dress suggested she had been overseas.

"Seth?" she repeated again.

And then from the recesses of his memory, a name emerged.

"Zayra?"

She smiled while Isaac looked on with a grin.

~

AT HOME THAT night, Isaac stashed the plastic bag with its tin of cookies under the wooden table in their room. Seth had bought two towels, both broadcasting color from atop Isaac's faded bed sheet.

"So funny that we should run into someone you went to primary school with," Isaac said, stretching his skeletal frame. From the depths of the house, they heard the familiar sound of clanging pots and running water—Aunty Sia at work in the kitchen.

"True."

"And what a coincidence that she's here to do that kind of work."

With an unexpected thud, Isaac sat down on his bed and splayed his legs in front of him. "You know I believe, Seth. I believe things happen for a reason, God's invisible hand and all that."

"What?"

"Never mind." But Isaac looked pensive.

Seth cast about for something to say. "You've told Hakim we're coming?"

Isaac seemed not to have heard him. "For a long time, there was nothing happening," he said, his speech halting. "Or it wasn't that there was nothing, because even during the war years, you know we Sierra Leoneans, we're all about enjoyment. So there were some events, some parties. And the beach was always there, and not even the war could change it. But it changed us. And those of us who were left would get together, but so many of you were gone, almost all my friends. It was never the same."

Seth watched him.

"You know, Seth, there are some people, like you, who want to *do*. They want to break things and maybe make some noise. And I'm not blaming you or saying it's bad. But I know how long it takes to put something together again. Anybody who was left behind knows." He stroked the towels absently once more and rose, leaving the room.

The next morning, Seth found the bag with the cookies next to his bed. He greeted Isaac and motioned to them.

Isaac smiled. "They're for you."

Seth looked at him in confusion. "Why?"

"It will make it much easier to talk to teachers and principals about the camp when you offer them something to munch on."

~ TWENTY-FOUR ~

SETH PICKED UP the sheaf of papers from the teacher's desk at the front of the class where he had turned them upside down. The children's eyes were on him. He gave Isaac, who was standing next to him, the papers to read before anyone noticed them shaking in his hand.

The exercise they had given the children was simple enough—to write one dream they had for their grown-up selves, but whether through worry, lack of aspiration, or something else, they seemed unable to carry out the exercise, giving each other worried stares instead. Completing the exercise had taken what seemed like a year but was in reality something like ten minutes.

Ettie, sitting within the group, had escaped as usual into another world, staring blankly ahead. There were seven boys and seven girls, including Ettie, ranging in age from thirteen to sixteen. Ettie was one of the oldest. The eighth boy on the roster hadn't shown up.

It was the exercise that would take a measure of why the camp mattered—at least to Seth. As Isaac read the choices out, Seth's heart sank: doctor, president, lawyer . . . Seth could have predicted these choices with almost one hundred percent certainty. These were their parents' and society's choices for them. Isaac kept reading, more of what Seth had dreaded—businessmen, computer professionals. He perked up, though, with one answer:

"I want to be an architect when I grow up."

"Why?" Isaac pressed the girl.

She wagged her pencil back and forth and sighed, as though she had known she would be punished for her outlier response.

"My uncle is an architect."

"Do you know what an architect is?" asked Isaac.

The girl looked around with uncertainty; her peers smirked. "He builds big houses."

"Oh, I see," Isaac said. "Well, actually, that's not true."

Seth had told Isaac that the camp had to be different from anything the kids had experienced before. "I want them to think about options beyond being a doctor, lawyer, or engineer. All those other choices no one told us were out there. Because what if you want to be something else? It wasn't until I got to the States that I realized how many more options were out there."

"You mean out there in the U.S.," Isaac said, his tone flat.

"And here too. We just don't think about them."

Isaac had run the idea by a few of his fellow teachers and elicited some brokered connections with school principals. Seth had made several visits to schools to talk to principals, cookies in hand, created brochures, and read resources on doing summer camps. They would take the kids to visit various professionals at work and have them try their hand at some crafts. In between, they would have sessions that sparked the kids' creativity and taught them about people who had changed the world.

And yet, if he and Isaac had not bumped into Zayra at the supermarket . . . If Seth had not remembered her from their school days—her litheness, neatness, and childlike smile—and beamed recognition at her . . . If Isaac had not marveled at the miracle of the chance encounter with a teacher—from abroad, no less—who understood Seth's vision and decided to put his faith in the idea . . . If Zayra had not brought concrete ideas where Seth and Isaac had had wispy notions . . . the camp would likely have never gotten off the ground.

Zayra taught middle school in Kentucky but had just returned to Sierra Leone to conduct some research on the educational system for her master's degree. With uncharacteristic boldness, Seth had told her, on the spot, about his idea for the camp. With her, unlike with Isaac, it did not seem to matter what was left out.

Then when Isaac came around, together they reached out to her, persuaded her to meet with them. Slowly they reeled her in and got her agreement to volunteer, helping Seth and Isaac as much as she could with the camp, while incorporating the venture into her research.

Seth grabbed Zayra's agreement with relief, for not having worked with children or taught before, he had few skills to make the camp a reality. And as he did so, he took a measure of his unbelief that things might finally be going his way, understanding as he did so that he had lost faith in goodness.

Seth tried to put the children's canned answers in perspective. He, of all people, should have expected this. Because even though he had gone to a good school, the teaching style had not been too different from what these students must be experiencing. The less-inspired teachers would intone the teachings from the textbook like scriptural readings requiring no other response than a congregational "amen." The students were expected to recite back what they heard with canonical fidelity. Imaginations were checked at the door.

Isaac looked at Seth with raised eyebrows. Now what? Seth looked back helplessly, lifting his shoulders in a half-shrug. This was the arrangement they had come up with, that Isaac and Zayra would be the faces of the camp, while Seth would feed them his vision from behind the scenes. Except he could barely call it a vision. What he had had was a conviction, a strong urge that he must do this camp. But no direction on how.

When he tried to imagine getting the children fired up, like in the movies where one good speech saved the day, all he could conjure was a feeling of longing for something indefinable and a hope that others would simply tune into this longing and feel it as he did. But he was a fraud. If he spoke to them, they would find out that he had built the camp on nothing more than an itch that insisted on being scratched. And yet, as wonderful as Isaac and Zayra were, they could not save the day when things faltered—they would look to Seth to lead the way. But how could they believe in him if he did not believe in himself?

Already, it was hard to push away the fear that Isaac had been right about which kids to pick. Isaac had wanted to pick the smartest kids through an essay contest. "You'll set yourself up for failure if you don't." But Seth hadn't wanted to. He wanted to pick the kids who needed the most help.

Ettie, when offered to attend the camp, had accepted without much display of emotion, as if she felt it had been decided for her and she would simply step into this decision the way she would step into a pair of shoes. And Aunty Sia's voice had quivered when she looked from Isaac to Seth and said, "You know Ettie hasn't done well with private lessons before. Will the camp be different?"

Seth felt an uncharacteristic conviction and said, "Yes."

That morning Aunty Sia, with three large steps, approached the girl from behind and put a hand on her shoulder. The girl had stopped in her tracks without turning, while Aunty Sia reached two coarse, quivering hands to fasten the eyelet loop at the top of the girl's blouse. Then she straightened the petal-like collar and held the girl's braided extensions in one hand for a few long moments before letting them drop on her back. Ettie held still, as though she were in a trance. Seth was reminded of Mr. Ba, one of the ginger-colored mongrels they had had when he was a child that used to rest his snout in Seth's hand and close his eyes.

Zayra pulled her chair closer to the kids, away from the front of the classroom. She smiled at them like a conspirator and switched to *Krio,* hoping this deference to their mother tongue would loosen their inhibitions. *Le we talk an pan Krio.* 'Let's have a conversation," she began. "Tell us one dream you have for when you grow up. Maybe someone wants to own a restaurant. Maybe someone wants to work on a ship."

The kids visibly relaxed but resumed the worried looks.

Zayra turned to Seth. "Seth, maybe you can tell them *why* you think it's important for them to do this," she said with the learned evenness of a teacher.

They all looked at him with expectation. But he could not think. He could not speak. He had been deluded with the idea of the camp. He looked around at the dark, cramped room and its oily green walls. *You don't know it, but you have a choice to do something different with your life,* he wanted to say.

"Why don't I tell you after the break?" he said helplessly. *Coward,* said a voice within him. Zayra and Isaac looked at him with furrowed brows, but for the first time, the kids sprang to life, relieved that the pointless inquisition was over.

During the break the boys wasted no time in organizing themselves for a game of football they would play over lunch. The girls congregated in another corner, looking at something on one of their cellphones. Peals of laughter shot out of the gatherings.

Seth wandered outside after them, still stinging from his earlier stumble in front of them all. He wondered at the energy now flowing from the children like soda fizzing from a bottle. They called to one another, made daring passes, coordinating themselves like air traffic controllers. Perhaps their dreams were there after all, darting about subtly like fireflies in the undergrowth of a forgotten forest.

When they reconvened, warmth, sweat, and vitality continued to issue from them. But as they settled into their chairs, their mood turned somber again, and the energy leached from the room. Seth looked at Ettie. Her head was turned in an awkward way so she could look out of the window.

Seth exhaled and tried to believe again. But instead, he was seized with a certainty that he would not be able to provoke the light he had seen on the playground and that the camp would fail.

~ TWENTY-FIVE ~

"Do you want to know why my name is Lucky?" The boy looked slyly at Seth. He had been the eighth boy, the one who didn't show up on the first day of camp. Seth looked down at the roster as he registered the boy. Adolphus Rogers. What an unfortunate name.

"Because your real name is Adolphus?"

The boy looked at him, quizzical.

"Never mind," continued Seth, holding back a smile. "I'm not a curious person, so I wasn't going to ask, but tell me."

The boy's eyes were like new marbles, bright and unscratched. He was thin with a puppet's loose-hanging limbs and dusty brown hair, patchy as a coconut husk. As he put down his enormous backpack, he sighed as though it were a load he had been bearing from a far country. Seth wondered what could possibly be in there.

"My mother wasn't happy about me going by Lucky; she asked what was wrong with the name they gave me."

Seth could think of plenty wrong with Adolphus Rogers.

"I had been going by Lucky for a year before she realized that I expected everyone to call me that. In fact, my friends had been using it all the time when they came over to my place. She thought it was just a nickname, you know. But I meant it." The boy nodded solemnly in affirmation.

The other children were coming in, and Isaac and Zayra were greeting them. Seth tried to catch their eyes and smile at them, despite being occupied with Lucky. The sun was already throwing sharp blocks of light upon the untiled floor.

Lucky had yet to tell Seth why he had missed the first day of class. Seth began to get the sense that this conversation might go on for a while. He picked up his pen and made a show of going through the registration form to make sure all the information was there.

"So why did you change your name?" he said, looking back at Lucky.

Lucky gave Seth a patient smile. Even with Seth sitting down, he was still not that much above Seth's eye level.

"I changed my name so no one would forget me."

Isaac called to Seth, and it was a moment before he looked in his direction, suddenly not ready to end the conversation with Lucky.

~ TWENTY-SIX ~

FOR THE FIRST activity of the day, Zayra taught the kids a simple game, the first of many she had planned to get them out of their shells. It consisted of having them form two lines, girls against boys, and then compete to pass a ball of crumpled paper using only their chins from one end of the line to the other. Seth watched them laugh, shake their hands with impatience, and fidget in anticipation for their turn with the ball.

The kids took to it right away, calling out to one another, "Hurry up! Look, the other group is getting ahead."

Seth watched Ettie closely, worried about how she would take this exercise, but she displayed no signs of nervousness. She took the ball expertly with her chin from the girl in front of her. And she passed it on calmly too.

It was over in a few more seconds, Ettie's group having won. Seth, Zayra, and Isaac applauded.

"You guys did great," Seth chirped.

"Can we do it again, Miss Zayra?" called one of the boys. "We have practiced now."

She nodded. "Okay, once more."

Their feet shuffled quickly into line like a well-coordinated millipede. A hawker passing by on the street that bordered the yard stopped to gawk, his tray of goods lying still on his head.

Seth caught himself smiling—at Zayra and Isaac, at Ettie and the other kids, and at no one in particular. He refused to think of the next day or the one after that and the final destination of the camp. For now, there was laughter and children with glowing eyes and an energy that could not be denied.

But in the afternoon, just like the preceding day, the kids were quiet once again. They slumped on the table, even though Seth, Isaac, and Zayra kept admonishing them to sit up straight. It was hot in the room that was certainly too small for eighteen people, and the heat only served to weigh them all down further.

One of the posters on the wall, a fine-printed elaboration of the parts of a plant, became unfastened and fell to the floor with a rustling exclamation, and they turned to watch it with tired eyes.

The afternoon break was a mercy. Seth stood outside on the small porch, arms akimbo, trying to conjure up the lightness he had felt that morning. He looked beyond the gate at the passersby without really seeing them. Lucky came up to him.

"You are worried," he said.

"What do you mean?" Seth was taken aback.

"You are worried about how things are going."

"What makes you think that?"

"Because you are the one in charge, and the ones in charge are always worried."

Seth thought to ask Lucky how he knew Seth was the one in charge, when all he had done was lurk in the shadows, allowing Isaac and Zayra to be the visible ones. But he thought better of it. Just as well that the boy hadn't been there yesterday to see him tongue-tied when Zayra asked him to explain the exercise.

He studied the boy with caution. Kids could be cunning creatures, this one in particular. They knew where tender veins throbbed beneath placid surfaces.

It was as though Lucky sensed this reckoning within Seth. He stepped back and clasped his hands behind his back, a diffident smile on his face.

"Don't worry about the others," he murmured, looking out to the yard where his companions had coalesced into clusters. "They are shy, but they will talk more soon."

"How so?"

"Oh, leave it to me," he said, and with that, he walked away.

Seth watched the boy's retreating back in fascination.

"Wait!" he called. *What do you have in mind?* he wanted to ask. But the boy didn't turn, and Seth wasn't sure if he hadn't heard him or, in his cunning, was pretending he hadn't.

~

IN ITS SECOND week, the camp stumbled groggily into a rhythm of sorts, like a marching band creaking out a valiant tune through a sun-induced afternoon stupor. They went to one of the two florists in the city and watched her at work. She let them make arrangements from her reject pile, which they took back to the camp and found wilted the next day. With the white sun dominating the sky, they had an astronomy day, where the kids solemnly listened to Zayra describe planets shrouded with mystery and gases (all this without the aid of a projector, just some grainy computer printouts).

Much to Seth's surprise, on Tuesday evening, he got a call from Saj's assistant, saying Saj would be there the next day. Saj was a well-known Sierra Leonean musician whose music Seth had been familiar with even in the United States. It was unrelentingly rollicking—the kind of Afro-pop-calypso fusion that got rotund, bobbing middle-agers and twerking teens alike up on dance floors. But some of his songs were more strident in theme and tone. They decried the gangrene of corruption in the country, the abandon of sense and compassion in the name of greed:

I wake in the morning and the first thing I see
Is that the world fell apart overnight
The old have forgotten the lessons of the past

And the young don't know how to dream

Seth had been seized with the possibility of getting him to come speak to the kids, even though Zayra and Isaac warned him it was a long shot. A vision fired him up: Saj at the camp working the deep magic of music, soothsaying with his story to coax the children from their cocoons.

Armed with nothing more than a vague connection to Saj (he could say he knew Zayra, who was a friend of a friend of a friend), he decided to stake out Saj's studio. But standing in the shade of a hardware store across the road, he thought of what he would say, and a predatory inertness engulfed him. Simply unable to cross the road, he went home. The next time he tried, he made it across the street and, amazingly, into the studio, where he made straight for Saj. He was much shorter in person than he appeared in pictures, though he clearly tried to make up for it in musculature. His hair was in short locks dyed a rust color, and he sported ample bling around his neck and on his fingers. Displeased by the unsolicited encounter, Saj blew him off with a vague agreement that he would come speak to the kids. Fat chance, thought Seth upon leaving.

But now, here was Saj's assistant on the phone. Once he got over the shock, Seth managed to say, "But we haven't planned . . . never mind. One o'clock, you say? We'll be waiting."

When he told the kids the next day, they dropped their pencils and looked at him in disbelief, the same way Isaac and Zayra had.

"Are you sure he's coming?" said one of the girls.

"He said he would."

Their excitement filled the room. They couldn't sit still or concentrate on the morning's exercise, a rather tame one of reviewing an assortment of modern-day careers—a presentation Seth had found online. Seth couldn't remember seeing Ettie so animated as she looked around her and chatted easily with her classmates.

By 11:30 p.m., Seth and his companions gave up and left the kids to their own devices, calling an early lunch. Seth wished he hadn't told the kids Saj was coming—because what if he didn't?

By 12:50 p.m., the kids were back at their desks and composed, their eyes trained on the door, waiting for Saj's supposed arrival at 1 p.m. Not that anyone actually expected him to arrive at 1 p.m. This was Sierra Leone. It was punctuality rather than lateness that caught people by surprise. But he hadn't shown up by 2 p.m. or 2:30 p.m. either. By 3 p.m., Seth began to lose hope.

Zayra tried to call Saj's assistant. No luck. Seth looked at Isaac for facial cues on when to break it to the kids. But then Isaac's eyes shot up as he looked toward the door. It was Saj.

Saj's effect on the kids was nothing short of magical. Their faces were incandescent, their voices like wind filling sails as they greeted him and spontaneously began singing some of his songs.

Seth and Zayra pulled Saj outside.

"How long can you stay?" asked Seth.

"Forty-five minutes."

Seth looked at Zayra, who rubbed her chin. "Can you give the kids a chance to perform with you?" she said. "Maybe come up with new lyrics to one of your songs? We're trying to get them to be creative," she added, looking at Seth. "Seth is worried everyone does their thinking for them; no one encourages them to think on their own."

When Isaac had asked the kids earlier in the day if they would be up to performing in front of Saj, there were smirks and smiles. "You'd be amazed," Isaac had told Seth. "When it comes to music and rapping, heh, they're not so shy after all."

"What about using the time to tell them your story?" Seth said now.

"It's either-or, I'm afraid," Saj replied. "Tell them my story or help them perform for a bit. Can't stay long."

"Seth, I think working with music and lyrics would help them be creative," Zayra said, crossing her arms.

Saj looked back and forth between Zayra and Seth, a faint smile playing around his lips. With Saj and Zayra looking at him and over the sounds of Isaac doing his best to keep the kids' excitement at bay, Seth heard himself say, "Tell the kids a true story."

"Eh?"

"Your story, how you became a musician."

"You don't want them to perform with me and I give them tips?"

Isaac came to the door and gave them a quizzical look.

"Are they going to perform with Saj?"

"Seth asked him to tell the kids his story instead," Zayra said, her tone flat.

Isaac and Zayra frowned.

Saj's hand went to the pocket of his jeans, perhaps groping for a pack of cigarettes. But then he brought it back and folded his arms instead.

"Okay." He looked up at the sky, gave it a brief scan. He shrugged. "Okay, I'll tell you my story," he said, catching Seth off guard with the ease with which he agreed.

~ TWENTY-SEVEN ~

"THE WAR TOOK everything from me and left me music," Saj said to the children. They looked at him with large eyes in the poorly lit room that became darker still as clouds drifted across the sun. "You must understand, I didn't have much to begin with. I was poor, a nobody. So insignificant that people didn't even think they owed me truth. So when I was growing up, I learned not to believe anything I was told, especially if it was something good."

Saj told them of his father's first lie about his mother—that she had disappeared running into the bush because she heard a voice speaking to her from the river. And of the second—that she was living in a different town, married to another man with two children younger than him, but that her voice still grew hoarse when she spoke of him. Finally, his father told him he did not know where his mother was, nor did her family, and he thought she had died many years ago, perhaps not too long after Saj was born. This, at last, stung like truth.

He went on to live with his uncle, a good man, who asked his sons to call Saj brother. Whereas Saj's own father came to visit him less and less over the years, his uncle and aunt, struggling themselves, gave him daily bread, paid his school fees, and even gave him love, which leavened everything.

"Then the war happened," Saj said, his jaw tightening. "We ran to Freetown, like everyone else did, without hope of staying alive or a life worth being alive for. When we moved to Freetown, I told my aunt and uncle I didn't want them to spend any more money on me (and they didn't have it anyway) because I wasn't going to go back to school. I can still remember the strain in my uncle's face when he heard this."

Though he continued living with his aunt and uncle, Saj found odd jobs and made the kind of friends that tuned him in to the worst aspects of life in the city—stealing, drugs, a suffocating rage.

Then music began to speak to him—American hip-hop, dancehall reggae, soukous. When he listened, danced, sometimes the anger rose like clouds of dust from the floor. But when he rapped, wrote his own lyrics, he could think a little more clearly, and some of the anger laid itself down. He began to write lyrics about corruption and the injustice of children dying in the streets while the ministers sent their money to secret banks in faraway countries. He wrote too about love and voluptuous women, but it was the lyrics about their society, their country, that woke him up in the middle of the night, twitching and restless for morning.

Inevitably, poverty dogged him and the ragtag band he formed. Often they performed for food alone, until eventually a tourist gave them some money—just enough to make recording an album seem like a possibility. Something to go hungry enough to save toward.

"The rest is history, as they say," said Saj, smiling at last. He uncrossed his arms, looked at his watch. Seth leaned forward, a growling want within him. But Saj was standing, reaching into his pocket for his keys, saying, "So that's my story, boys and girls. I hope this was helpful. Peace."

It took Seth a moment to realize the story had ended. "Wait!" he said. They all turned to look at him. The kids were not used to him speaking in the room. Most of the time he lurked in silence in the back. He grasped for words. After opening and closing his mouth a few times, he walked toward Saj and held his hand out as if in appeal.

"Lots of people came to Freetown with nothing to do. Lots of people rapped for fun and sang happy songs. What made you different? What made you stand up against corruption?"

He walked to within arm's length of Saj and motioned to the chair.

Saj looked at it but did not sit. "I have to go."

Seth stepped even closer to Saj. "Please," he said, his voice coarse.

The musician looked at Seth through squinted eyes, then looked at his watch. He stretched and asked them to excuse him while he went outside. Seth watched as he walked away. After a few moments, he followed him outside, worried that the musician had planned to simply escape. But Saj, when he locked eyes with Seth, seemed to yield to his determination.

He followed Seth back inside and sat down again, pensive. They all looked at him, their eyes consuming him, their ears tuning to his voice. Outside it started to rain. Tendrils of softer, fresher air crept into the warm room, and the light waned even more, so as Saj spoke, nimbuses of dark and gray emerged in the far reaches of the room.

"Well, there was that day under the mango tree," said Saj, his voice trailing off as he looked at them. He cleared his throat and steadied his voice.

"That was the day I peeped around the side of the house and saw my uncle sitting with my other uncle."

"Under the mango tree?" Isaac said somewhat unnecessarily, perhaps afraid that Saj would falter if they did not remind him that they were listening.

"Yes, the mango tree." Saj's gaze was growing distant again, and he trailed off into silence.

"So you had another uncle?" offered Seth.

"I had another uncle; I'll just call him my other uncle. Or at least I was told that he was my uncle, but it turned out we were not even related."

The other uncle came once a year, around Ramadan, Saj continued. He was a minister in the president's cabinet. Saj's aunt would cook for hours, and the house and yard would be swept with extra vigor. When the uncle came, if he noted their labors, he seemed to think nothing of it. But the household was left better each time the uncle departed. There was beef in stews and crates of soft drinks, and his aunt and uncle's laughter was a bit more loose. Saj didn't know what ministers did, but he wished with fervor to be one.

His uncle was nothing but grins and smiles when the other uncle was around. Only one time did he observe any tension between them. His uncle had been having trouble with his oldest son. One of the worst times was when the boy and his friends broke into the shop of a well-known Lebanese trader and stole a lot of expensive merchandise—watches, jewelry. There was no way Saj's uncle would come up with the money to pay the trader back. That was one of the few times Saj could remember the other uncle coming to visit at a time that was not Ramadan or another important holiday. Being the curious boy that he was, he sidled around the house to eavesdrop.

"The boy knows you are soft. That is the problem," said the other uncle.

Saj's uncle bowed his head and said nothing.

"But don't worry. With the diamond contract we will get Hedjazi, he will wish for those boys to rob his store all over again. You know these Lebanese; they would sell their own mothers for diamonds."

"I can't thank you enough."

"Your chance will come. If we are ever forced to return to the multiparty system and hold elections, I am counting on you to deliver votes for us."

"Of course. You know these people would trade their votes for a cup of rice."

Here Saj's uncle bowed his head low before his "brother." And Saj ran away from what he had just seen, hating it with a ferocity that hurt.

From that time on, Saj made it a point to be out of the house whenever his other uncle came to visit. His aunt scolded him and told him to make sure he was around because he liked to see them all. Because he was the one paying for the kids' school fees and uniforms in this bone-dry country. Saj found himself hating school and wishing for the day he could leave.

He got his wish. A year later the whole family ended up moving to Freetown to escape the rebels, and that was the end of school.

Isaac fidgeted and darted glances at Zayra. Seth discerned his unease. Was Saj going to admonish the kids that they should not do like him and should focus on their studies instead? Isaac shot a glance at Seth, and Seth could only look back at him, helpless, not able to intervene, because he had caught Saj's eye before he caught Isaac's, and in Saj's eyes and words, he understood that they were brethren. That they belonged to the tribe of wild souls for whom destruction, and the sudden interruption of placidity, was their terrible and secret yearning.

By the time Saj and family moved to Freetown, the military junta had overthrown the government. His other uncle was no longer in his old, fat position; in fact, he and members of his family had fled to Guinea because the military men now in power were persecuting members of the former government.

Freetown was starting to stink in the same old way because the young military boys got stupid with the same power and corruption they had been fighting against. Foreign aid was used to build houses for mistresses. People were saying, "They are just the same as the ones before them. Only God can help us."

Then power changed hands again, but it made no difference to the people. Corruption was as ripe as ever before. From time to time, Saj went back to visit his uncle and aunt, who had moved back to the provinces. During one of these visits, his uncle told him that influential people in government had come to visit them. They told him they were approaching him softly, carefully, so he would influence Saj. No one was arguing in favor of corruption, they said. However, his lyrics were making things worse. Student unions who loved nothing more than to make trouble were inspired to demonstrate and were disturbing the fragile peace.

Nobody knew what it was like to be in the hot seat of a post-war government: the debt, the donor demands, the shattered infrastructure of the country. Saj's lyrics were raising unfair expectations.

Saj said, "What do you want me to do, uncle?"

"Your father always said how he didn't want you to get into trouble," he replied.

"But what do *you* want me to do, uncle?"

"Remember your older brother," the shop robber, he meant, "and do not make a mess of your life like he did, moving from place to place to run from his crimes. There is no glory in being a troublemaker."

Saj listened to the man he loved and respected, the only true father he'd ever known. But even his uncle's words couldn't keep him from performing, talking, and singing about corruption and how Sierra Leoneans must change to save their honor, their country; though each time he thought of his uncle, something tore inside him.

His uncle summoned Saj a few months later, told him they had been given new warnings to make him stop. His aunt pleaded. That night Saj pulled a cap low on his head and walked the streets. Twice he heard his band's music blaring, carrying those words that the government hated so much. Smoke from night fires stung his eyes, and as they smarted and ran, he thought of how his love for his country brought him so much pain. Finally he understood why blatant self-interest was an easier way to live.

He determined to give his aunt and uncle more money for security. Or have them move in with him. But then they refused to see him and stopped accepting the money he had been sending them. Then his aunt sent word that his uncle was ill, and would Saj stop now. Before he could figure out what to do, she sent word again that his uncle was dead.

The rain had stopped, but the sky remained a folded petal, a tender closed eyelid over the brilliant light of earlier. Saj's voice became softer. He leaned forward in his chair, looking at the children with intensity, as though through this story, they had become brethren. Then he stood up quickly and walked outside. Seth felt the silence settle like smoke from a dying fire. The children sat with hunched shoulders and did not look at each other.

Isaac and Zayra looked at each other, each reading the others' minds: *What do we do now?*

In a couple minutes, Saj came back in. "Don't do things because they look cool. As we say in *Krio*, 'All lizards rest their bellies on the ground. Only they know if they have a bellyache.' The war took everything from me, and then music took some more. But I had to do it that way."

And with that, he was gone.

~ TWENTY-EIGHT ~

"Granny, do you want to see Samantha?" Stella asked.

"Who's Samantha?"

The child looked up at Evelyn with a grin girded with tiny scalloped teeth.

"My cat."

"I didn't know you had a cat. Where have you been hiding her all this time?"

Stella threw her head back and released shrieks of laughter that sounded like hiccups. She had been expecting this very reaction.

"She's online, Granny. She's a virtual pet."

Evelyn's granddaughter had decided to like her, had decided that for better or for worse, Evelyn's presence in the beautiful, quiet house made things more interesting. That morning Stella had waited outside the bathroom for Evelyn to emerge. Evelyn nearly bumped into her as she stepped out in a cloud of steam.

"What are you doing here, child?"

Stella smiled and ran away.

As she slowly followed the child and found that she was being led to the computer, she was reminded of how far apart their worlds were in every sense. Evelyn still had difficulty remembering when you were supposed to left-click and when to right-click. Stella used the mouse without awareness, as though it were an extra hand. Evelyn observed as the child pulled up the website where the cat lived.

Samantha was a delicate Abyssinian that uncurled herself, walked toward them, and put her paws up against the screen as if it were a glass cage. She made purring noises and twitched her bat-like ears. Witch animal, thought Evelyn. Like others of her generation, she had never understood the appeal of cats beyond keeping a home free of mice. When the creature meowed, Evelyn started, causing Stella to seize with laughter.

Now Stella was pointing to her animal and saying, "Granny, isn't it awesome?"

"Yes, dear," she said with as much enthusiasm as she could scratch together. "It surely is."

Unfortunately, other times did not go so well. One evening she offered to braid Stella's hair. She figured Joanna had never braided it in small, tight plaits before and thought it might be a treat for the girl and her mother. But Evelyn had barely done a fourth of her head when Stella began to squirm and fidget.

"Sit still," she hissed.

Stella began to whimper, which annoyed Evelyn to no end. She prodded the child's shoulder with the comb.

"Stop it!"

At this, Stella began to bawl, wriggling her way out of the brace of Evelyn's knees and running off to find her mother. Evelyn expected that Joanna would quiet her down and send her back to get the rest of her hair done, but she didn't. They had dinner with part of Stella's hair lying in neat plaits and the rest of it sticking up like stalks of corn.

Sometime that night or morning, Joanna must have undone the plaits, because by morning, Stella's hair was back to its usual few twists. Evelyn could not help but feel slighted. She had only been trying to help.

Her impatience was growing. How much longer was she going to look across the table at her daughter-in-law and pretend to like her? It was taxing to maintain this farce, and yet do so she must until she got confirmation of the truth about Sam.

Once, as they drove, she made it a point to look out the window and say with studied distraction, "What a shame that you and Sam didn't come for my sixtieth birthday party. What was the reason again that you couldn't make it?"

Joanna stiffened. "You don't remember?"

"The old brain. You'll see when you're my age, you don't remember anything."

"Funny, I don't either . . . except that he felt terrible. He'd really been looking forward to being there."

"It's too bad. It was one of the most important moments of my life, and he was not there. And of course, it would have been good to have you and Stella there too."

"It must have been disappointing. But at least you had Seth."

"Seth?" Her blood ran hot at the mere mention of the name. "Seth is a different story. He thinks only of himself, and he wonders why the whole world does not understand him."

"And how is he doing in Freetown?"

Did Joanna take her for an idiot? Did she think Evelyn was too dimwitted to figure out that Seth and Joanna probably talked from time to time?

"I really don't know. He decided to move out and since then hasn't made any effort to contact us."

"That's a shame. I hope he gets things figured out."

She would play along. "Yes, you should check on him every now and then. Maybe you can talk some sense into him."

Alfred had tried to talk with her about Seth the last time they spoke to each other on the phone.

"He hasn't come by," he said.

"Did you expect that he would?"

"I was hoping so."

She had shared with Alfred some of what she had learned from a colleague of hers about Seth's camp. The colleague had shared some concerns, but Evelyn thought it best to keep the full details from Alfred, in the same way she had not troubled him with all her reasons for coming to the United States. These were the roles that had been set for them long ago—she the memory-keeper, he the peacekeeper. He was so guileless that her affection for him made her want to protect him from information that might rupture his innocence. But at other times, she felt contempt for his ignorance, his smooth-cheeked placidness, and was overcome by an unholy urge to hide from him information that would have made him glad.

"How much longer will you be there?" Alfred had said, his voice crumpled by the phone line.

"Just a few weeks more. Stella and I are getting along well now, and I want to make the most of it."

There was a long silence from him.

"Joanna has been through a lot, Evelyn."

"How so? Yes, she lost her husband, but we lost a son. And you should see how she lives, no doubt in part because of Sam's life insurance policy."

More silence from Alfred. She pretended like the minutes on the phone card were about to end, even though that was not the case, and they hung up.

~

SHE SAW IT in the den one day when she went in search of a pair of scissors. It was an ebony carving of a woman holding a basket on her head, bare breasted, knees bent in the pose that was typical of such carvings from Sierra Leone. A hollow had been carved into the basket to make it a receptacle, but anyone could see that the piece was too beautiful to be used as such.

The wood was smooth to her touch, as smooth as it had been then, but she needed no aid for her memory. She could see them now with the same crispness she had seen them with then through the slit between the door and the frame, their voices clear, as if they were speaking into her ear.

Sam had his back half-turned to Evelyn. He partially obscured Joanna. Joanna had been fanning herself with a newspaper in a show of how she was wilting in the heat and couldn't wait to go home.

"How are we going to transport this back with us?"

It was the first and only trip Sam and Joanna had made to Sierra Leone as a couple. They were merely engaged then.

"We'll have it wrapped up and checked like a piece of luggage."

"But it's so bulky. Why would we go through all that trouble?"

"Sweetheart, we really have no choice. My mother bought this for us. We can't leave it here. How do you think she would feel?"

Silence.

"Where shall we put it?"

"I'll leave it up to you."

"Well, I'll put it close to the door, perhaps. It would make a good receptacle for keys and things."

Some tension crept into Sam's voice. "It is an ebony hand carving from my country, Joanna. It's not a dollar store basket for tossing paper clips and those used batteries you seem to be forever collecting."

Joanna had not given the carving away after Sam died as one might have guessed; instead she had kept it. It was stashed behind a pile of newspapers and magazines, furry with dust. Nothing in the house was neglected in this way; everything else was impeccably clean. In the basket on the woman's head was an assortment of paper clips, screws, rubber bands, some googly eyes and bits of felt, perhaps the remnants of a craft project with Stella.

Evelyn ran her fingers over the woman's sightless eyes, the rounded nose, the ridged lips. Her fingers left trails in the garment of dust.

"We will have the last word, my dear."

~

THAT EVENING THEY had salmon and mashed potatoes for dinner. After weeks of eating such bland food—more suitable for babies than adults—she could barely stand to shovel the white mass into her mouth and was almost past bothering to hide her disdain.

"When you and Sam came to visit and you spent some time with me in the kitchen learning how to make that food, were you ever able to try some of the recipes over here?" she said with a forced lilt in her voice.

"Not really. They looked hard enough that I was sure I would never quite get the hang of it, and I didn't want Sam to have to pretend each time that they were even half-edible." Joanna let out a half-laugh. "You made it look so much easier than it actually was."

Evelyn said nothing. Perhaps what most irked her about Joanna was that as she made utterances like this, there was not a trace of embarrassment or regret, just the even, unflinching gaze. Evelyn refused to look away, and eventually Joanna turned to Stella to monitor her progress on the food.

"Eat up, sweetie. Only three spoons left."

How different the younger generation was! Foreign wives of Sierra Leonean men of Evelyn's generation had quickly figured out that learning how to cook the cuisine of that country was as essential to keeping their husbands happy as sex. But perhaps Joanna's indifference to cooking was not generational; it was more to do with the hold it was clear she had had over Sam.

And Evelyn was sure now that in his final years, Sam had not been happy. Men with such wives never were, for nothing was ever enough.

She decided to change the subject.

"I should have brought more handicrafts with me so Stella could see around her a few things from her homeland. Did you and Sam have any in your old house?"

Joanna looked at her curiously and paused before answering. "We had a few pieces here and there. Very few though, and I think they might be in storage along with some other things I didn't have room for in this smaller place. I'll have to take a look and see though. Perhaps Stella could take them to school sometime for show and tell."

~ TWENTY-NINE ~

As THOUGH FALLING through a door that suddenly gives way, Seth was cast into the swamp again one night. He couldn't name the emotions he felt at being sucked into its rot-infused depths. It was not one thing but rather several—relief, perhaps, that he could stop dreading whether *The Thing* would come for him again, and a cutting sadness that he would never be free. The sadness sharpened, and he wished for the swamp to swell and flood its bounds, carrying him to the sea, where he could be lost forever, disentangled from the noose of hope.

But then he peered as best he could through the billowing sediment at what looked like a glowing coal, as mesmerizing as the eye of an ancient and omniscient dragon. He wondered if, at last, he was looking into the eye of his foe. Then the sediment parted, and it appeared to be an underwater flame, flickering and folding, flaring and thinning with such rhythm and power that it caused the caverns of his heart to swell and shrink to the same music. And for the moment, he could rest in the brace of that meter.

Then he felt a coming to and realized he was sitting in the kitchen, not lying in his bed as he had thought. He was pretty sure he had gone to bed and covered himself up to the waist until the vision of the swamp consumed him. How had he ended up in the kitchen?

From outside, the sounds of traffic had thinned. It was the dead of the night. He could almost hear his own breathing, and if he listened even harder, his living—each cell quivering within its membrane, opening and closing its stores, shuddering and dying or breathing anew.

For a while it seemed sufficient to sit in darkness and witness the symphony of his body. And so he sat, unaware of whether it was hours or mere minutes that passed while he sat immobile. Eventually he began to hear the sounds of traffic thicken outside, and he perceived that dawn was emerging. He stood and, with some effort, moved his limbs as though learning how to walk. He began to look for matches to light the lantern.

Saj's story burrowed into his mind like a mother tongue. Surely, it had also lit up the children's minds. Three children had dropped out of the camp that day, but this did not bother him nearly as much as he thought it would.

Isaac walked into the kitchen, startling Seth. "How long have you been up?" he asked.

Seth thought it unwise to respond that he wasn't sure if he had gone to sleep at all. He tried to use his voice and found it sounded like a rustling leaf. "What are *you* doing up so early?" he croaked, deflecting the question.

"It's 5:45, nearly time to get up." Isaac pulled up a chair. "I don't think they're coming back—Foday, Isatu, and Eric. And to think Foday was the one who started dancing after Saj left."

"Dancing?"

"When you walked out after Saj. First there was this silence, and Zayra and I tried half-hearted attempts to get them to talk about what Saj said, and they just sat there—you know how they do. Then Abdul started beatboxing, and first all the kids were looking at him, amused. Then they started tapping along—"

"All this happened while I was outside?"

"Well, you were outside a long time."

"Not that long," Seth said, running his hand over his head.

Isaac looked at him with a furrowed brow for a minute.

"Anyway, it was Foday who got up and started dancing, you know. He was being so real. Nobody asked him or gave him permission or anything. But there he was, so in the moment. And the kids started clapping along. And I thought the mood would catch, would take, but just like that—quick as how it started, the clapping stopped, and Foday sat back down. It was like something had leaked out of the room. But the disappointment from Saj leaving was still there."

"This happened while I was outside?" repeated Seth, his voice seeming to come from far away. "I didn't hear it." Something rustled in his brain, like the uneasy feeling of something forgotten.

Isaac went to the sink to get himself a drink of water. He drank it slowly. "So I was thinking—maybe we could switch things up with the camp," he said, turning around to face Seth.

"Switch things up like how?" Another time, Seth would have been intrigued, but now he could barely pay attention to Isaac while replaying the scene over and over in his mind of what happened after he followed Saj out.

"I'm in the educational system, and what I see over and over is that kids lack the basics. Like reading and maths. I'm talking how to construct simple grammatical sentences and properly understand what they're reading. You've heard these kids talk."

"We talked about this already when the camp started, and I told you this was not a camp about the basics. They can get private lessons for that."

"But many of these kids' parents can't afford private lessons."

"Why are you bringing this up again?

Isaac half-smiled. "Did you meet Abdul's mum when she came?"

"No. I wish I had."

"Well, she has really high expectations for the camp. She believes the camp is going to turn things around for Abdul. I worry about whether we can do that."

Isaac, in his winning way, had been able to find out much more about the kids' stories than Seth. He told Seth now about meeting Abdul's mother, who had come to drop him off on the first day of camp, a peasant woman, unsmiling and thin. The woman had offered Isaac a weak hand to shake along with a few halting words in *Krio*. She had walked away right after meeting Isaac. Although she was not the only parent who had come on the first day of camp, Isaac had been intrigued by her and had sought out Abdul, a large-eared boy with a shy smile and grubby clothes, to find out more about the family.

"My mother lives in Makeni with the rest of my family," explained Abdul. "I live in Freetown with my uncle. I am the only one of my brothers and sisters who is going to school. The rest are working on the farm. My mother came down from Makeni the night before the camp, and she went back right after you met her," he said.

Often illiterate themselves, poor rural families rarely became this involved in their children's education because they were diffident and unsure of how to interact with the school system. To have made the half-day trip from Makeni just to come to the camp was highly unusual.

"I didn't advertise a camp for the basics," Seth said, wincing at the inadequacy of his response. "I told Aunty Sia that too at the outset."

"I know, but they may still not understand that. That's what has me worried. It's not just Abdul. I wonder about some of the other kids' parents as well. They're probably hoping this camp will help their kids be better at taking tests, and that's all they want."

"All these kids will eventually learn how to read and do arithmetic, but not all of them will get the space to think about what they want to do with their lives."

"I'm just saying, well—I think we all know Saj's visit was somewhat of a disaster. You know they had their hearts set on rapping with Saj."

"Disaster?" It was all too much to comprehend. Seth was desperate to get away from Isaac, to puzzle over the events again, decipher what they meant. But this much was true—the kids had been bitterly disappointed not to rap with Saj. And the day after, the three kids had failed to turn up. God, how could he have been so self-absorbed? Of course, Isaac was right—Saj's visit had been a disaster as far as the kids were concerned. But then there was the kindling it brought, a slow heat winding its way through Seth's entrails, flooding out of him as though the borders of his being had dissolved and all was liquid fire. Could it be he was the only one affected in that way?

"I'm sorry, tell me again what you're suggesting."

"I'm saying we hedge our bets, focus on basics. You do maths for a bit, and Zayra can do reading. We've still got time. Enough time to give the kids something of a boost if we give them lots of one-on-one attention."

Seth bristled. "That means axing a lot, everything. Like the *gara* making and meeting with the agronomist and the field trip with the NGOs to the water and sanitation project and all those other field visits and activities. And this without any proof that parents are complaining. What else did Abdul tell you?"

Isaac told Seth of Abdul's tragic yet ordinary story. Of how, like many others, he used to work on the farm with his father. They barely made enough to send him to the Muslim school where he and the other boys had sat gripping wooden slates laced with Arabic, repeating the foreign words like recordings.

The war had interrupted his schooling. Yet he and his family were among the lucky ones. Though rebels had come to their village and burned down houses with people inside and killed family members in front of each other, Abdul's family had remained intact, and together they fled to Freetown. When the fighting ended, they went back to the province and resumed farming. There was no time for anything else but hard work on the farm, which had been neglected.

During that time, one more baby was born to the family. Abdul's father named her Peace, because the war was over. When Peace was one, grasping and tottering, they sent Abdul back to the city in the hopes that he would become educated and change their fortunes, or at least assure a future where there was enough food for everyone.

As Isaac finished telling the story, its weight smothered them in silence.

"Okay, let's give the basics a chance," Seth said. "Remedial education, as you say." He was surprised at the bludgeoning this concession brought.

"Okay," said Isaac, his voice quiet. Seth was surprised at his joylessness.

The dark had begun to lift; the sky was pierced with the first sparks of day.

"Do you really think the session with Saj was a disaster?" Seth said. "I thought his story was so powerful—what he saw under the mango tree that day?"

Isaac looked at him, his face quizzical. "What mango tree?"

"You know, how he talked about the deals his uncles were cutting . . ." Seth's voice trailed off as a feeling like a lump of wet clay began to expand in his stomach.

"Maybe you and he had a separate conversation? He didn't say any of that when he was at the camp."

"He did! Don't tell me you don't remember?"

Isaac sat down and was silent for a long time. When he spoke, his voice was grainy and dry as a wrung washcloth.

"It's like I told you, Seth. After he left and you went after him, you were gone for a while, fifteen minutes maybe. And then you came back in the room looking kind of dazed. I thought you must have gone to see him off and then had a difficult conversation with him. While you were gone that's when—"

"That's when Abdul started beatboxing and Foday started . . ." Seth's voice trailed off as though his breath had run out.

There were times when he had seen a task before him, whether small or large, and chosen not to do it. Fall into bed dirty and clothed with unwashed teeth rather than prepare for sleep. Blow off the term paper. Forget to call his parents. And another such task arose before him now—reconstruct his memory of what had happened with the understanding that some of it hadn't happened. It seemed far easier to believe that two events had indeed happened—the presence of one did not negate the presence of the other. Just as it had been easier to ignore what had happened with the men he had spoken with who did not remember him. Isaac was speaking now, but he needed great effort to tune him in.

"What did you say?"

His friend held an onion in a tight grip, which he slowly released to let it drop to the table. "I said maybe it's time for you to go back to America where there are people who can help you."

~ THIRTY ~

AT THE END of the camp later that week, Seth couldn't wait to leave. He quickly inverted the chairs on the tables and grabbed the palm spine broom to sweep. Instead of going home with Isaac and Ettie as usual, he made a pretense of having to go shopping.

Lucky had overheard this conversation and asked Seth if he could come along. Seth, caught off guard by the request, hadn't been able to come up with an excuse swift enough to refuse the boy. Feeling a prick of guilt, Seth looked around to see if the boy was in sight, thinking he might slip out after all and pretend he had forgotten about him.

"Mr. Thomas wants to see you," Isaac said now, perching himself on a table by Seth.

"The principal at Bai Bureh School? The school Abdul is from?"

"Yes, him."

"Why are we talking about him? Thought he was old news."

"Well, today I had a phone call with him," Isaac said.

"Huh. Why didn't you tell me earlier?"

"There's not much to tell. It's not like he ever says anything new, so what's to tell."

"What did he say?"

"Well, I know it's bullshit, given how much we tried, but he's still saying we didn't consult him about the camp. So he 'invited' you to come see him."

"When?"

"As soon as possible."

Seth began sweeping, and after a minute, Isaac walked away.

Seth and Isaac had been mainly silent toward each other since the night when Isaac had suggested Seth return to the United States, and when they did speak during the day, it was about matter-of-fact affairs of the camp. At home, they avoided each other as much as they could. Isaac had come into their room late the last two nights and slipped into bed without speaking to Seth. Seth would have been grateful to once again talk with Isaac had it not been for the unpleasantness of the subject matter.

Lucky turned up and grinned at Seth. "Ready?"

"I was just looking for you," Seth sputtered. As they walked out together, he looked down at the boy. Surely if he mentioned how Saj had told a story of watching two men sitting beneath a mango tree, spending trust like worthless coin, the boy would nod in recollection. Surely.

At the park Lucky looked around with a commanding air. "What did you come to buy?"

Buy? Ah, yes, he was supposed to be here to shop. The park was much like Seth remembered it. Even back in his childhood, much of the park and its environs had long ago been overtaken by market stalls that sold everything from local crafts and clothing to cellophane-wrapped Chinese goods.

"A shirt or two, I hope."

The boy visibly crackled with intent, looking around for the best place to start shopping. "Come. This way."

Seth followed him, his mind elsewhere. He chose some words, forced them out of his mouth. "Great discussion with Saj, eh?"

The boy nodded but seemed distracted. Seth felt bold; he would press on.

"I'm so glad I urged him to tell his real story, his true story." He held his breath, but at this too, the boy nodded. Seth suddenly felt too scared to press further. He changed topics, thinking to find out more about the boy. "Are you expected home at a certain time?"

Lucky shrugged. "Not really. I can go home whenever I want."

Seth guessed that the boy had intended this statement to be bait for Seth to pick up, but still preoccupied with working up a flash of nerve to lay bare his experience of Saj, Seth left the bait dangling.

They passed makeshift stalls of knobby wood covered with black and blue tarps strung together with nylon strings. The traders sat together on the platforms alongside their merchandise, chatting with one another while keeping a predator's eye out for prospective customers.

"I saw you standing up for Abdul the other day," Seth said, the event having suddenly come to mind. "When George and Nimata were making fun of his English, and you reminded them of the mistakes they'd made."

The boy broke into a broad grin, his head boulder-like upon his scrawny shoulders. "Really?"

"It made a big difference for Abdul."

Seth looked down at the boy, at the rust-tinged hair, the protruding shoulder blades evident even through his oversized shirt. He wondered as he had many times what Lucky's agenda was.

As if the boy had read Seth's thoughts, he said, "I can help with the camp too, you know."

Seth stopped. "What . . . how?"

"Are you giving up on the camp?"

"I'm sorry?"

"You don't have to answer. I'm sorry for asking. My mother says I'm too uncivilized."

Seth changed topics.

"Are your parents both here in Freetown?"

"Only my mother. My brothers and sisters and I, we live with my mother. And my father is in Germany."

"When did he leave?"

"Two years ago, once his papers came through."

"Will you guys join him there later?"

"Yes, of course."

"I see."

They sunk into silence once again. A little girl in a torn dress crossed their path selling plastic bags stuck together in silky sheaves. She looked askance at them, but they shook their heads. Much to his surprise, Seth saw a shirt he liked and bought it. They continued walking.

Last night he had seen the flame in the swamp again, and it ravished him, lured him, making him despise his own need, his hope that if he drew to it, it would yield something true. And even though his rational mind knew that it could be nothing—a paper cutout of his dreaming mind—he felt it, or rather something it portended, straining against the membrane of another realm to come into fuller existence in this one.

Perhaps Saj's story had caused this flame to appear in dead water. When he was a kid playing in the garden, he had pulled out tufts of grass, only to discover they were connected with other tufts at root level. Saj's story had canvassed him and become rooted. It was a true story.

"What do you want to be when you grow up?" Seth said to the boy. "We asked this question on the first day of camp, but you weren't there yet."

"Me? I want to be a politician," Lucky said, his voice eager.

"A politician. I see." The boy was clearly cut out for it.

"Why do you ask?"

"It's a big deal. And it seems you're the only one who has your own idea of what you want to be when you grow up and why. Everyone else seems stuck with the same ideas teachers and parents and everyone else gave them." It felt good to let out his frustration, but he immediately regretted confiding in Lucky. He still wasn't sure whether to trust the boy.

The boy took it with solemnity. "I'm different. No one gave me the idea of being a politician. I want that because I'm good at managing people."

"I can see that," Seth said, smiling despite himself.

The boy smiled back. "When my father left, he put me in charge. Let's take a right here," he interjected. "This would be a good place to find more shirts."

Lucky seemed to display no urgency in continuing his story. Seth took a deep breath, trying to be patient. The boy was not shy and would speak at his own pleasure.

"He said, 'Lucky, I am putting you in charge around here. If even the dog bites someone as they are walking down the street, I will hold you responsible.'"

The boy seemed to throw his shoulders back and grow taller at the mere recollection of the event. Yet he was so thin and patchy-haired. Seth tried not to show his amusement at the paradox of authority in such a scrawny figure.

"Did he call you Lucky?"

"No, of course not. But in my mind, everyone calls me Lucky."

"So were you cool that he said that?"

Lucky conceded the briefest of smiles.

"Actually, it didn't make much difference because I knew I was already in charge."

"Is that so?"

"Yes, but of course I didn't tell him I knew that."

"So how do you manage things at home?"

"Oh, I do it in all sorts of ways," Lucky said nonchalantly. He looked into the distance, as though casting about in his mind for something. "When my older brother was misbehaving, my mom was so frustrated, and she didn't know what to do. I took care of it."

"So what did you do?"

Lucky looked pleased that Seth had asked. "I simply told her what to tell him. And it worked. I told her to tell him that if he wanted to cause trouble, he had better do it really well so the street would kill him before my father did when he got back."

"Did it work?"

"It surely did. But it wouldn't have worked so well if I hadn't changed my name to Lucky just before that. She doesn't know that's a reason, but I do."

Seth stopped in front of a stall and faced Lucky. The boy gave him a fond smile, like an elder to a younger.

"If you've never changed your name before, I recommend you do," said Lucky. "Even if it's just for fun." He winked at Seth. "So will you let me help you with the camp?"

"I still don't know how you intend to help, but sure, we need all the help we can get."

"Okay. What do they say in America? I'm your man." He held out his hand for Seth to shake, and for some cloaked reason, Seth thought of The Mayor and couldn't bring himself to shake the boy's hand; he opted for a pat on the back instead.

"So, tell me. What are you planning on doing?" Seth asked, trying to sound casual.

"Relax! Everyone likes me. I wouldn't do anything to change that." He looked up at Seth with glinting eyes.

Night was unfolding its blankets in the sky. It was time to head home. Seth stopped walking, the worry of not asking the question overpowering the fear of knowing the answer. "Lucky, what do you make of the story Saj told, of the day he spied his uncle and other uncle sitting beneath the mango tree making a deal?"

The boy stopped walking. He looked back at Seth with eyes lit with intelligence. Seth felt his muscles stiffen. Perhaps Isaac had been right, and yet, he couldn't be. He was ready to swear on it.

~ THIRTY-ONE ~

"I USED TO be ugly once," Madame Tarawally said, lowering her bronze-lidded eyelids. "Can you believe that?"

Seth looked away and waited for the clothing designer to continue. Out of the corner of his eye, he saw a fly land on the table between them.

"Can you believe that?" she repeated.

He snapped his head back toward her. Increasingly he'd become paranoid that his distractedness was a visible tell that all was not well within.

"Of course not," he said.

"Not truly ugly. Maybe only some stupid people thought that," she continued. "Whatever they say about beauty being in the eye of the beholder, maybe it works the other way too."

He had sought Hawa—Madame Tarawally—out and compelled her to make a deal with him. All the while he was thinking of Isaac and how the fabric between them had torn further, into ragged strips, when he had told Isaac that he could not bring himself to continue with remedial education after all.

He had *not* told Isaac that Lucky too had heard the story of Saj witnessing betrayal under the mango tree. Or of how the boy's eyes had flared open and drifted into remembrance. For it *had* to be remembrance; Seth was sure of it. Of how shortly after Seth had felt the beckoning of the flash of flame in dead water and the compulsion to bring forth the camp as he had intended at the outset. Indeed, he had chosen not to think of why Isaac had such a radically different account of what had happened than he did.

"Have you ever thought you were ugly?" Hawa continued. "Do men think that way?"

To be unloved is to be ugly, he thought. "You are beautiful now," he said. He stole a glance at her purple fitted blouse with its abstract pattern of gold ink branching through it, the plum-painted lips raised portals on her dark-honey skin. In another time, he might have been overtaken by lust; its absence was more disturbing to him than *The Thing* itself.

She looked at him. "Shouldn't I just tell my story at the camp?"

"The deal was you would tell me now."

When he had showed up at her boutique for the first time, she was stressed and distracted. Her boutique manager had failed to show up that day. She urgently needed to deliver a clothing order but couldn't leave the store. Seizing his chance, Seth had offered to deliver it—on the condition that she would grant him an audience later.

"Yes, that was the deal," she recalled. "But you've only bought me one drink so far, and the food hasn't come."

Without a word, Seth got up and walked from the outside table toward the restaurant. He grabbed a waiter by the arm. Shortly after, he returned to the table and sat down. Right behind him, a waiter came bearing a plate of chips.

"We didn't order this," said Hawa.

"I know. I asked them for any food they could bring right away."

She smiled and then lifted a clump of chips onto a plate. Her bangles clamored on her wrist as she poured a generous dollop of ketchup alongside them.

"So your story . . ."

She smiled. "You don't miss a beat. There isn't much to tell."

"I've come to believe that when people say they've got a story, that's like a cat in a bag, meowing like crazy to get out."

She laughed and then said in even tones, "Well, this cat won't come out easy; you'll have to get it out of me."

Seth took a gulp of his pineapple juice. "Tell me how you got your inspiration then."

"I got my inspiration from magazines. Nothing surprising there. I used to look at models and what they were wearing and wonder why everything was so boring."

"Boring?"

"Well, you know the White people. It's white and gray and brown, and that's the palette—maybe it's the weather or something. Oh, and then they'll use a bright color, but it's like there's a quota, and you can only use one or maybe two strong ones at a time. Ridiculous! You walk the streets in a country crying poor like Sierra Leone, and the streets look like one big catwalk. Africana! The colors, the patterns, the designs. I thought, why does the fashion world not know this?"

"So that's what got you going? Showing the world the African side of design?"

"Something like that."

"How did you make your dream come true?"

She shot him a sly glance, and he began to think that she had decided not to divulge her story after all. But then she looked into the distance for a moment and began talking of how she used to walk up and down Thorpe Street and other streets in the East End like a beggar sniffing out loose change. It was a veritable tailor alley, and she got to know all the tailors who had shops there, their floors littered with colorful fabric.

First, she was ever so shy and aware of her youth and coarse hair, her plainness.

"Speak up, child," they would say. "What do you want?"

She wanted material, as much of it as they would spare. Even scrap fabric the size of a hair ribbon or handkerchief would do—whatever they had. But material was just the beginning. She wanted someone to teach her, but it was an ask she didn't know how to make.

One day one of the tailors asked as he handed her his scraps, "What do you do with all this material we give you? I don't believe you use it to stuff cushions as you told me earlier."

"I sew. I try to," she stammered, looking at the floor.

"Well, bring in something and let me see. I could do with an apprentice."

His name was Foday—a rail-thin man with an intermittent hiccup and a kind smile that he trained, along with smacks on the head, on his three snot-nosed children whenever they came into the shop. He taught Hawa everything. How different types of fabrics behaved and how to care for them. How to use the machine. From his hands, dresses with sleeves like wings and skirts like crests of ocean fluttered forth, as butterflies from cocoons. More than anything, she desired to learn his mind, how he could see a dress before it was born, pattern be damned. She studied the intake of breath of his clients when he brought forth his designs, and she felt like someone who had awoken from a dream of a faraway land.

Later she would think how in other countries he could easily have been a high-end designer himself and lament how much natural talent went to waste in the country.

"I was the lucky one who made it," she said, a catch in her voice.

Seth pondered the odds of this fortuitous pairing happening. "How fascinating. You stumbled upon the perfect teacher."

"Yes, that part of it was amazing, incredible. The rest is boring. Sewing became what I did when I had any free time. I went to university in England and went from studying finance to fashion design and broke my parents' hearts. At that point they had to admit that it was more than a hobby, and they weren't happy because, of course, all they could imagine was me poor and living with them until they died."

Seth wiped the last trace of ketchup from his plate with the fat body of the last chip. The sea air and afternoon sun were beginning to make him sleepy. He suddenly missed being at the camp. "Maybe when you meet the kids, you can tell them more about how you knew you were on the right track and what doubts you had. If any. Just flesh out the story a bit?"

"Uh-huh, okay."

The waiter came at last bearing their order. Hawa cheered, clapping her hands, bangles jangling some more.

"So what about you? What made you decide to do this camp?"

In his mind, Victor's silly grin. Damn the boy. Damn his happy eyes, now hurt, now smiling because what else was there to do when everyone thought you were an idiot, and that's what idiots did, anyway—grin and smile and hope to at least be thought muzzled and benign, without prickliness of thought.

"Well, there was this boy in my class in primary school who everyone thought was stupid, and somehow that stuck with me."

The mention of Victor—to someone other than himself—was like thrusting a trowel in earth and bringing up a clump to see worms and all manner of life wriggling in it.

"We used to sit together, and I would whisper answers to him. The teachers thought I was stupid too, or at best mediocre, and had sort of given up on both of us. I guess with the camp I'm trying to fight back a little—for kids like me and Victor." He saw the shame coming from afar, welling up from his past. He braced for it, and it broke over him. He closed his eyes and thought of the camp. When he opened his eyes, Hawa was frowning with concentration.

"That one boy? From so long ago? What an experience that must have been."

The air became heavy with foment. The next moment, the breeze coming in from the ocean became more muscular, and they held down their napkins and turned their faces into it. He closed his eyes, letting his mind flirt with sleep, with expectation.

Hawa said, "Why did you care so much about Victor?"

Seth opened his eyes and turned to face her.

"I was ugly too."

"What? You couldn't have been."

"I was the ugly stepchild, so to speak." When she looked at him with a furrowed brow, he told her of not-beingness, of languishing in Sam's shadow.

"I understand," she said and then took a breath and pursed her lips. "You wanted my story, right?"

His own breath quickened. "More than anything."

"I guess you could say I had a Victor too."

He put his fork down. "Tell me."

It began with her little brother, she said.

"I have a secret to tell you," he had said, dropping it in a casual way as he watered the plants and she swept the front verandah of their house.

He was born a politician. At seven he knew her better than she knew herself.

"What is it?"

"What will you give me for it?" her brother said, knowing her curiosity put her at his mercy.

"Keep dreaming. A big fat nothing," Hawa countered, feigning indifference.

He made a point of huffing in displeasure and then decided to spill anyway. "I heard two boys talking about you. They were buying something at the *Fullah* shop when I was there. Batteries, maybe."

"I don't care what they were there to buy. What did they say? And how old were they?"

Her brother told her of their conversation, with one boy telling the other how girls from his school were snobbish—with one exception. And the teller described this singular girl, who happened to go to his school, to no avail, as the other boy registered no recognition. Then the boy said he had pointed her out one day to his companion as she walked by wearing a purple dress. Recognition dawned in the other boy's face as he exclaimed, "Oh, her! I remember her now. Yes, that girl is something special."

She gave her brother some money, and he ran off. Her head was spinning; she felt like it was her birthday, and everyone she knew had come to her party. In a life otherwise without remark, somebody had called her special.

She began to get lost in her imagination. No one noticed. In her daydreams, she turned them into onlookers, overhearers of the boys when they had that conversation, the onlookers' faces seizing with shock as they heard her described that way. She imagined the boys with clear, kind faces.

Eventually, though, she did not get that same tingle in her stomach when she imagined the scene. But she wished, with every breath, for the specialness to remain. She had avoided wearing the purple dress again, or even looking at it, but one day she put it on, wondering how it would make her feel now.

But when she started to pull it over her head, everything changed. She smelled a perfume on it that was unmistakably her sister's, her butterscotch-skinned, fine-haired sister. She knew then that her sister had worn the dress and that the boys had been talking about her.

"How could you wear my dress without telling me?" she shouted at her sister. Both her sister and Hawa herself were taken aback by the strength of her anger.

"I'm sorry, okay? It's just a dress." But she did not know what she had taken from Hawa.

Hawa let sadness take her, falling into it like a wet mattress. Still, no one noticed. So she vowed never to be betrayed by vanity again. But that wasn't the end.

Her voice softened to a near whisper. In the distance, Seth heard the cries of children flying kites, until like the kites themselves, the wind appeared to lift their voices away. He leaned forward to hear every word.

"Sometimes the world notices you, even if people don't," she said. "I could speak of God too because the world is the hand of God."

She was walking home from the bus station one day, passing by the traders who lined the streets as usual. "*Sista, cam buy granat,*" called one trader to her. She didn't want roasted peanuts that day, so she shook her head and walked past. But then she thought of her little brother and retraced her steps. The trader made a cone out of a magazine page as they always did and put the peanuts inside.

At home, her little brother hugged her when she handed the peanuts to him and wasted no time popping them into his mouth as he slipped off the dry skins. When he had finished them, he came back and handed her the magazine page they had been wrapped in, now stained with oil spots.

"This is for you," he said with a smirk.

He and Hawa often teased each other like that. "To this day, I don't know if he was joking or not, but I know he was meant to hand me that page," she said. "Now he claims he doesn't remember it," she said with a chuckle.

The page was oil stained and wrinkled, but on it was the most beautiful woman Hawa had ever seen. Yet she was as dark as Hawa, startlingly so. Her features fit together like they'd been made from seamless cloth, and her skin was velvet. She wore a bottle-green sheath dress with gold jewelry and green eye shadow. Hawa couldn't take her eyes off her. She kept the page tucked in her statistics book, and when she thought of the woman there, lustrous and dark, she felt like she was cheering her on—her black sister. Restless thoughts stirred in her mind. Clothes were meant to cover, but suppose instead they revealed, like putting a gilded frame on a forgotten painting?

It was then that she got interested in clothing, her desire overpowering her shyness as she began to visit the tailor shops. One day, many years later, after she became successful, she made a dress for her sister. Her eyes flashed like Christmas lights when she saw it, and when she tried it on, it was stunning on her. As Hawa looked at her, she felt no envy in her heart. She was a free woman.

As he took in Hawa's story, a crevasse opened within Seth, and he knew he would not fall in because he had been cleaved already, but he perceived the size and hunger of the void. He gripped the table without thinking because the solid world outside surely could not help but be sucked into such a crevasse. But nothing changed except Hawa looking at him, and he realized he was to say something. Because he could not think of what to say, he simply said again, "I don't believe you were ever ugly."

"I know."

"What you just told me, that's the story to tell the kids."

"Are you kidding? I can't."

He said nothing because he wasn't even sure anymore anyone but him felt the emptiness of abandoned caverns within that cried for stories of creation.

~ THIRTY-TWO ~

ON SATURDAY, SETH stepped into the backyard to seek daylight. He thought to himself how nice it was to have a reprieve from the daily stresses of the camp. On the ground was a basin full of wrung clothes that Aunty Sia must have been planning to hang. He was strong, so he wrung the clothes even tighter, until every last drop of water dribbled to the ground. Then he carried the basin to the clothesline and began to hang up each piece.

Air and sun were one substance, inseparable, that broke upon him until something primal leaped up to taste it. The wind-sun lifted a shirt he was hanging up, and it flapped in his face. He smelled the sweet freshness of laundry soap, yet a faint, lingering odor of perspiration also. An emotion he could not place arose in him; he knew only that it was welcome.

"Will you help me light the fire, Seth? We are out of kerosene."

He turned around to find Ettie watching him.

"Sure," he said, pleased every time she overcame her shyness to ask him for something. After hanging up the last of the clothes, he set himself to the task of assembling the charcoal rocks on the coal pot, stoking them with some kindling, lighting a plastic bag to slowly melt and burn until the coals caught on and began to grow red. He watched his own hands, aware that he had never done this before, only watched as a little boy as their houseboy, Mustapha, had done it before he had gone off in search of love.

Seth and Sam had watched Mustapha's oversized hands, disproportionate to his small frame, fascinated by his thick fingers holding the kindling gently like feathers. Once Sam had blown out the flame as soon as Mustapha padded away on his large bare feet. But Seth had been watching the precise assembly of the kindling, the tease of the melting plastic bag twisted into a point, the first timid curl of fire, then the spire of smoke before Sam blew it out.

Now it was his turn. It pleased Seth greatly when the fire awoke and danced gingerly among the glittering black coals. But there was this sudden ache of knowing his brother would never be there to remember Mustapha's fire making or see that somehow Seth had retained the knowledge all these years, even though if he were alive, they would never have discussed it. As he watched Ettie fan the glowing coals with the flap of a cardboard box, Seth could somehow picture her in the scene with himself and Sam and Mustapha, even though she hadn't even been born yet.

He felt overcome by the soddenness of the memory, the burden of carrying it forward without Sam. For that reason alone, God must watch earth, if only to know that the little boy watching the fire, never touching the coals, would pass on the gift of fire making to this girl with the shattered soul. And though, by the time they were born, her children would no longer need to know how to coax a fire from coal, the knowledge from Seth would stay nestled within her, feeding into the web of rivers and oceans that were her life.

What was life, then, but the passing on of fire? It was the flame that Saj and Hawa had passed to Seth without knowing it, and perhaps to the kids. It was the dimming memory of Sam blowing out the flames and the air-sun spilling over Seth and the laundry and Ettie, so incandescent that he could hardly believe this moment too would one day be a husk but for the seeds it would scatter into the future.

~ THIRTY-THREE ~

ZAYRA HAD THE kids making pinhole cameras out of light bulb boxes. And though she had to explain each step multiple times, they were attentive enough. Each day he was made keenly aware of how limited their education was, yet he kept pushing Zayra to procure projects from her seemingly endless bag of tricks that involved insipid art or craft projects that seemed of marginal use to the children. Why couldn't he yield to the basics Isaac had requested? Help ensure that these children would be able to read with some competence after graduating from school?

Out of the corner of his eye, he saw movement in the doorway and turned to see a woman dressed with incomparable elegance appraising them. He looked to Isaac and saw recognition take hold in his face.

"Madame Tarawally! We weren't expecting you. But welcome!"

The children looked up, taking in this fascinating development.

Hawa looked past Isaac, straight at Seth.

"Seth didn't tell you I was coming?"

"Well, eh," Seth stammered, "I didn't think it was agreed."

Isaac looked toward the kids and motioned with his hands, and they rose to greet her. Hawa said something about Seth having requested her to tell the story of how she became who she was.

She told the story she had told Seth. All of it. And when she was done, she looked into the distance as if in a trance, and the silence became long and doughy. They all sat, looking at her—

the impeccable makeup, the almond-shaped lips, the brightness and sheen of her clothing. Then there was the fragrance that emanated from her—a combination of soap and spice and forests drunk with fresh rain.

After Hawa left, there was silence, even though Zayra tried to resume the exercise of making pinhole cameras. At ten minutes to three, Seth, Zayra, and Isaac could bear the silence no more and ended the camp for the day.

The next day a driver came with a package. Inside was a glossy coffee table book, and in it were photos of sapling-thin women feathered with clothes so beautiful that all the kids clustered around, raptured. And even after they had all seen it, they kept passing the book around until the beauty seemed to rise off the pages like the fragrance of Hawa herself, that forest of unbruised flowers and wet smells arising Lazarus-like from its leaf-veined soil, life awakening and giving off scent and spirit that would move where it pleased, hypnotizing those it would.

~ THIRTY-FOUR ~

STELLA GOT THE idea while watching dolphins cavorting through sprays of ocean on TV. "I know, Mom! We should take Granny to the aquarium!"

Evelyn had settled into something of a rhythm in the home, waking up in the morning to sit with them during breakfast before they left for work and kindergarten, and then taking a walk, followed by a nap, while they were gone. She didn't know why she joined them for breakfast as she said little and did not eat with them, only drank tea and watched them eat.

In the evenings, watching TV with them, she observed Stella plead with her mother for toy after toy that she saw advertised. Usually Joanna resisted her firmly. Then Stella's eyes would shift to Evelyn, as though trying to discern whether Evelyn would argue in her favor. One time Evelyn did offer to buy something for her, in this case a gnome-like figure that grew grass out of its head like hair. Joanna turned to Evelyn.

"She'll lose interest before the grass even grows, you'll see." But she nodded at Evelyn and said to Stella, "All right then, you lucky girl."

After that little victory, the girl's curiosity about this new person grew even more. Stella would run up to Evelyn's room after kindergarten, wanting to show Evelyn what she had drawn, offering her scented markers to smell. Evelyn was often stiff in her responses, working an unpracticed smile, though making an effort to take interest. The girl reminded Evelyn of Stella's father, Sam, in her eager, unwilting love.

Now it seemed the girl had gotten into her head that they should give Evelyn a tour of the city. It occurred to Evelyn that Joanna had not thought to do this, not gone out of her way to take Evelyn sightseeing or even to ask about her interests. How pitiful that it was a mere child who had thought of this. Joanna should be embarrassed.

"Granny will love the aquarium, Mom. We could go this weekend."

Joanna smiled. "Maybe your granny prefers a more mature type of entertainment, Stella, not to be run over by a thousand screaming kids like yourself at the aquarium."

In that instant, Evelyn saw a possibility—one so obvious that she was surprised it had not presented itself to her before. She would conquer the mother through the child. It would be that easy. The child was softening already, drawn by something not of her choosing: the power of blood and the longing for a father. Evelyn would become indispensable to Stella, and Joanna would recognize her amplified purpose in the girl's life. But to do so, she would have to open the memory vault. Was it worth it?

"That's a fantastic idea. I'd love to go to the aquarium with my granddaughter." And here she gave Stella a conspiratorial look.

"Maybe the two of us should go alone to give your mother time to herself."

Stella's transparent face suddenly looked unsure. She looked at her mother.

"Can Granny and I go together, Mom?"

Joanna seemed to have weighed the thought already.

"Sure. I'll get some errands done in the meantime."

~

AT THE AQUARIUM, Stella pulled her grandmother's hand with surprising strength. Evelyn had never been to an aquarium before, but she had been to zoos and botanical gardens. She had been wowed in the past at the things that people could create in rich countries to amuse, to entertain, and hadn't expected to be overly impressed this time. But she found herself watching with interest the exotic fish with their paint-box colors. Then there were the whales, the penguins, the iridescent jellyfish, fragile as flowers, gracefully suspended in the water.

"There's a beluga whale, Granny. The last time we came, it did a flip. When we went to its tank, we couldn't see it, and we waited and waited. Mom wanted to go, but I told her we should wait longer. I knew it was coming." She smiled proudly.

She had worked hard to forget Sam, blindly swinging at the memories that had crowded in on her, turning them away with an animal ferocity. And they had succumbed. But now, a new and powerful fear took hold of her, strong enough to constrict her chest—the thought that one day the memories would be gone from her entirely. If they languished and dissipated in the vault, if they were no longer hers to summon and banish, then of what meaning was her life? Surely this was an even greater loss.

"Too bad you were never able to come here with your father."

Stella looked up at her, standing still for a minute, and then tugged on her hand. "Let's go to the Wonder River part, Granny. We haven't gone there yet."

"No, wait, Stella. Granny's a little tired. Why don't we sit down in that cafeteria over there and have a bite?"

Stella didn't look too pleased, but she complied and even brightened up after a while.

It was time to make a move. Joanna would be coming within the hour. Perhaps if she could make only a fleeting entrance into the vault, then the memories would stay tamed, but not disappear. Perhaps.

"I've never had the hot dogs in the cafeteria before. Can we have some?"

"Yes, whatever you want, dear."

The girl squealed, and Evelyn marveled at how easily she became excited. It had been so long since the boys were children that she had forgotten the simplicity of a child's mind.

Stella munched happily, looking around her and swinging her legs as they dangled off the chair. Evelyn felt a little guilty, taking advantage of the child's guilelessness, but none of this would hurt the child.

"Do you remember your father, Stella?"

The munching stopped.

"No."

"Would you like to remember him more?"

The child looked at her round-eyed.

If she could paint a picture real enough, perhaps the girl's imagination would coalesce into something like true memories.

"Does your mother talk about your father?"

The child thought hard, pouting her lips in concentration.

"Umm . . . yes."

"Well, what does she say?"

"That he was tall . . . and that he loved me."

"What else?"

"That he was from Sierra Leone."

"What else?"

"That he had to have rice every day, and it would take him half an hour to take the bones out of sardines."

The memory vault was open, and around her, it felt like the heaviness in the air and the shudders of wind just before a storm. She could see Sam now, carefully lifting a sardine from its bed of oil in the newly opened can, painstakingly pulling out the softened bones without breaking the spine.

"Did she talk about things they did together?"

Stella seemed to be getting bored. She shook her head and tapped her feet together.

Evelyn clasped her hands and leaned across the table, bringing her face close to the girl's.

"Do you know you walk like your father?"

"Really?"

"Yes. And the way you pulled my hand through the aquarium is the exact same thing he used to do. Remember, I knew him when he was a little boy of your age. I can tell you all sorts of things that he did as a child." But even as she said this, she wondered how far she could reach into the memory vault without having the memories turn on her as they had before she left for the States.

The child stopped swinging her legs and looked solemnly at Evelyn. "Mom says he didn't like to talk about his childhood."

Evelyn studied her face, taken aback by this. But there was no questioning on the girl's part, only the regurgitation of something discussed between mother and daughter.

"I find that hard to believe. Sierra Leone is a very interesting place to grow up in."

Suddenly she couldn't wait for Joanna to pick them up, to be alone in her room, where she could review this information like some hoarded morsel. Of course, as she suspected, Joanna had told the child things she was too young to evaluate for herself now and would not have the evidence to do later. What inner churning had led Joanna to say such a thing to a child? Beneath that cool exterior bubbled the discontent Evelyn had suspected.

She looked at the child with pity. Stella could see the most beautiful fish in the world, even a whale, but only behind glass. Sam and Seth had caught fish with their bare hands, river water licking their ankles, mud squirming through their toes. They had cut through undergrowth like explorers penetrating the primeval forest. It had been their birthright to disappear for hours on end, wandering, playing, exploring. Joanna would be there to pick up

Stella at the hour. They would go home, and Stella would have no one to talk to or play with but the two women.

Evelyn felt for Stella who would remain forever disconnected from the world her father had inhabited. If the memories could be tamed, ruled again, then in the telling of them, the girl would see Sam, his body becoming the semblance of the words, his form being built from her breath.

Evelyn's cellphone rang. It was Joanna.

"Are you ready for you mother to pick us up?" she asked the girl before answering.

"Yes," the girl shrieked.

"Good."

~ THIRTY-FIVE ~

SETH SLIPPED OUT the door without telling Isaac that he was leaving for his meeting with Mr. Thomas, the principal. He reasoned that Isaac knew of the meeting, remembered the agreed time. And he knew full well under different circumstances, he would have told Isaac.

Isaac remained reserved with Seth, his demeanor always concerned, even cagey. The joking and sparring were gone, replaced by a strained politeness. Seth realized he hadn't heard Aunty Sia mention or ask about the camp as she used to. He thought to ask Isaac about this and realized he no longer felt comfortable asking such a question or hearing what Isaac had to say in return.

He felt the old anger kicking up in him like a cloud of dust. Tired—of fighting, of doubting, of hoping most of all—he decided instead to welcome its stinging breath, its seismic roar. He marinated in the rage during the taxi ride to the school where he was to meet Mr. Thomas.

There was at least reason to be angry with the man, Seth told himself. It wasn't as though Seth and Isaac hadn't tried to consult him before, as he claimed. In truth, when Seth and Isaac had first gone to the principal's school, well before the camp started, they had not been granted a meeting. After a subsequent try, Isaac simply went about handing brochures to teachers he knew. Two kids from Mr. Thomas' school had ended up in the camp, one of whom was Abdul.

A bowed, gray-haired caretaker let him in through the pedestrian gate and into the empty schoolyard with its graveyard aura.

With a grunt, he pointed a gnarled finger in the direction of Mr. Thomas' office.

When Seth entered, he found the principal talking on his cell-phone. He motioned to Seth to have a seat. The office was stifling. Seth felt the damp creeping out from his armpits and the small of his back. And there was a heat within him too that caused his pores to dilate, his blood to rush fast and unfettered through the gulleys in him.

Mr. Thomas was a slender man with fingers as thin as birds claws, Coke bottle glasses, and a large garishly colored paisley tie that drew inordinate attention as an accessory to his nondescript school teacher shirt and slacks. When he at last got off the phone and turned to Seth, he offered him a lifeless hand like a dead fish and cast him a squint-eyed, puckered mouth look. He was younger than Seth would have thought—in his early forties, per-haps, though he was doing his best to project an august air. Seth detected a faint Britishness to his accent. Perhaps he had been educated overseas.

"How is the camp going?" asked Mr. Thomas as they settled themselves into seats, Mr. Thomas in his faux-leather chair and Seth in the metal chair on the other side of the desk. The princi-pal's chair had once aspired to majesty with its faux leather and high executive back, but now the arms had holes in them from which white synthetic stuffing tumbled.

Why do you ask? Seth wanted to shout. *Get to what you're really after.* He tried to slow his breathing and dispel some of the anger into the armrests of the chair he was gripping as though they were guardrails. "So far, can't complain. The kids seem to be slowly coming out of their shells."

The principal thrust himself back in his chair, which creaked, as though in alarm. "What can I do for you?"

Seth looked at him in confusion. "You requested this meeting. What did *you* want to see me about?"

"Ah. So you got the message, and you took it seriously?" he said, trilling a light laugh and making a waving motion, as if to dispel any seriousness of the matter. "Why should you listen to me or consult me? I just mentioned the meeting to Isaac in case there was anything I could help you with."

So there it was. Mr. Thomas was nothing more than an African "big man" whose carnivorous ego must be satiated at all times. Such men demanded titles, obeisance, and respect. Seth knew the way forward—flattery, deference, and assurances to the man of his omnipotence and Seth's gross negligence in not paying heed to it in the first place by failing to seek his blessing about the camp.

But the rage rushing through him would allow none of it. During the best of times, he disliked such men. Now he loathed them. He chose his words unwisely yet with intent, like one deliberately driving into oncoming traffic.

"I think we're fine, but thanks for asking." He rubbed his chin and looked at the man straight on. "Is there anything else?"

Mr. Thomas cocked his chin, smiled at Seth, then trilled an artificial laugh.

"Well, now that you've taken the trouble to come all this way, maybe you can tell me a bit about the camp?"

"What have you heard so far?"

"I've heard you want it to be different. God only knows how inferior any extracurricular activities in this country must seem to you," said Mr. Thomas with a straight face. Seth didn't fail to detect the lurking sneer.

"Different in this case doesn't mean superior," Seth said. "I just wanted the kids to think differently about their futures and possible career prospects—and also think a bit 'out of the box,' to use the cliché."

"I see. How's that going?"

"Well," Seth said, holding a steady gaze.

The principal pressed the tips of his fingers together and looked at his desk for a moment. "Great that the boat has washed you in from America with all the enthusiasm and ideas."

So now the gloves were off. "What's wrong with that?" Seth said through gritted teeth.

Mr. Thomas smiled. From within his desk drawer, he procured a tissue with which he began to wipe the edge of his desk.

"Nothing, of course. Nothing's wrong with trying. I tried too, years ago. I was already a principal and frustrated at the kind of students we were turning out. Illiterate bumpkins, ragamuffins who picked their noses and couldn't manage one straight sentence in English.

"So I determined that even if I couldn't change the masses I would try to make a difference for a few. Because I couldn't do this in my school, of course, I identified a few students from other schools who I heard were somewhat promising but were from very poor families. Out of my meager salary, I paid for their schoolbooks for the year, took them out to eat with my family so they could learn how to behave in public, let them play with my own children so the whole family could get to know them. I even paid for private lessons for them.

"Would you believe that those ungrateful parents turned on me?" he said, his voice climbing. "They began to complain that I was corrupting their children—filling their heads with bad ideas and teaching them to be disobedient to parents and lazy at home. Worst of all, these allegations filtered to me secondhand through the children. I asked for a meeting with the parents to hear their side and explain my intentions. But they didn't even give me the courtesy of an audience. Nothing," he spat. A droplet of spit landed on Seth's hand. He pointedly wiped it.

"So I entrusted those kids once again to the care of their illiterate parents and this vagrant society. It was only years later that I was able to put things in perspective and realize that it was too much change for them to handle. We Sierra Leoneans like suffering."

Despite himself, Seth smiled.

"Do you think I'm joking? Years ago, I would have been scoffing too like you at the mention of that, but not anymore." He paused, waiting for Seth's reaction.

"I'm sorry to hear about your experience," Seth said, his tone flat.

Mr. Thomas gave him a gracious smile. "I don't tell you this for pity. Pity those poor children instead, progeny of nincompoops, vagrants, and half-brains. I told you this for your benefit. Let me ask you this. Are the kids faring as you would hope in your camp? Are they animated?"

"They're opening up slowly." Seth said.

Mr. Thomas leaned back in his chair and pressed the tips of his fingers together again. He smiled in a dreamy, melancholy way, like one caught in the blush of the memory of a first kiss.

"Heh. Slowly. All these new methods you are trying might be intimidating them. And the expectations too. They live in mortal fear of expectations because they're sure they don't have what it takes to meet them. And this is why this country never goes forward. It's the backward mentality of the people. So suspicious, so comfortable in primitiveness that they will snarl at you even when you try to give them a hand up.

"So why don't you adjust your expectations—for the good of the children and for your own good. That way they won't feel as stressed out about meeting them, and you won't be in for a big letdown."

With this pronouncement, he leaned back even farther in his high-backed chair, which groaned as though bearing the weight of a much heavier man.

Seth thought of all the teachers in his life issuing edicts of what was right and wrong, who was worthy and who was not.

"Someone has to expect something out of them," he seethed, "or else they will think they are worthless. I know the feeling."

Mr. Thomas cocked his head slightly as he looked at Seth.

"You, eh? You from your privileged background know the feeling."

Unable to contain himself any longer, Seth rose to his feet.

"I must take my leave," he said. What would Isaac have said instead? He would have started by talking about the remedial education, which wasn't.

Mr. Thomas refused to stand up with Seth. He looked up at him coldly, ensconced by his long-suffering armchair. "Good. All the best with it."

Seth thanked him and walked out, his steps quickening, anxious to get out before his rage erupted into something worse.

But the principal was not yet done with him.

"Mr. Walker," Seth heard him call.

Setting his jaw, Seth retraced his steps and stood in the doorway of the man's office.

"Do you mind if I come by to visit the camp sometime? I'll be very careful not to bother you."

He loathed the thought of laying eyes again on the man, but he would not go so far as to refuse him. "Suit yourself."

Mr. Thomas flashed him a satisfied smile.

~

THAT EVENING, AS Seth sat on the kitchen steps, Isaac, without a word, pulled up a chair behind him. Seth didn't have to turn to know it was him.

"Did you see him?"

"Yes."

Seth gave Isaac a factual account of the encounter, leaving out his anger, Mr. Thomas's cloaked arrogance, the undertow of emotion in every sentence.

Isaac said nothing in response. Then he moved his chair, making an unbearable grating sound. "The other night I went to the kitchen and saw Aunty Sia stooped over some documents on the table. They were Ettie's old report cards and even some handwritten essays. And I could see some of them had wax splotches, maybe from when she'd been reading them before by candlelight.

"She saw me and said, 'Is Ettie learning at this camp, Isaac? I keep asking her, but she won't talk to me. Do you think it will help her pass her exams?'

"Then I went to find Ettie herself and I asked, 'Is everything okay at the camp?'"

Seth held his breath.

"She shook her head but wouldn't say more. And I said to her, 'You know, you can leave if you want to, Ettie.' And she shook her head again and said, 'I can't.'"

"Why? Is it something Aunty Sia said?" Seth asked. "Is Aunty Sia making her stick it out?"

"No, I'm sure of that. There's something else going on, but I couldn't get it out of her."

And Seth couldn't help but imagine Mr. Thomas advising Aunty Sia to lower her expectations of Ettie.

~ **THIRTY-SIX** ~

ABDUL CAME DOWN the few steps from the balcony wearing
dark glasses, his face clenched with pain. For once, the other children did not snicker at him; instead, they watched him,
enthralled. He walked onto the space of the yard that served as
the stage. Seth had never seen sadness cloud Abdul's features for
even a moment. Now the boy put a blind man's trembling hand
forward and took some unsure steps. When the blind man called
out with a weak voice, one of the smaller boys came onto the
scene to take him by the hand. Gone was the adolescent awk-
wardness; on stage Abdul was a different boy.

After the performance, as they had talked about, Seth would
lead the children in a discussion of careers—the first real session
he would lead with the kids.

Isaac was watching the skit, his face enraptured. The acting
had been his idea—an acquiescence to (or perhaps quiet resigna-
tion to) the exploration of other livelihoods and loves that Seth
was intent on making the camp about.

"Isaac, I'm sorry," Seth had said. "Perhaps we can still do some
remedial education, just not for all the remaining time."

Isaac produced a smile that stretched his skin taut. "It already
wasn't that much time to begin with—for either purpose. No, it
was wrong of me, Seth, to hijack your vision."

But their old sparring did not resume as before.

~

Now in the fourth week of the camp, they had dived into acting with the aid of a drama instructor, and a couple days into it, the kids were ready to put on their first skits. Seth, Isaac, and Zayra were happy to sit back and watch for once.

The story of the blind man unfolded: He was living happily when a cobra spat in his eyes, blinding him. He then began to rely on his small son to be his eyes, to guide him. But his wicked ex-wife took the boy away from him and replaced him with another one.

The man was troubled because he knew it was another boy, even though his body, face, and voice were like his son's. But fearing the ex-wife, everyone around him denied that such a thing had been done.

He ended up contriving a test whereby he solicited a friend to pay a surprise visit to his ex-wife who lived far away. The friend did so, where he found the son living unhappily with his mother. The friend returned to report this to the blind man, who, in the meantime, had come to love the other boy as his own. Conveniently, the wicked mother died unexpectedly, the son came back to live with his father, and the two boys ended up living as brothers.

Seth was very impressed by the story, but what took his breath away was Abdul's acting. His character's face cracked with inner groaning when thinking of his boy. Joy lifted his features when he heard that the boy was alive and living with his mother. During one particularly stunning moment of contemplation, Abdul took off his dark glasses, his dead gaze swinging hither and thither.

Many of the other children did well too, but Abdul stole the show.

Above all, they loved putting on the skits. They cackled, they shouted at each other, they let their mouths fall open, rapt with attention and sometimes amusement, as they watched each other perform.

When they were done, Seth began:

"Throughout the course of the camp, you've learned about some different careers and had different professionals come in to speak with you," he said, trying hard to control his nervousness. "That was the fun part. But now we want to take it a bit further and see if you have new ideas about what you'd like to become—in the future, in your careers. Can you tell me if you have a better idea of what you'd like to be when you grow up?"

The children looked at him with cocked heads. And then in unison, they all turned toward the door as a figure appeared. It was Mr. Thomas, wearing a fixed half-smile and the long-sleeve cotton shirt and tweed trousers of a technocrat.

He stepped over the threshold, and the children rose like a gathering wave to greet him. Seth stole a glance at Isaac, then looked toward Mr. Thomas, realizing he must greet the man, afford him the welcome he was awaiting, but his throat had contracted as though he must retch.

Isaac sprang forward, exclaiming with forced enthusiasm, "Sir, you are welcome."

"Thank you so much, Mr. Sesay. My profound apologies for coming unannounced. I was nearby and thought I would just come by for a quick visit to see how things are going and learn how I can be of further assistance," he said with an amenable expression. "Carry on as if I weren't here. Although . . . I do very much want to hear the answer to that thought-provoking question Mr. Walker just asked."

So he had been eavesdropping outside the door—for God knows how long. With that, he insisted on installing himself not in front, on the chair they offered him, but at the back of the room where he sat looking around with a plastic grin that seemed to have been manufactured for the occasion.

Isaac flashed Seth a warning look. It was totally unnecessary. Seth already knew he would have to choose his next steps with care.

All eyes turned to Seth.

"We were talking about what you want to do," he said in a faltering voice, pausing as one does at a fork in the road. Before *The Thing*, when his mind was his own, he could easily have parried and thrust, appraised the choices before him with lightning speed and charted a way forward. Now he could merely grope in the dark reaches of his mind for a doorknob that would creak and turn.

Out of the blue, the memory of Saj flashed before him, after the telling of the story that happened with the mango tree and how his stomach had turned at what he saw. He saw again, clear as a shard of glass, Saj saying, "I hated it and wanted no part of it," and understood in the pit of his being the loathing that had torn Saj away from his old life. It was what had torn Seth away from even the memory of Sam.

"Sometimes it's what you don't want that can define who you are, who you need to become," Seth said to the children. They looked at him, perhaps surprised that he had recovered the powers of speech. Mr. Thomas' expression was inscrutable, Isaac would not meet his eyes, and Zayra was leaning forward in her chair.

"Can you think of a time, maybe during these few weeks, that you realized, that's something I don't want to do with my life?"

A stony silence enveloped his question. This was not what they'd expected, not what even Seth had expected. Absently, he put his hand to the side of his neck and felt his pulse strike back at him. He would proceed.

"Do you remember when Saj told the story of his two uncles beneath the mango tree?"

Although Seth wouldn't look at him, he could tell Isaac was leaning forward. He could sense his alarm.

He looked to Lucky, but the boy returned only a quizzical look.

"Lucky remembers the story, don't you?"

There was no response from the boy from whom words normally poured like oil.

Mr. Thomas stared at the scene with the unblinking eyes of a raven. There was a silence like the falling of dust after an explosion. The kids looked at one another in confusion and then at Zayra and Isaac, who looked as though they had been unexpectedly charged with a crime.

"I want to be an actor," burst out Abdul, stumbling on his words somewhat. As after any pronouncement of his, the whole class broke into laughter, tinged with relief this time.

"I want to be an agronomist," said another boy unexpectedly.

"I want to be a pilot," said one of the girls.

The other kids were raising their hands. Seth was taken aback.

"A computer engineer."

"A geologist."

Not all the kids spoke, but a few more mentioned careers that they heretofore would not have mentioned. Then they looked around at themselves, pleased.

~

MR. THOMAS LEFT at the end of the session. Seth walked him to his car, a decrepit Nissan Sunny missing its rims. Seth planted his eyes forward, barely aware of the principal's presence. His face, his very entrails, burned as though he'd had a double shot of whiskey. So had Saj truly never spoken of the meeting under the mango tree? But instead of answers, there were only feelings within him.

Mr. Thomas too seemed strangely quiet. "Good work, Mr. Walker," he offered at last in the stiff manner Seth was accustomed to.

"Sorry?"

"Those kids seem to be learning something." The principal pulled his keys out of his pocket and looked at them.

"I must ask you though, it seemed there was a moment of confusion when you brought up that incident the kids didn't seem to remember?"

"I don't recall," Seth said, doing his best to wrinkle his face into uncertainty. Fool. Even the feebleminded would have been able to deflect better than that.

Mr. Thomas looked Seth straight in the eye. His gaze was inscrutable.

Seth looked away and opened the car door for the man.

When the car was out of sight, Seth walked to the main road to hail a taxi, unable to bear the thought of returning to the camp.

~ THIRTY-SEVEN ~

JOANNA WAS BUSY in the kitchen drawing chicken parts through a honey mustard sauce for baking while talking in soothing tones to a friend on the phone. Evelyn patted the space next to her on the couch and the child levered herself onto it.

She looked up at Evelyn sideways, shy, as Evelyn put her arm around her.

"What did you do today?"

"I drew three drawings. One was a boat, and then a salt and pepper shaker, and then there was one of the three of us. Do you want to see them?"

"I'd like to, yes."

Stella brought her three sheets of heavy-grade paper and pulled out the family portrait.

"Can you guess which one is you, Granny?" The child looked up at her wide-eyed, no trace of mischief in her face.

Evelyn would not have had patience for such a question from Seth or Sam when they were little, but now she was able to find the humor in the moment. The figure of Evelyn had been depicted by two egg-shaped mounds, one on top of the other. The arms were long and snakelike, ending in fingers that sprouted like a bunch of bananas. In contrast, the taper-like form of Joanna was delineated in elegant lines, her blue dress shaded in, and Stella had taken the time to impose upon the blue a string of pearls colored with silver crayon.

"This one," Evelyn said pointing at her crayoned likeness.

Stella smiled. "How did you know?"

"I can tell by my burgundy handbag that you've drawn here."

"I knew you would know!"

She lowered her voice and pulled the girl close. "You must draw a picture of your father."

"Why?"

"Because he is part of you, even though he is not here. You must think of him now so it becomes something you do always."

"I don't remember him, Granny."

"Then you must come visit me in Sierra Leone, and I will tell you stories about your father. You will see the room he had when he was a little boy, the garden where he and your Uncle Seth used to play hide-and-seek, and the river they used to escape to without telling me. It is called the Matenge River."

"Did Uncle Seth and Daddy live in the same house?"

"Yes, they did. Their rooms were as close together as your room and your mother's room." She watched the girl picturing this, the workings of her mind transparent.

"Your father was brave, he was special," she continued. She entered the memory vault, afraid but resolute. Its cold familiarity enveloped her. There was Sam's voice, his laugh . . . she must focus. "There was one time when your father and your Uncle Seth went to the river even though I had warned them many times not to. I remember it like it was yesterday. We hadn't seen true sunshine for days, for in Sierra Leone, the country where you are truly from, it rains so hard you think the rain will never end, and that even if it does, surely nothing will ever be the same again. Every time the thunder cracked, the cat would dash across the room and startle us."

The child giggled.

"What type of cat was it, Granny?"

"It looked like Samantha," she lied.

"One rainy day, the scariest sound I heard was not the thunder but a scream so loud that even though I knew it was coming from far away, I could feel the fear and danger right in my stomach. I just knew it was one of the boys—your father or your Uncle Seth—so I ran to the river as fast as I could."

Stella watched her wide-eyed, hardly breathing.

"There used to be rocks in the middle of the river that you could walk to in the dry season. Now, the river was swollen, and only the tops of them were visible. The water that was normally green and fresh was brown, so full of dirt that God knows all the other things that flowed inside. There, on the banks of that river, so close that their feet were muddy, I saw your father holding your Uncle Seth tightly, comforting him as he cried. And they were both wet. They had disobeyed me and gone to the river. And they had been playing games until your Uncle Seth threw your father's slipper into the water. Then they must have started to tussle, and because the banks were so slick and muddy, your Uncle Seth slipped in. Your father got him out quickly before it was too late. He could have died, you see. Seth would have died had your father not been brave. That was when I knew for sure that your father was special."

Stella considered this, her eyes small, round lakes. "Uncle Seth could have died?"

"Yes, if your father hadn't been brave." It seemed lost on the child that had her father died, she would not exist today. "And not only was he brave, he had a big heart. I have never told anybody what I saw at the river, not even your grandfather, but I am telling you, your father's only child, my only grandchild. And now that I have told you, this story connects us forever like a rope that no one else can see. Do you understand? Just like I will not forget, you must not either."

Stella looked at her, unblinking, silent.

From the kitchen they heard the squeak of the oven door being pulled back on its hinges and Joanna's velvet voice. "You should just have walked away. You know the moment you did, he would have come down on the price . . ."

"Do you understand?"

Stella looked at her, solemn and alert. Then without another word, she ran to the kitchen, and Evelyn heard the flow of Joanna's conversation staunched as she looked to the child.

~ THIRTY-EIGHT ~

FROM THE COTTON tree, the bats winged their way into the purple sky. Down below, Seth wandered in the heart of the city, while others strode past him, trying to get home or to some other destination. Traffic thickened around the roundabout circling the landmark tree as the sounds of the city swirled about him.

He groped in the dark of his mind for a passage, a certainty. In the morning, he would have to face the children again. They had greeted him with blank stares at the mention of Saj's other story, after Seth had revealed himself for the lunatic he was.

And yet, they had voiced the new careers he longed for them to want. Their very destinies were beginning to change—but could he truly believe that when his mind had proven itself to be so thoroughly unreliable?

He thought of Dr. Holland and his solemn prognosis, prophecy perhaps, of what would happen if Seth neglected to take his medication. And Seth had resisted, then and later, throwing the medication into the river. Allowed himself to be dissuaded by Joanna from sending for more. Wanting to believe anything but the obvious about his mind.

He should fade into the background once again, before he had another episode. Before that ugly word—violence—came to be. But where was there to go now? Looking back, even the desire to die, to expire under a bridge, had seemed surgically clean and clear, a blessing almost. But now he neither saw nor felt either the creature in the swamp or the flicker of fire.

Perhaps the flame had been a harbinger only of rage. A rage that would consume him like a sunset bleeding over the land. Then there would be a time when he would be drawn into the swamp once again. It would close over him for a final time as the creature dragged him deeper and deeper into the clotted world of sediment.

"Aberdeen!" shouted a bus conductor hanging out the door of an overburdened *poda-poda*. Aberdeen was in the direction of his parents' house. If he went there, he would have but one more taxi to take, and he would be within walking distance of his old home. He hadn't seen or spoken to his parents since the night he left. If he went to them, Alfred would be sitting on the veranda, no doubt, surrounded by the sweet smoke curls of mosquito coils, the transistor radio pressed to his ear. If he was lucky, Evelyn would be off attending a meeting of her women's club.

His eyes and the conductor's met. Such people could sniff out even a hint of intent from a potential passenger. For a moment, Seth stared at him. Then he shook his head, and the bus continued in its labors along the street.

He wandered about until the crowds thinned and darkness settled upon the city. At last, he worked up the courage to return to the place that, for now, was still home.

~

UPON APPROACHING THE house, he heard voices that were slightly raised: Isaac's and Aunty Sia's.

"It's clearly stressing the girl out."

What was?

"Aunty Sia, Ettie is going to be exposed to all kinds of stresses in life. We cannot shelter her from everything."

"Isaac, I can't let the girl can't take any more. She's been through enough for five lifetimes."

Silence from Isaac. Seth's hand hovered over the front door handle.

Aunty Sia's voice grew more muffled. "You know I want that girl to be a lawyer."

"But, Aunty Sia, suppose she is not able to do that?"

"So you're just like everybody else. Believing she's slow. I'm surprised at you, Isaac."

"I'm not saying that, Aunty Sia. It's just—"

"And I thought she would be learning, anyway. She comes home, and the most I can decipher is that she listens to a bunch of people all day go on and on about what they do."

"There's much more to it. We go on visits; they try their hand at—"

"I thought she was going to learn things that would actually help her in school, like maths, science subjects, composition. You told me she would, Isaac. I even asked Seth about giving her maths lessons a while back, but he's been preoccupied with this camp."

More silence from Isaac. Seth could take it no more. He walked in.

They looked at him, then Aunty Sia put her hand to her head. "I must go to bed now. I wake up normal time tomorrow."

Seth felt an unbearable soaking of his body, as though it were a sodden loaf of bread good for nothing but being thrown away. He could barely stand the thought that he had brought discord to this family that had been so good to him.

When Aunty Sia had retreated to her room, he looked at Isaac.

"What was that about?" he croaked.

"Ettie seemed bothered this evening. Aunty Sia kept questioning her, and she finally burst into tears and said she doesn't want to go back to the camp."

Seth took this in. "Did she say why?"

"No, we tried to get it out of her, but it was next to impossible to get her to stop crying long enough to talk. She wouldn't talk the last time I asked her how the camp was going either . . . but then she insisted on staying—"

"And now something's changed." Seth bit his lip. "I am so sorry to have brought this on you guys."

"Seth, I told Aunty Sia the things I knew she would want to hear about the camp."

"What?"

"Well, I didn't give her details, but I led her to believe the camp would be about, well, remedial education. I did a bad thing, Seth—to you, to Aunty Sia, to Ettie."

Seth took this in, surprised that among the jumble of emotions he felt, there was a cord of relief—that he was not the only one to have failed in their friendship.

"You thought the camp *was* going to be about that."

"No. You made that clear." There was a bite in Isaac's voice.

"Then why?"

Isaac pulled his cellphone from his pocket and smacked it, distracted, against his open palm, a look of queasiness on his face.

"I really did think Ettie would benefit . . . or at least I hoped she would. And when I saw how much hope it brought to Aunty Sia . . . and then I thought you might be persuaded to . . ."

"To change to remedial education." They both stood in silence, not knowing what else to say.

Doors opened and closed, and then they heard sobs coming from the room that Ettie shared with Aunty Sia. They thought to leave the woman and the girl alone. But the sobs continued, and they stood hesitantly outside the door until at last Isaac gave it a timid knock, then a more insistent one, and finally opened the door, unbidden.

Aunty Sia was sitting on the bed, Ettie sitting on the floor with her head in Aunty Sia's lap. Aunty Sia rested one hand awkwardly on Ettie's head of braided hair. Seth and Isaac stood in the doorway, unsure of what to do.

They couldn't make out what Ettie was saying in between the sobs muffled by Aunty Sia's lap.

"What is she saying?" asked Isaac.

"She's saying she can't do it," said Aunty Sia.

"Can't do what?"

"The camp, I guess."

Aunty Sia spoke in low, liquid tones to the girl. "I've told you, child, it's okay. You don't have to do anything you don't want to do. You never had to go to the camp, but we all thought it would help you."

Aunty Sia's strident tone of earlier had softened. She turned to look at Seth and Isaac now, her face a mixture of bewilderment and empathy.

The girl raised her head.

"But I can't do it, Aunty Sia."

Isaac said softly, "I don't think she's talking about the camp."

"Do what, child?" Aunty Sia asked.

The sobbing intensified.

Aunty Sia let the hand on the girl's head slide downward, the beginning of a stroking movement. She sighed and closed her eyes. Even in the dark of the room, Seth could see her pressing her eyelids together, tight and tighter. Heat and a smell of Mentholatum emanated from the room. He could see this picture etching itself into the spool of time, Aunty Sia's head whiter, bending still over the girl, grown to a woman by then, yet still broken apart by sobs. The old woman's dreams would remain as hidden as the few bits of gold jewelry Isaac told him she kept in boxes under the bed.

"Child, there is nothing I will make you do if you do not want to."

Seth felt a confusing urge to both comfort and yell at the girl. *Do what, Ettie? What is it you can't do?*

The sobbing intensified and at last began to subside.

Isaac retreated, and Seth followed. They closed the door gently behind them.

~ THIRTY-NINE ~

"STAY HOME," ISAAC said the next morning, his voice tinged with guilt. Seth, aflood with a sense of loss, nodded his aching head. As Isaac left the house, Seth remarked that they had not even discussed what had happened in Mr. Thomas' presence.

Around midmorning, the phone vibrated angrily. Seth ignored it, but it kept vibrating as though incensed that Seth hadn't picked it up the first time. It was Mr. Thomas, wanting to see him again, right away.

"I can't," Seth said weakly.

"You must." Even over the phone Seth could hear the menace in his voice. "Tomorrow."

After he hung up, Seth considered his options. Isaac had made clear to him how influential the man was in the educational system. He took a shower and put on a dress shirt. What was the point of waiting for tomorrow? He would go today.

~

MR. THOMAS WAS on his cellphone when Seth arrived, nodding as he listened to what appeared to be a monologue on the other end. Finally, he ended his call and called Seth into his office from the anteroom. When Seth entered, the principal lifted himself slightly from his chair, not quite rising to his feet. He offered his hand to be shaken. It was no firmer than before, and this time Seth made no effort to pump life into the flaccid fingers.

"Seth, I have some concerns about the camp."

"How so?"

"I have wondered for a while about your intentions. This is a poor country. Many people come here with bold intentions, foreigners who think, 'These are Africans, they'll settle for anything.' But they do things more to feel better about themselves, than to really help . . . well, you know those types. Then there are the ones like you who moved away to America or France or wherever and then come back, and when you're sitting in your air-conditioned houses, you think about Sierra Leone. You think when you come here you can change everything because you know so much, you have all the best ideas, no?"

"What is your point?" Seth asked, a tinge of frost in his voice.

"Let me remind you that we are talking about young lives, children going through a critical period in their development. One of those young lives just happens to be Abdul. I was quite stunned to hear that the boy wants to be an actor, thanks to the guidance he has been receiving at your camp."

"Why not? He's very good at it."

The principal smiled once again, as though Seth's unreasonableness had left him no recourse but to find humor in the situation.

"I hope you can hear yourself speaking." A misting of sweat appeared on Mr. Thomas' forehead, and he seemed more animated than Seth had ever seen him.

"You know that the boy's parents are poor!" he spat, causing another globule of spit to land on Seth's arm. "They have very high expectations for him. You cannot help him entertain thoughts of some no-use career just because at fourteen he happens to think that's what he wants to do."

"I can't tell children what to do or discourage them from doing what they want to do. I don't have a right to do that, and neither does anybody else."

"But that doesn't mean you should encourage them either," Mr. Thomas said, his voice ominous. He pressed the tips of his fingers together and smiled a smile as though battered by the relentless years of accommodating the dull. "I know your mother and father, Seth. They are good people. And I was sorry to hear about your brother. But let's face it. Coming from your family background, you cannot possibly begin to understand the tremendous obstacles facing a boy like Abdul."

Seth felt hot all over. "With all due respect, you know nothing about my childhood or who I am now. Nor do you know what kind of obstacles I faced."

"Seth, I have to get to the point here. I don't like to tell you this, but I'd advise you to make some serious changes to the camp, or I will have to advise the parents of the children I have there to withdraw them. Including Abdul's parents, of course. And then I will have to advise my colleagues in other schools to likewise seek to withdraw their children."

Seth looked at the man, noting the subtle smirk on his face. He wouldn't gratify the man by betraying his anger. "What sort of changes?" he asked calmly.

"Well, for one thing, this whole business of encouraging children to think about a different future. This is not America. Those options might be possible there but not here."

Seth worked on steadying his voice. "We have less than three weeks to go. Is the camp that much of a threat that you are asking me this?"

"Yes. I'm afraid I'm going to have to ask you to promise that there will be no unwarranted fanning of the children's expectations and putting undue pressure on them."

Seth considered this for a moment and what it might mean if Mr. Thomas were to make good on his threat to advise parents to withdraw their children from the camp. "Mr. Thomas, I don't like to be threatened—"

"I'm meeting with some colleagues in a couple days about the matter and would strongly suggest that you attend."

"I have a camp to run," Seth said. And he got up and left.

~

THAT NIGHT HE sat on the steps at the back of the house thinking about the disturbing meeting. There was no electricity, only a lamp in the kitchen that cast a shadow of Seth, his head large and monstrous, into the yard.

He heard a noise behind him. Ettie stood there looking down at him with uncertainty.

"Hello, Seth."

He smiled at her. "Hello, Ettie." He made room for her on the step, but she remained standing, rubbing her hands on the sides of her jeans. Finally she sighed, then sat down as far away from him as possible. Now she rubbed her knees with her hands.

"I told him I didn't know anything, but he didn't believe me," she said, looking down at her hands.

His legs tensed with a feeling of unpleasant anticipation.

"Who are you talking about, Ettie? What happened?"

"Lucky. He wanted to know why you are doing things. I mean, what you are doing with the camp. And I told him I don't know, but he didn't believe me."

Seth saw Lucky's face in his mind, the pebble-small eyes, the hair as brown as dry bush.

"I have to go now," Ettie said.

"Wait, Ettie. Please stay. What you're saying is important to me. Was he mean to you?"

Her eyes were glassy.

"I didn't want to tell him anything, that's why I said I didn't know. So then he made up his own stories and told the other kids the reason why you were doing the camp was that you had scholarships and maybe those who did well in the camp would be selected to go to America."

"Do you know why he told them that?"

"So they wouldn't drop out. He told the kids they should stay so they might be picked. All the kids wanted to know what you wanted from them. So he said you would want to hear that they wanted to be different things when they grow up, not the usual things. And then he told me not to tell you. And I told the kids the part about the scholarships wasn't true. I think some believed me and some believed him."

He let the truth pierce him, and he felt something leaking out, and it kept leaking until he wondered what would happen to him after it had finally spent itself in the outflow. But here with Ettie before him, he couldn't survey the damage of what had been lost.

"Ettie, I'm very sorry this happened. And thank you so much for telling me. Did he scare you?"

"He told me I wasn't cooperating because I was stupid. But I'm not, Seth, I'm not," she said, her voice fluttering like a flame.

"You are the smartest and kindest of us all," he said, his voice fierce. "Aunty Sia and Isaac and I know who you are."

Anger rose in him at the thought of Lucky trying to intimidate her. But Ettie did not need him. While he and Isaac had carried on, oblivious, she had resisted Lucky to shield them from the deception he had hatched.

He went into their room to tell Isaac this news. Isaac let out a small sound like an animal caught in a trap and looked at Seth with an anguished face.

"And there's something else, Seth."

"Yes?"

"I was the one who told Mr. Thomas he should summon you that first time. Yes," he said, his voice hoarse as he began to weep. "I did that behind your back."

~ FORTY ~

"I'VE BEEN WATCHING you with my child, Aunty Evelyn," said Joanna. She was perched on a barstool at the kitchen counter, her back ramrod straight, her legs entwined elegantly. Evelyn was seated at the dining table across from her. Stella had long since gone to bed.

"What do you mean?"

"I think you know what I mean."

Evelyn was truly astounded. A Sierra Leonean girl would never have talked to her in such a fashion.

"Joanna, I have never been so offended in my life. She is my grandchild."

"Well, I'm sorry to be so frank, but I still don't understand why you came and why you're still here."

In Evelyn's mind flashed the thought of being back in her own house once again, the memories issuing from the walls to reach for her.

"I came to see you and spend time with Stella. I don't see why that should be so hard to understand. And it appears that I'll have to leave if this is the way I am to be treated."

Joanna had a bunch of keys splayed on the counter radiating from the ring that held them, and she prodded each of the keys in turn as they lay in formation.

"I want Stella to know her grandmother and for you to be a part of her life, but I need to know what your intentions are."

Evelyn said at last, her tone lower, dark and smooth as oil: "Well, I wish I had been around to watch you with *my* child."

Unflapped, Joanna continued fingering the keys as though trying to decide which one would open the floodgates of Evelyn's wrath. This nettled Evelyn all the more.

"Sam changed while he was married to you. He used to be so loving, so open; in no way would he hide anything from me. And yet with time, I saw him withdraw. He even lied to me about not being able to attend my sixtieth birthday. Yes, don't think I don't know. Don't think I don't know he was working his fingers to the bone to keep you happy, to buy nice things for you—that old house he never liked, the art."

Joanna gave Evelyn a steady look as if Evelyn had merely been explaining the difference between various brands of toilet paper. Then she abruptly swept up the keys and put the bunch in her handbag, which she then let drop to the floor with a thud.

"I'll tell you why your son was not at your birthday," said Joanna, her voice even, "though it's not the answer you're looking for.

"Sam was a firecracker when I met him. He was like an overeager little boy, always happy, bouncing off the walls. But early on, I sensed that restlessness. Like an earthquake waiting to happen. The night I agreed to marry him, he phoned all his friends, and I watched his eyes shine as they congratulated him. Then he phoned them all a second time out of pure excitement.

"He was always loving—but he was also obsessed. With having a child. No sooner were we married than he began badgering me to have a child."

Stella had come quickly, Evelyn remembered. "You look too young to be a grandmother," Sam had teased her when he shared the news. She found this ironic. When she was young, people had always thought she was older than she was. Then there had come a point when she had apparently ceased to age. People told her she looked good, but she interpreted it in a different way, as though something vital that surges forward with the passage of life was missing in her.

"When I did get pregnant, it only got worse," Joanna continued. "His anticipation and obsession grew, and everything was 'the baby this' and 'the baby that.' He tried to pretend, to ask how I was doing, when I knew he really only cared about how the baby was doing. There came a time, during the sixth month or so, that I'd had enough. I almost wished I could pull the child out, hand it to him, and walk away. I felt like saying, 'Carry your own damn baby!'"

"Joanna, what does this have to do with him not coming to my birthday party?"

"I'm getting to that." She stretched her neck, curled her hands one inside the other on her lap, and carried on unperturbed.

"The day she was born, I realized that I had lost him. I felt somehow that the man I had married was a persona that he had put on at will to suit a purpose and that that purpose had been achieved with her birth. I was a means to an end that I had not seen coming.

"If somebody had asked me, 'What's different about him?' I would have had a hard time answering. So I told myself that we were new parents and that things would sort themselves out. Then, when Stella was about seven months—only a few months before he died—we had a nasty quarrel because he wouldn't let me leave her with my mother while we went on a brief vacation to the Tennessee mountains. We ended up taking her, and we drove in silence while she cried all the way.

"The weather turned on us while we were there. One day there was this loud, driving rain with thunder booming, so scary that Stella cried and cried. I remember standing outside on the porch of this beautiful log cabin, and it was only about noon, but the sky was dark with the rain. I looked in through the door of the cabin, and there he was, sitting in this armchair with her, and everything looked beautiful and yellow inside, and he was bouncing her in his arms, and she was gurgling. And that's when I noticed, from the expression on his face, that he wasn't happy, even in such a beautiful moment."

Joanna looked intently at Evelyn as though studying her reaction.

"I don't know why I hadn't noticed it before—maybe it was the strain of new parenthood—but the irony is that after Stella was born, he gradually became an unhappier person, even though he seemed to love her more than himself. It was as though in being born, she had inflicted a strange illness on him that made him a tormented, moodier version of his former self.

"He joked around less often, he wanted to spend more time alone or with her. He would lock himself in the office. I tried to give him his privacy, but I would work myself into tangles wondering what he was doing in there.

"The more he withdrew, the more jealous I became of the baby, of his playing with her, his time with her. One day I put it to him point-blank. 'I feel like there's a wall between us, Sam, and I feel like as hard as I try, I'm not getting through to you.'"

"So what did he say?" said Evelyn, her voice rising, doing her very best to hold herself back from shaking Joanna with impatience.

"I don't remember his exact response. But I do remember that we argued long and hard and that he told me I was overreacting. And then my jealousy spilled out, and I told him that the only thing he seemed to care about was Stella."

"He got angry, saying that, well, she was his firstborn, so what did I expect? Why couldn't I be happy that he was a good father? I pressed on and told him it seemed to be beyond being a good father. He seemed to be obsessed with being a father."

"So what did he say?" hissed Evelyn.

"He turned to me with a bitter look and said, 'You have no idea the hell I went through as a child. You had a happy childhood. If you even had one iota of understanding of what it was like for me, we wouldn't be having this conversation, and you would be happy that I'm doing everything to ensure the same thing doesn't happen to Stella.'

"I was stunned and couldn't say anything in response to that. And so Aunty Evelyn, when we started this conversation, I said I would tell you why he didn't come to your birthday, but I think I've told you enough."

Evelyn wanted to give a quick and cutting response, but too many words were swirling around in her head like leaves whipped up by a storm. And then she was caught up in the storm itself, spun around and around until even her breath was snatched away and she couldn't feel level ground beneath her.

Joanna looked at her coolly, and it was this that helped her regain her bearings. "And what of you? What of your coldness to me, your persistent pushing me away, keeping your child away? Do you mean to tell me you have been this way to me, yet an angel to my son?"

For the first time in her life, Evelyn saw Joanna look flustered, something she had not even seen at Sam's funeral. She stumbled on her words.

"I have been wrong on so many things, Aunty Evelyn. You are right that I tried to create distance between us, but not for the reasons you might think. At first it was because I wanted to protect Sam from you, though I didn't try to dissuade him from going to your birthday party. And then, even before she was born, I wanted to protect Stella from you."

Evelyn waited for an apology to follow, but there was none. The story was told, and she had been cast as a villain. The outrage lashed her like the tentacles of a jellyfish. But now Evelyn noticed that the smooth planes under Joanna's eyes were damp. She lifted her manicured white-tipped nails to wipe them, passing under the rims of her eyes slowly in a manner that reminded Evelyn of Stella. She was but a child after all.

~ FORTY-ONE ~

AFTER TALKING TO Ettie and then Isaac that night, Seth went to his room and prepared for bed. He took off his shoes and placed them on the floor near the bed. He took off his watch—9:27 p.m.—and put it in one of the shoes. Into the other he placed his silenced cellphone. Then he closed his eyes and called for still water.

He soon found himself suspended within the swamp, his back to the distant light. As he looked down, he saw no trace of the flame, only the darkness that cloaked *The Thing*.

Anger rose up in him at the thought of the beast. He sank lower and lower, and when he felt himself grow afraid, he thought of how its tentacles had ensnared him before, and the anger devoured his fear. He would fight until the end.

A scent of rot—that of dead animal and plant flesh left to fester in dank water—became so overpowering that he thought to be overcome by such a stench was akin to drowning.

He became aware that his flesh, too, was falling away, crumbling. His fingers dissolved, his limbs became flaccid and soggy. He felt his eyeballs roll out of their sockets and his tongue fall from its anchoring. Bit by bit, he became sediment. And yet, he could still feel, think, see even, to the limited extent possible. But that was little comfort.

Then it occurred to him that there was none of the familiar movement from *The Thing*, no churning of the waters below him, no stirring of the sediment, no grasp of tentacles. Like one realizing he had been stabbed only when the blade has exited the flesh, he realized, without being sure how, that *The Thing* was not in the swamp. It had lured him into his death, not into combat. Seth had plunged into the swamp with bravado, exchanging courage for stupidity. He had been seduced by the siren song of the hero's journey, the James Bonds of all his years of movies burning this slick deception into his soul, that he too would prevail against injustice.

If he could not fight, he would resist, cry out and curse with what remained of him. From his earliest years, this strength of turning away had defined him. But now, rallying what remained of his essence, a new knowing surged up within him, and he realized that to fight in this way would be foolery. He was in the thrall of a tarry vastness, an ancient and troubled sea that could not be traversed by human strength.

It felt like a betrayal of himself at first, to surrender to the water, to abandon himself to the depths. But let go he did of the fragments that were himself, and the sludge around him became thicker and denser with the particles that had once been dreams. He would fight no more. Instead he would wait until the last fragments of consciousness bled from him. Until it was clear that there was nothing more for which to wait.

All of a sudden, from far away, a voice was speaking, and he knew the voice was from up above. It was his ex-girlfriend, Gaia. Seth could not hear what she was saying, but upon hearing her voice, he felt the sadness of thousands of sea turtles leaving the sand for an unbound and violent sea.

He called to her, but she did not hear, and he realized his voice, too, was fragmented across his million parts. Then he willed all those parts to hum together, and slowly, a keening reverberated across the swamp. He willed his parts to say her name again, and this time there was a coordinated voice that said, "Gaia."

Though he could not see her, he could feel that her attention had turned. Then he saw a sinewy gray cord descend from above and sway before his fragmented parts, strong and rubbery. He understood it to be his umbilical cord and realized that he had seen it before. In the moments after his birth, straining to make sense of the moving shapes, he had noticed the glistening tether attached to him. There was Evelyn, dazed and covered with sweat as the attendant said to her, "Mrs. Walker, we can't find your husband. He must have left the premises."

Seth had watched them cut the cord and put it in a basin and had known they were taking away a river of life that could water any kind of tree and beast. Seeing it before him now, he knew he could flow through it, reach Gaia perhaps, remake himself in some fashion even.

But suddenly a faint glow illuminated the swamp, and it grew like a sunrise until it had kindled the darkness and seared the shadows. He felt the heat and the glare of red light, and all of a sudden he could see all the way to the top, and there indeed was Gaia on the bank.

He called her name again, and she answered, "Seth," and reached her foot into the water. But suddenly the swamp caught fire like a pool of magma, and he cried out to her to not step in any farther. But he was being consumed by the fire, and his last thought was, "We have been dead from the day we were born."

When he came to, he was holding himself and trembling on the back steps of the kitchen, the moon casting a speckled light upon him. For the first time in many months, his thoughts were clear, his mind a broad path. In the end there were worse things to lose than one's mind. In truth, he had disintegrated long before *The Thing* began to throttle him. He had been terrible to Gaia. He had left Isaac few options but to undercut him.

You wanted remedial education so badly that you had to call Mr. Thomas to force me to do it?

Well, I did want it—at least for Ettie's sake. But also, I could see that your mental state was not good. I didn't know if you would be able to follow through on your vision. At least with remedial education, Zayra and I knew what to do. We could take over if suddenly you couldn't do it anymore . . .

His delusion had bred a delusion that the children were truly transforming. It had been a show of smoke and mirrors that Lucky had put on. Even though Abdul really did seem to want to be an actor, there didn't seem to be any other fruit.

And yet he believed, as sure as he could still feel in his heart a blacksmith pounding away in an inner forge, that he had experienced a story from Saj that was true. He could not turn away from that.

~

AT THE CAMP the next day, Seth moved about dazed and slow in his grief as though drifting in that same cloud of sediment. He noticed strange looks from the kids and remembered his moment of lunacy before them. But now he was beyond caring.

Isaac and Zayra too were downcast, for he had told them everything, both Mr. Thomas' threats and Ettie's revelation. Isaac had warned of Mr. Thomas' influence, his ability to make good on his threats. Zayra had felt that if no one challenged the status quo, things would never change in this country that seemed averse to progress. In the end, they left it to Seth to decide the way forward.

Yes, Seth would speak to Lucky. At least there would be answers. He asked him to walk with him down the road. The boy looked up at him, hopeful, with shining eyes. At first, they walked in silence, navigating their mud-stained shoes carefully around puddles.

"Why did you lie, Lucky? You know I have no connections to any special program in America."

Lucky looked at Seth, his mind no doubt calculating with its lightning speed. His smile faded.

"So you're not happy?"

Seth's laugh was bitter. "Why would I be?"

The boy frowned. "You were struggling with the camp. Remember, you said how all the kids seemed stuck, when we were in Elizabeth Park? I wanted to help you, that's all."

"I didn't mean for you to do it this way. You can't manipulate people just because you want them to do things a certain way, Lucky."

Lucky looked at him with a puzzled expression. There was no trace of sarcasm in his voice when he said, "But isn't that what you were trying to do with the camp?"

Seth did not answer. As they walked back and the building loomed larger, his throat constricted with the responsibility he felt for the lives inside, the people who had followed him, trusting. He had thrown them a tightrope to walk on, a mere spider web spun from the delusion of his mind, and had been surprised when it could not bear them to the other side.

"It was wrong of you to pressure Ettie, and you know that," he said at last to Lucky.

Lucky sniffed. "I know. I just thought what I did would make you happy." The boy's head drooped on its sapling-thin neck.

Long before he came to the camp, Lucky had already known what he wanted to do. What had Seth, Isaac, and Zayra been able to offer the boy? Surely the most important thing they could do would be to, in some small way, try to mold the boy into a more upright and kind person.

"I need you to apologize to Ettie and tell the other kids what you did." Seth clapped him on the back, feeling his angular shoulder blades. "You'll make a good politician someday—by 'good,' I mean one with a good heart."

~

BACK IN THE room, Seth made no attempt to quiet the children. He simply leaned against the table at the front of the room, his arms folded, watching them chatter until they noticed him watching and eventually quieted down. Zayra and Isaac shot him looks of encouragement from the back of the room.

The monster opened its maw and moaned from the midst of the sediment. Its claws, its barbs, its great creaking voice were near now, so near that it seemed as though it was speaking directly into Seth's ear. But it could not pierce him for he had already been broken and threshed, subsumed by the swamp.

Now he faced the children. He smiled at Isaac and Zayra, hoping his eyes could tell them how much he appreciated them.

"Let me tell you a true story," Seth said to the kids. They looked back at him, their eyes like open doors. "Once when I was even younger than you are now, I got in trouble at school, and on that day my life changed. There was a boy named Victor."

As Seth spoke, it was as though the story began to tell itself—not to the kids, not even to Isaac, but to him. It was as if it was being explained to him for the first time, and he himself was unsure of what would proceed from his mouth.

"Later in life I became an actuary because it is one of the professions where you can use strong skills in maths. My parents made sure of that. I don't regret it; it paid all the bills, got me some respect from my parents, and made other people admire me. I can't hide the fact that all these things were important to me.

"It's only here in Freetown that I've realized that what made me whisper answers to Victor all those years ago was not just that I wanted to help him—though in a way I did—but that I was angry he was accepting what everybody thought of him—that he was stupid. I wanted him to prove them all wrong, like I wanted to prove everyone wrong about me. And I've wanted you to prove wrong those in your life who don't think much of you.

"Now I know I needed you more than you needed me. I don't have any special connections to schools in the U.S., no scholarships or exchange programs.

"You have to figure out how much you want to change your lives. How much to accept and where you have so much fire in you that if you don't change things, the fire will burn you from the inside out. And if there's no fire, then maybe you're lucky and maybe life will be peaceful and kind, and you can forget this conversation.

"It's true that you have to think about how you're going to eat, and the people who depend on you, and maybe sometimes you can't have it your way. Just don't forget to ask yourselves what you really want to do."

Seth looked down at his hands after this, unable to bear looking at a room of stony, uncomprehending, or worse, smirking faces.

Isaac finally came to the rescue again with their perpetual face-saver: "Why don't you all take a short break outside?"

While the kids were outside, Isaac and Zayra came to him.

"Glad you got that out," Zayra said. "Now, when you go see the principals, whatever happens, happens."

"Me too," Isaac said. They left him and began tidying up the classroom, pushing bags out of the way, straightening desks. Seth felt numb.

He heard sounds coming from the yard, louder and louder. The children were shouting, screaming, their voices unfettered. Sound tumbling over sound. Laughter and words shimmering and riding on the breeze.

Seth went outside and joined Isaac and Zayra on the balcony to watch them. The three of them stood looking at the children who were complete in their abandon, lost in movement. The kids had never played in that way before. They were like dancers in the sway of drummers who beat faster and faster, weaving hypnotic rhythms around them, until the dancers let everything go—shame, worry, sadness—to succumb to the dance.

"Come back in!" Isaac yelled from the balcony when break was over. But they ignored him and continued playing an elaborate game called touch. Seth was reminded of his childhood, of the days at the end of the school term when they could barely concentrate on anything and the teachers went lax on them, abandoning them to the whirlwind of play.

Isaac cupped his hands to his mouth again. Zayra put a hand on his arm.

"Leave them, Isaac. They will get tired eventually. At least let this game end."

"It's a long game, you know. What if it doesn't end soon?"

She smiled mischievously.

"Then we'll join them."

~ FORTY-TWO ~

SETH WENT TO Mr. Thomas' school the next day and found his way to the classroom where the principal had asked Seth to meet him. There were three principals from schools the kids attended and a board member of Mr. Thomas' school. Seth was told that a board member from another of the schools was on the way. Only one of the group, a middle-aged matron, smiled at him.

Mr. Thomas was there. A stiff smile crossed his face. Seth nodded but did not smile back. He thought of the faces of the children, and the image filled him with both strength and anger.

The most senior-looking principal started.

"Mr. Walker, thank you for coming," he said, pleasant enough. He was Alfred's age with a crop of hair and a beard amply specked with white. Seth sensed no antagonism from him.

"I think you already know some of our concerns about the work you're doing. Rather than repeat them at this point, I think it would help all of us to understand a little bit in your own words about why you are doing this camp. Would that be okay?" He smiled, reassuring.

Seth cleared his throat.

"When I first got the idea for the camp . . ."

Someone entered the door to his right. He turned.

It was his mother.

Evelyn's face was somehow less creased than the last time he had seen her, like a face resting in sleep or death. She looked at Seth without expression before taking a seat at the edge of the circle.

"I apologize that I'm late, everyone." They were all smiles.

"No problem at all, Mrs. Walker. We are just getting started," said the friendly principal with the frosted hair.

Seth saw a smirk on Mr. Thomas' face as he studied Seth's shocked reaction. He had known that Evelyn had connections in the educational system, but Evelyn a board member? That he had not known.

After a loud scraping of the chair on the concrete floor as Evelyn took her seat, the friendly principal turned to Seth once again.

"Seth, I understand that you and your mother have not been in contact recently. Nonetheless, we invited her because as a member of our board at Hastings School and as your mother, we thought this would afford her a unique position to observe both points of view and therefore come to an acceptable conclusion for everybody—especially our children. She graciously agreed, even though she is still readjusting to being back from her trip overseas."

Seth tried to keep his legs still and his face impassive.

"You were about to explain the steps that brought you to this unique place of sitting here with us," continued the friendly principal.

A moment passed. Two. Who could tell if they were seconds or minutes? A voice sliced the silence. His voice.

"Mr. Thomas has already made his concerns known to me. I'm pleased to inform you all that I have taken his advice into account, and for the remainder of the camp, we will focus on the basics, reinforcing the subjects already taught in your schools."

Mr. Thomas stiffened momentarily, and the principals cast brief glances at each other. The man must have been spoiling for a fight.

Mr. Thomas clasped his hands together on the table in front of him. "It's great to hear of this about-face, but I wonder if there have already been some ill effects of your camp. You and I have already spoken about Abdul's circumstances and his newfound desire to be an actor despite the impracticality of such a choice, given his family's circumstances. What is the point of telling these kids to think about things they may never be able to do?" asked Mr. Thomas, looking at his peers. They murmured and shifted in their seats while Evelyn maintained her impassive gaze.

Seth felt some relief that the frontal attack he had been expecting had come. "When I was a child, no one encouraged me to find out what I was really good at. I didn't care about any of the things that other people thought were important—law or medicine or engineering. I've tried to do it differently with these children. I wanted them to have a choice, rather than have it forced upon them. Most of all, I wanted them to *realize* they have a choice. I think our educational system, our culture, robs children by not recognizing their ability to choose." He looked at Evelyn, but her face remained expressionless.

There was silence for a while, then some throat clearing. Evelyn made no motion or sound.

Mr. Thomas spoke again. "Mr. Walker, based on my own observations, I've had, er, how shall I put it? One does question your, er, emotional well-being . . . Is it wise for you to continue to work with our children in this way?"

Though not surprised that Mr. Thomas would bare every claw, the directness of the attack still wounded Seth, but Isaac had prepared him for this possibility.

"My colleague, Isaac, who is an experienced teacher in your school system, has been leading the camp this whole time and going forward will take over."

When they had discussed this, Isaac had shaken his head, made shooing motions with his hands.

"Isaac, I should have done this long ago."

"It's too late for remedial education now, Seth."

"No, it's not. We still have a third of the camp left. Please take it over . . . for the sake of the kids."

And Isaac had reluctantly agreed.

"Sounds reasonable to me," murmured the kindly old principal, nodding his head rhythmically like the orange-headed lizards Seth had grown up with. "I don't see the harm in letting the young man continue on with the changes he has made." He looked around at his colleagues for affirmation.

As if drawn by an unseen magnet, all turned to look at Evelyn. Seth too. She in turn looked into his eyes and his alone. There was no anger now, no animosity, just a gaze of appraisal.

~

That afternoon, long ago, the slices of pineapple were like yellow suns on a plate. The pineapple was sweet to its core. Seth tried to be careful, but the juice slid down his chin, and he dabbed it with the collar of his T-shirt when Evelyn wasn't looking. They sat together on the verandah on the day he had carried the pineapple home. A breeze parted the curtain of heat, and Evelyn said, "Mercy, doesn't that feel good." Her feet were propped up on a stool in front of her. They both sat on cane chairs with a table in between them, and on it, the large plate of sliced pineapple.

Lunch was not ready yet; the servants were still laboring in the inside and outside kitchens. Hungry, they devoured slice upon slice of pineapple, even the hard centers. Seth reached with his fork for one more but thought better of it.

"You can have another one," she said.

"But what about Sam and Daddy?"

"Don't worry about them. It will be our secret." She smiled at him as though he were the only child in the world. It was a smile he clung to in remembrance, even in the years of distance that were to follow.

~

SHE LOVED HIM despite herself, Seth thought as he returned Evelyn's gaze. Of this he had no doubt. Try as she might to shun him, she was a mother, when all was said and done. Why else would she be here? There was no Sam now, only Seth. He looked into her eyes, and he thought he saw the faintest lifting of the corners of her mouth as the principals turned their gaze from him to her, from her to him.

At last, she spoke. "Gentlemen—and lady—obviously I have known this young man for as long as he has been alive. Though he is a passionate person, he is also extreme. There is no middle of the road for him, no compromise. But he is my son, and I think what he is doing is commendable. I would only question, perhaps, whether he has been mistaken from the beginning. He suggests that he was, well, failed as a child by his parents, the educational system. I wonder if he has stopped to consider that he is a unique case.

"Perhaps not all of his peers feel that they have been wronged in this way. Most of his peers are doing well with good jobs, good lives. They don't seem too concerned that they have somehow missed their calling. He may be projecting his own biases onto these poor children. I also wonder, if these are the messages he has been giving to the children so far, if it might do more harm than good to try to switch the format of the camp at this stage."

Another long silence ensued. Finally, the elderly principal cleared his throat and said, "Well said, Mrs. Walker. I don't think any of us can disagree with that assessment." The principal asked Seth to step out. When they called him back in, he said, "Seth, we are going to have to advise you to stop the camp, or we will compel our parents to withdraw their kids."

~

WHEN SETH TOLD Isaac and Zayra, they patted him on the back, and he stiffened, not wanting to be pitied. Yet as they looked at him, he could see from their expressions that they thought a terrible thing had been done to him. But what was one more disappointment, one more lost love?

He asked them whether they should resist, and they thought about it, but they knew there would be a fight, and the kids would come in the middle, as would Isaac. So they told the kids, and they accepted the news in silence, some nonchalant, some visibly sad. The kids did not ask why, as though they, unlike Seth, had known that a bird fattened with ideas of rebellion would always be too heavy to fly.

~

IT WAS DARK by the time Seth and Isaac finished loading the bins into the borrowed van. Seth told Isaac he was going inside to take one last look around. He lingered more than he expected, even though it was too dark to see much.

Isaac came in behind him.

"Seth, there's somebody here to see you."

Seth walked out and pulled hard on the door, closing it for always. Outside in the mottled dark was a silhouette that was featureless but at once familiar. His father.

"I'll be in the truck, Seth," Isaac said, walking away.

They were alone.

"Hello, Seth."

"Hello, Dad."

As if by arrangement, after a pause, they both sat down on the steps. Neither said anything for a while.

"I wish I could have seen your camp."

"You could have. It was here all along."

He thought of Isaac, waiting and worrying.

"You know your mother is unhappy, and sometimes she takes it out on other people. Sometimes I think it's a bit out of her control. There's so much that's out of our control, don't you think? Maybe to some extent your decision to come here was out of your control."

"Don't make excuses for her, Dad. She knows exactly what she's doing."

They said nothing more, for neither one of them knew the way forward. Then Alfred's arm was around his back, heavy and quivering. Seth felt shudder after shudder course through Alfred's body and realized his father was weeping in his own tearless way.

Seth continued to sit, immobile, realizing that pity, the one thing he hated receiving the most, was what he now gave his father.

~ FORTY-THREE ~

ALFRED DESPISED THE ride home from work. The traffic was incessant. It wasn't just the cars, but the people, everywhere people, threading their way through the cars without regard for whether they were in motion or not, milling about in throngs— a perpetual crowd. It had been that way since the war when those displaced from all over the country fled to the relative safety of the capital. And they had remained even after peace had returned. Now Freetown was staggering under its human burden.

In Alfred's childhood, Freetown had been a different place— quiet, orderly, lined with august trees, swept streets; a world removed from what it was now. He looked at his watch. A half-hour had gone by, and he was still waiting to enter the roundabout. A man passing in front of him thumped on the hood of the car with his open palm for no apparent reason other than he needed something to do with his hands. It was a common occurrence, but it riled Alfred more than usual this time. He lowered the passenger-side window, lunged toward it, and shouted with all the air in his lungs.

"Bloody hell! Why can't you hit yourself instead of my car?"

He sat back, his breathing heavy, feeling shaken from the energy exerted. And scared of his outburst. It was so unlike him. The man hadn't even turned. This damned city with its crumbling roads and crammed streets. It would drive him to his grave. These things had always bothered him, but today they were more than he could take.

Most of all he was angry at Evelyn. She had walled him off with her silences and forced demonstrations of indifference, the way she always had. When he asked her how the trip to America had been, she had told him that she got what she wanted: to connect with Stella. More lies. Even her silences were the highest form of lies, robbing him of the truth of what was going on in her world, within his very family.

She had refused to tell him the whole truth about Seth as well. Her informant about Seth's camp had been the principal of a school where she was on the board. It was an act of desperation, she told Alfred. Seth was obviously trying to prove something to them.

He asked her for more information about the camp, but she said she knew little else. Lies. Just the other night, as they were getting ready for bed, she had mentioned that she had been at a meeting earlier in the day with principals of schools that the children at Seth's camp attended. They had met to discuss the future of the camp, given the appalling way Seth was running it.

"What was the decision?"

"To advise him to end it right away."

"Has he been informed yet?"

"He was at the meeting."

Stunned by this revelation, he walked to the bathroom, hung up his bathrobe, and went to the sink. He squeezed a bead of toothpaste striped aquamarine and red onto his brush. It was beautiful—a glittering, translucent marvel. Beautiful as so few things in life are when all is said and done.

In the mirror was his face; in his mind was Seth's face. Seth, his son with the curly lashes. Seth, who at this very minute was probably no more than thirty minutes away in this city. He was not used to this, only to Seth being far from them.

Seth. Alfred wanted to fling this name at her like a curse.

She sat on the bed wiping her glasses with her skirt hem.

"Did you talk to him personally?"

"Who?"

"Seth."

"Only briefly."

His hands tightened around the steering wheel as he thought back to that conversation. When Alfred went to see him at the camp, Seth had had so little to say to him, and he so little to say in return.

On the night Seth was born, Alfred left the hospital to catch some air, feeling claustrophobic and trapped by the weight of second-time fatherhood. Outside, he looked at the stars that seemed to be the only constant in the blanket of night. When he returned, Seth had been born. Evelyn had never forgiven him for being absent, even though men were not allowed in the delivery room in those days.

A narcotic sadness descended on him. It was like that first ripping sense of loss at not being there when they looked for him to tell him his son had been born. Then, he had been distracted for what seemed like a mere moment, and both Seth and Sam were gone. It was as though they had floated up and away and fixed themselves like strange lights in the sky, far from his reach.

He had lost them all.

There were things he remembered effortlessly, usually events in places far away. Like the name of the town, Timisoara, in Romania, in which a priest had cried out against the regime of the dictator Nicolae Ceausescu in 1989. And how protests and bloodshed in Romania had erupted over the ensuing days so that in a matter of mere weeks, the iron fist of the dictator had been pried open and he and his wife shot after a hasty trial.

In the sweep of horror and mayhem that unfolded, no doubt few thought about the priest. But Alfred did. How rebellions began was interesting to him. Like a slender match to tinder, it took but a lone person to light the fire. So it was when the Rwandan president's plane was shot down in 1994. Though the conflict had been brewing for decades, who would have known that one event would open the maw of hatred, leaving nearly a million people dead within three months? He thought of the plane, even now, falling through the sky, and how it stirred the winds that became enraged and devoured the souls of eight hundred thousand people.

Perhaps he liked the beginnings of rebellions for their purity, sacred as the water of baptism, in which a new birth glimmers for a moment. News of rebellions in other countries made him feel alive as nothing else. But rebellions were like solitary flames that pointed north but for a stroke in time before all erupted into the fire of war. War was a different matter altogether. In his own country, the years of struggle had not left him feeling alive but rather desolate, even though he had lost no one directly to the war. If rebellion was a quickening of the heart, war was its very evisceration.

But though he could remember with great clarity the days in which he heard of the protests of priests and the falling of planes, the years of his family were a mystery to him, lost forever. He could remember little. There were periods of noise and periods of silence. And these were dictated by Evelyn's moods. Later there was nothing but the granite sullenness of the empty house once the boys had left. This was about as much as he could remember. Except one memory that he had never been able to put from his mind.

The boys and their sad-dog eyes, holding spoons dripping with milk, the joy of eating cornflakes, a rare treat, gone. Evelyn had stormed from the room because she had found their swim club bag in Sam's closet, wet towels and bathing suits never hung up to dry, never sent to the wash, now stale and smelling. In departing she had screamed at them like a banshee.

They had cowered, wondering (how could they not, even at that age) from whence came this relentless rage.

"For God's sake, Evelyn," he said, following her out, mainly to get away from the boys' eyes.

And so, when Seth sat on the steps with him the other day, the closed door of the camp behind them, there were no questions. It was too late for answers.

But this time it would be different. She would give an answer, for he would accept nothing less.

~ FORTY-FOUR ~

STELLA LED SETH through the aisles, his hand curling around the toy-like fingers.

"Don't you have a list, Uncle Seth?"

"No, I don't."

She looked at him with disapproval.

"My mother always has one. We make one together."

"Well, let's just say I made a mental list."

She considered this.

"You mean a list in your head?"

"Yes! How did you get to be so smart? I'm worried."

"Why?"

"Because you're already smarter than I am!"

But he had made no such list. If not for the small hand tugging at his, he would have gone back to his apartment after five minutes in the store.

Ever since returning to the United States, he had struggled to pull his fragmented pieces together in a world that required wholeness. What brand of laundry detergent had he used before? Now the rows upon rows of it intimidated him. Detergent with bleach, without bleach. With a touch of fabric softener. Lavender scented. Clean rain, scented. Eco-friendly. What was the point of all these differences? And when they stopped in the detergent aisle, feeling overwhelmed, he turned to his tiny assistant.

"Mom goes with Tide," Stella said sagely. "It smells really good."

Smell. The smell of clothes. He understood that he was supposed to care about this. That another time, not too long ago, he had cared about this.

"What else do you need?" the little voice asked.

He saw his new apartment in his mind. The empty entertainment console, the fridge with a few hardening slices of bread and green apples with brown bruises on them. There was nowhere to sit. Whenever he was home, an overwhelming tiredness came upon him, and he went straight to bed. Whenever he was hungry, he ate out or brought food home to eat, standing in the kitchen or looking out the window at the cars sliding into fishbone formation in the parking lot below.

Sometimes he would lose track of whether he had eaten and would check in the kitchen for signs: the crumpled bag from the fast-food joint in the trash can, the ketchup-smeared dishes in the sink.

At night he lay in bed thinking of Isaac and Ettie, Aunty Sia and the kids, Zayra and the principals. They floated through his head in no particular order, strange pairings of people and memories. He thought of Abdul and the blind man he had played, the trembling hand reaching out to perceive the world before him.

He no longer dreamt of or saw the swamp, but often he awoke in the middle of the night and felt a loss so crushing that he would turn in the bed as if a new position might ease the pain. Ever since he had dissolved in the swamp, he felt as though his mind had been returned to him. But the terrifying thing was that this healing, if that's what it was, brought little joy, as if his illness had broken something irremediable.

He had begged Gaia to see him, and when she agreed to, he had begged further for forgiveness, and she gave it. Yet he could tell that she was looking at him as though through a sliding glass door—a barrier that offered both clarity of sight and protection.

No doubt he didn't look much different to her than when he left, and she had kept him at arm's length.

The quiet in his apartment unnerved him. He was afraid unwelcome noises would rush into it, as into a void: fragments of unfinished conversations from the previous occupants, the gnawing of termites working their way into the wood. He realized how much he missed the sounds of traffic in Freetown that had lulled him to sleep at night when nothing else would.

But ironically, it was for quiet that he had come. All he wanted was a place to be still and feel darkness and emptiness wash over him. A place where curtains could stay drawn as long as he wanted and he need not talk to anyone—not his housemates nor gregarious neighbors congregating on their front porches.

"I need hand soap," he said to Stella now, and she sprang forward with renewed purpose.

"I know where that is." She towed him with a preternatural force.

Who was to visit him? What did he care whether they washed their hands? But the girl's excitement was not to be denied. He would let her choose the soap while he thought of the next thing he would ask her to get. It had to be something she was familiar with, something she and Joanna went shopping for on a regular basis.

She had chosen the soap and was pulling him in another direction with a purpose of her own. She stopped in front of the flowers, bright-faced arrangements sheathed in cellophane, standing upright in round black bins.

"Are you going to buy some flowers for Mom?"

Heat swarmed over his face. Words rolled about in his mouth like marbles before he got them under control.

"What—I mean—think—do you think I should?"

She looked at him quizzically, as if he had forgotten that it was the first thing on his list.

"Mom's last boyfriend bought her flowers all the time."

"Well, maybe he didn't buy them at the grocery store," he mumbled.

She put three fingers out, delicate as sea anemone tentacles, to touch some pink tulips. Then she moved closer to Seth and wrapped her arm around his leg. In the first week after he came back, she had done this every time she saw him. And then less so, until just now.

"Can we call her now?"

"Why?" he said, suddenly terrified.

"Because I want to go home."

He felt irrational jealousy of her guaranteed and eternal access to Joanna. For the tether of love.

~ FORTY-FIVE ~

CASSAVA LEAVES. THE palm oil stained the white rice a dark orange as he churned it with his fork. Even in anger, Alfred could eat. In fact, anger made him hungrier, depleting his body to feed its voracious fire. He brought new spoonfuls to his mouth before he could finish chewing the previous ones.

Evelyn looked at him with raised eyebrows but said nothing.

"How was your day?" she asked him, picking out a slim red pepper from the stew and laying it to rest on the side of her plate.

How dare she ask without caring? When was the last time she had really cared?

"It was wonderful," he intoned in a low voice. "Everything went well in the office. And yours?"

"The usual. Too much work and too many lazy people around."

The girl stuck her head in through the outside door of the kitchen.

"I've finished, *Ma.* I've taken the clothes off the line and put them in the basin."

"You can go home then," Evelyn said. "Make sure you lock the gate properly behind you. Last time you didn't, and it swung open and the dogs got out. Very careless of you."

"I will, *Ma.* Good night, *Ma,* good night, *Sah.*"

He marveled that this girl had stayed with them so long. It was unusual for their household.

He used to ask her why every time she fired somebody:

"Too slow."

And another time:

"Caught him stealing."

Or maybe yet:

"So sloppy. Can't you see with your own eyes?"

And he thought nothing of it for a while, for who did not have these very same problems with their help. So it continued on and on, new faces arising like seedlings, so when he thought back over the years, he could barely remember distinct names and faces, voices and gestures. Who were the people who had cooked for them? Wiped the crumbs off their dining table, flung meat scraps to their dogs? Watched over their sons?

And her responses continued. Even with the man Alfred liked, the one who looked up from his work when Alfred walked into the house one day, and the man said, "Sir, I will break up some stones to fill that part in the driveway where the cement has cracked 'til you decide to fix it."

About a week later, swerving his car to avoid the hole as he pulled into the driveway, he realized he hadn't seen the man in days.

"Wasted too much water," said Evelyn.

Long ago, when her face was soft with youth and he had the hard hands of a young man who believed true strength could break anything, he had cloaked himself in the mystery of her. Her mother's shop had been the best of all the little convenience stores he knew. Because of Evelyn. He would go into the store and chat with her mother, and there Evelyn would be, silent, busying herself with arranging and rearranging the supplies until everything was in unassailable order. Her mother complained about the heat, her failing eyesight, the treacheries of trading with some Temne people. He would keep up with the conversation, maintain the banter with the deferential charm that mothers loved, meanwhile aware of Evelyn bent down, out of sight behind the counter, lining up the loaves of bread behind the glass pane, so every time he looked down, he saw row upon perfect row.

When he married her, he had expected there to be time to take apart the mystery like the segments of an orange, find out from whence came the perfection. And there had been time. So much so that he had forgotten to wonder. And those times he did remember, it seemed too formidable a task to try.

Now he was sweating so much that he took off his shirt, hung it on the back of the chair, and sat there in his vest. He felt dampness in the plains of his palms, something unaccustomed.

"Are you not feeling well?" she asked.

"No, I'm quite all right."

She had cheated him. After all these years, he could tell you the type of beer you must have at the ready for Evelyn and the preferred routes she would unerringly take to any given destination in town. But he knew nothing of any importance about the woman in front of him.

When he put his spoon down to drink some water, she lifted his plate to take it to the stove and top off the remaining rice with more cassava leaves. For some reason, this anticipation of need upset him.

"No! I don't want any more," he cried in a strained, choking voice.

She raised her eyebrows: a challenge, a rebuke, a question. He knew she was likely to get up and walk out of the room.

"Don't walk out! I want to talk to you about Seth. About what you did to our son."

His voice was dying to a whisper. He surrendered himself to a fit of coughing, while his heart labored to keep the mechanism of him going. Tears draped his eyes. There was a slight tingling in his fingers.

If his boys were there, they would have reached out to him, put their hands on his shoulders, thumped his back. But he had lost them long ago. He might fall dead on this floor, and she would continue eating.

There was no mystery. She was what she was.

And yet there was that time.

An evening at the store. He had been so poor back then, a student whose ribs could be felt through his shirt. Proud, though, proud as dreams will make you. He had done his best not to show his desperation. How had she known?

Do you remember, Evelyn?

All those times he had chatted with her mother in the store while she busied herself, she was listening, not allowing a single thing to escape.

She'd observed that he came every Thursday, paid attention to the things he bought. So when she saw him appear in the doorway, before he had a chance to recite his list, she would pull these items together with a deftness that never ceased to amaze him and a memory that was singular: five cups of *gari*, two cans of luncheon meat and a can of sardines, three cans of baked beans, and four loaves of bread. No one had ever paid such attention to the minutiae of his life.

When he cut corners here and there—a tin of sardines less, a cup of *gari* less—she said nothing. Then one week, when he arrived on Thursday evening, as was customary, he found she had already bagged everything up for him. She rattled off the list of what was in the bag. It was exactly the same as what he had been ordering for weeks on his reduced budget.

"That'll be fine," he said, and he paid and was off.

But oh, at home the contents revealed themselves to be more than he had paid for, more than she had rattled off.

Could the decision of a lifetime hinge on one act of kindness? They had never talked about it.

"Evelyn," he whispered to her now, his voice hoarse, "do you remember the time you put the extra groceries in my bag?"

She looked at him with brow furrowed.

"What are you talking about?"

"When I asked you, you pretended like you had no idea what I was talking about, just like now. But you did it to cover my shame, didn't you?"

"You should go for a walk and clear your head. I have no idea what all this is about. I remember no such thing."

"God damn it, Evelyn!" he whispered, shaking. "You remember everything."

It was no use. He had lost the battle long before he knew there was something to fight for.

~ FORTY-SIX ~

ONE DAY THE anger disappeared. The girl had thrown out Evelyn's avocado seeds—the two seeds she had brought all the way from America. The avocados had been so large and perfect that she immediately thought of how wonderful it would be to have a regular supply of such a fruit.

But the girl had thrown them out. She seemed to shrivel as she waited for Evelyn's response.

She opened her mouth to roar at the girl. But strangely, she couldn't muster the effort needed to get the words out. In place of the anger she had expected, there was only a sudden fatigue.

"Go finish the rest of your work," she said to the girl.

The girl looked at her with incredulity before leaving the kitchen.

Evelyn went upstairs to lie down and rest her eyes, which had been troubling her lately. But closing her eyes gave her mind no rest.

There had been so much to be angry about—first Joanna and her obtuseness, her outrageous mischaracterizations of Sam, then upon her return, there was Seth and his sheer idiocy with the camp.

Even when she returned from the United States, back into the house, the memories had not returned—for this she should have been happy. And she had entered the memory vault only carefully and sparingly. Yet a deep sense of dread infused her every hair. And there was this tiredness, as though whatever lay ahead, she was not up for it. She heard Alfred's car in the driveway and then, a little later, his voice as he talked to the girl. He would come upstairs, and even though she would feign sleep, in two hours it would be time for dinner, and she would have to endure another evening's portion of strained conversation.

The tiredness seeped into her blood like wastewater. If only she had never met Alfred. If only Seth and Sam had never been born. Evelyn was tired of the very thought of them all.

~

IN THE MIDDLE of the night, Evelyn woke from her dreams. Alfred was snoring beside her. He had never even woken her up for dinner. She couldn't remember what she had dreamed except that it had been of her father, and he had been so real that she could feel the touch of him warm as daylight. But when she awoke, the sense of his presence was still so strong that she grew afraid of the dark surrounding the bed as if he might appear out of it.

As she lay awake, she began to feel the memories issuing from the vault, first like innocuous wisps of smoke, then slowly thicker, corporeal. It was the damn house. She would talk to Alfred about moving. But where would they go? They were too old for a change so major. Steeling herself, she waited for the memories to coalesce around her, look at her with the shadowed eyes of beggar children. But like dark clouds portending rain but not releasing it, they didn't.

In the morning, with her head throbbing, she called in sick at work. Later in the day, the girl knocked on her bedroom door. She ignored it, but when the girl knocked again, she whispered, "Go away." She was shocked to realize that she had been weeping, her pillow wet. She hadn't wept in decades.

In the bathroom, she cupped her hands under the tap to drink water. She avoided looking into the mirror so as not to see the disheveled hair, the eyes red-veined with weeping. She went to Sam's room, put her hand on the doorknob.

Then, all of a sudden, there was a memory, and it shimmered like a bead of mercury. She did not know whether it would poison or heal, only that she would not be able to control what it did. She had never truly been able to control the memories; she realized that now. The memory: Her hand on this very door, laughter inside. Boys' voices. The life in the room so strong that even the wood of the door seemed imbued with it. She listened to the cadence of sounds, and when it crested, she entered so in the din they would be surprised to see her standing at the door. There were Sam and two friends from the neighborhood. Sam should be ashamed of himself, she told them. He had snuck off to a Tetteh Man concert behind her back. He must think he was big enough for a concert when up until recently he was still wetting the bed. Their sad faces sucked the life out of the room. The friends left early, and Sam refused to eat dinner that night.

Now her hand lingered long enough to turn the cold doorknob warm. She entered the room, pulled back the musty sheets from Sam's bed, and lay down under them.

A memory: A man called Moses smiling at Sam as he held out a white plastic container full of water with two gray fish, mere slivers of silver, darting about like lightning.

"I caught them with my bare hands in the river," he said.

Sam peered into the basin. "No, thanks," he said, "Give them to Seth."

Had Moses been the one to replace Alimamy? Alimamy whom Sam had loved? Alimamy whom she had fired because she found Sam laughing outside the kitchen, Alimamy's arm draped over his shoulder? It didn't matter because Sam had been sullen and surly with every houseboy after Alimamy.

"What a difficult boy," she had heard one say. She had marveled that he was talking about Sam.

Joanna had been right.

Now something else arose in her mind, not memories but the children of memories, strong and burnished with time, images sharp as noonday sun, clear as water, images of Seth and Sam's sad eyes, looking at her, images extending as far out to the horizon as her mind could see. And she understood this to be her future.

She emerged from Sam's room, shocked at how cool the air outside the room felt.

Alfred was on the balcony. He had already dozed off in the lounge chair, his head leaning to the side, held awkwardly in place by the weathered wood frame of the chair. She watched the blunted nose of the green mosquito coil grow red, its smoke breaking into wisps somewhere near Alfred's toes.

The radio station he had been listening to had become scrambled, and Evelyn heard voices and snatches of music tumbling together in a strange cacophony of sounds.

With effort, she lowered herself on her haunches next to the chair and shook his arm. He awoke with a start, blinking rapidly, his eyes red. Then he looked at her, and she touched her swollen eyes, imagining how they looked to him.

"About the bag of groceries. I remember," she said.

"What? Bag of groceries? Did I forget to pick something up?"

"No, I mean back then, in the shop when we were young. Of course, I remember."

She wanted to say more but couldn't. How could one begin to describe the burnt trail of a wasted life? Her life was drawing to its end, she knew. Even if she lived long, a life could be in a perpetual state of ending when it has harbored marshes of decay for so long.

He looked at her with a curious frown.

Pulling strength from her very bones, she said at last, "I've been so wrong, Alfred."

He looked at her from a million miles away, and she wondered whether she would ever reach him even if she walked toward him all the remaining days of her life. She would walk if it took the rest of her days. Trembling, she put her hand on his. She felt a slight tug, as though he meant to pull it away and then decided to leave it there. She reached out her other hand, held his with both hands, and he let her. Her hands released their memory of the rind-like hardness of his young hands, years ago. They were soft now with age and comfort. She held on and waited for the world to take form again around her.

~ FORTY-SEVEN ~

"Bra, you broke my couch," Isaac said.

Seth cackled, suddenly missing his friend intensely. In the two months since he'd been back, he hadn't spoken to anyone from Freetown, not even Isaac—until now.

"You're welcome! Now you can throw it in the Dumpster where it belongs." And so their conversation ping-ponged, the gentle heckling, the ribbing easing a tightness in Seth's neck he hadn't known was there.

"How are you?" Seth said for the second (third?) time, with intent, so Isaac would know it was less greeting than actual inquiry into his friend's well-being. He had already asked, apprehensive, about Aunty Sia and Ettie, but Isaac had evaded the question, filling Seth with foreboding.

"*Ah dae fodom en grap,*" Isaac said. The standard answer. Getting down and falling up.

Seth brought Isaac up to speed on what he had been doing for the past two months. It only took a few sentences because he hadn't done much at all, other than find a place to live and apply for a few jobs. Seth hated to admit once again the benefit of being pushed into maths, but as an actuary, he was eminently employable.

Finally, Isaac seemed ready to say more. After Seth left, Aunty Sia and Ettie had gone about business as usual. But sometimes Isaac would hear muffled cries at night from Ettie's room and then the older woman's gentle murmurs. Although he could not see past the door, he imagined the woman cradling the girl, absorbing her sobs into her own body.

Ettie went about her duties wrapped in a brittle silence, and when school resumed, she seemed to be gone from the house more than appeared to be necessary. Aunty Sia, too, cooked more than seemed necessary, as though her limbs surged forward with an automaton force.

Then one day, Ettie came home and said she had found an organization she wanted to be a part of, that was helping people overcome their trauma from the war.

"She used the word trauma?" asked Seth.

"Yes. Why do you ask?"

"No reason. Well, I guess that means she's conscious of what she's suffering from."

But within two weeks, Ettie announced that she wasn't going anymore.

"Why?"

"She wouldn't say . . . or maybe she told Aunty Sia, but Aunty Sia wouldn't tell me. In any case, everything changed after those two weeks." Isaac described how Ettie was different: less distracted, more animated, happier even, and how all of this was delighting Aunty Sia.

"You think those two weeks made a difference?"

"Who's to say. But she made a couple friends there. Girls who, like her, had suffered horribly during the war. And she still spends a lot of time with them. I think that's what's made the difference."

Seth let out his breath, relief spilling forth. "I was so worried. I thought the camp had hurt her even more—"

"I think the camp saved her."

"Eh?"

"Even though what she went through with Lucky was bad, I think somehow, through the process, something awoke in her.

Maybe standing up to him helped her regain some of her old confidence, become the Ettie we knew who took charge and was brave enough to trick the soldiers."

"Why do you say that?"

"Before the camp I can't imagine her finding out about this NGO and telling Aunty Sia that she wanted to go, let alone go on her own."

"And what of the other kids? Lucky?"

"Lucky stopped by the other day to say hi and to ask whether I'd heard from you."

"Really? I'll shoot him an e-mail sometime."

"Don't be discouraged. You did a good thing. It might not show now, but I believe somehow it made a difference to those children. I've touched base with a few of them, and they asked whether you were going to come back and do another camp next year. They want you to come back!"

The idea of going back to do another camp had never occurred to him. Was there fight left in him?

Freetown arose before him. The circus of sounds. The grimy beauty. The smell of sea, rot, and tropical sweetness. The weariness and exhilaration of sheer life. Had he really thought escape would be possible?

"I never told you this, but during the camp, I was summoned to go see the principal of my school," Isaac said. "He is usually a fair man. A bit hard to read, but I've never had any problems with him. Anyway, he told me to talk you out of what you were doing. And if I couldn't do that, at the least, dissociate myself from it. Well, I told him I believed in what you were doing, and that if I thought we were warping those children, I definitely would not be a part of it."

Seth realized he had been holding his breath.

"Seeing my response, his face grew grim. He told me that Mr. Thomas, though young, was a dangerous man to cross—as if I didn't know that. And he had influence. Word had it that he had close political ties with the party likely to win the next election and there was a chance he could end up as minister of education if they won. This is why the other principals kowtowed to him so much. Anyway, he didn't like to see things happening that he didn't approve of. It's some sort of a threat to his control, you see. And Freetown is still like a small town, and he makes it his business to know everything.

"My principal had been approached by him because of his 'concern' that I was involved in your venture. He didn't go into details, but I could tell he wanted to remain in the good books of Mr. Thomas."

Seth felt what had started as a vague dread draw itself up to its full height.

"So this guy strongly urged me to withdraw from your camp. I was made to understand, though the words were not spoken, that I might lose my job if I didn't."

"Despicable," Seth said.

"And that's what happened," said Isaac.

"What?"

"Yes. Shortly after you left, the school contacted me and told me not to return when the school year started. There was no reason given, just that it had been deemed to be in the interest of both parties."

"*Bra*, I wish you had told me. I would have insisted that you stop helping me with the camp. I would have managed on my own."

There was a noticeable pause before Isaac spoke again. Then, "The truly despicable thing is that I consorted with that bastard, Mr. Thomas, to get you to change course. Looks like he had it in for us from the very start."

"I don't blame you, bro. I wasn't to be trusted. I . . . I was a mess."

"And are you better now?" Isaac asked haltingly.

"Yes." It was the first time Seth had accepted or even understood that he was. "I can't believe you lost your job. I—I'm so sorry I put you in that position."

"I've found a job with another school, and it's working out just fine. Things are better than before, and even if they weren't, I don't regret doing what we did together, Seth. For you, my brother, I would do it all over again."

~ FORTY-EIGHT ~

STELLA HAD EXHAUSTED herself at the park climbing the jungle gym and throwing up leaves so they rained down in showers, and Seth worried about how he would pick leaf fragments out of her clothing to present her neat to her mother.

Joanna hadn't wanted to leave her, concerned that Seth might need the weekend alone to prepare for his job interviews the next week. But Seth insisted that he could think of no better preparation than spending time outside with his niece in the beautiful fall, thinking of anything but job interviews. And a client called with a rush request, so Joanna gratefully accepted Seth's babysitting offer.

At his apartment, Stella begged him to watch cartoons with her. So now they sat on the floor eating applesauce, Seth leaning against one of the armchairs he had finally purchased. He looked at the screen, unseeing, her laughter punctuating his thoughts.

"Uncle Seth, you aren't watching with me," Stella whined.

"How do you know?"

"Because you aren't laughing."

He was suddenly hungry. "Why don't we go out to eat?"

"But we just got home. Don't you have anything to eat here?"

"Not really. Take a look in the fridge."

She strutted over to the fridge with self-importance.

She called out her findings to him.

"Five cans of soda, four slices of bread, some carrots . . ."

She walked back over to him and gave him a searching look.

"My mother always has food at home," she said in an accusing tone.

"I know she does. That's why you're so lucky."

"Uncle Seth, why don't you marry my mother? Then you won't be alone." She looked at him as he sat on the floor. They were eye to eye. "You know what? If you did, you wouldn't have to worry about shopping. You could just eat our food."

She sat down now, all the while keeping her eyes on him to see what effect her attempt to sweeten the deal had had on him.

He thought of Joanna now, the curve of her shoulder, her even, unwavering gaze. She was not his, but something like desire overtook. He was alive after all.

"No, Stella. I'm not planning to."

"Why? Don't you love her?"

"I do. I love both of you."

"But you know what I'm talking about."

He laughed again.

"I told you you're getting too smart for me."

"If you married my mother, would you be my father or still my uncle?"

"Well, I'm not going to marry your mother, Stella."

She picked up the remote and pressed the mute button.

"I know, you can't be my father."

"No, Stella. I am not Sam," he said quietly.

"Granny said that my father was very special."

He put down his applesauce and patted the floor next to him. She settled herself by his side.

"He was one of a kind." His throat thickened for Stella and the father she would never know.

"But I love *you*, Uncle Seth," she said, her voice fierce. She was so close that he could smell the applesauce on her breath, see the satin finish of her skin.

He picked up one of her starfish hands and looked down at the tiny nails so she wouldn't see his eyes open to the years that were behind him. Putting her arm around his neck, she pulled his ear closer. She said it again, in a whisper this time, to keep it from the room and the walls and the things they held at bay.

"I love *you*."

~ **FORTY-NINE** ~

AT FIRST HE thought the sound was simply that of water stampeding with more vigor than the land could bear, eroding the banks, snatching every twig and crust of earth it came across. But then it became unmistakably different—a singing so sad and piercing that he woke up holding his ears. And then a second sadness hit him—like dreaming of a departed love only to remember, upon rising, that they were gone. Thousands of miles away, that same river an opaque trickle within its bed.

But even after waking, the singing didn't go away. Its plaintiveness haunted him, as though it belonged not to the torrent but to something captured within it—a prisoner's wail, a cry for help.

The damn river, he thought, remembering how he had been led astray by the signs, had gone to the banks of the Matenge River only to have to shutter his eyes from its disgrace. But against his wishes, he found himself on his computer, looking up the meaning of a dream of a singing river.

A client once heard a voice coming from within a river, he read. He clicked on the link. It was for a psychic. He slammed his computer shut. But later that evening, still unable to wrest the eerie siren song from his head, he clicked on the link again. Embedded deeper within the piece was a link to the Spiritual Emergence Network. *Find a practitioner near you.* He hovered with his mouse. The singing seemed to rise in pitch as he clicked.

~

EVERYTHING IN THE room was beautiful. There was a Persian rug, a stool made of intricately carved sandalwood, and framed pieces of exquisite embroidery on the walls. And everywhere, elephants—of clay, of stone, of cloth even.

"I have a bit of an elephant fetish," said Marian, noticing him take them in. "Maybe it was manageable enough when it started, but then my clients took note, and they started bringing me more," she chuckled.

Nothing about her seemed to give off an air of mysticism. Not that he had known what to expect. Bohemian skirts? A third eye painted on her forehead? Prayer beads around her wrists? Instead, she was the picture of White middle-class respectability with wavy, shoulder-length graying hair, lipstick, and a manicure.

"Tea?"

"Yes, please."

She returned in a few minutes with water steaming in a hand-made mug, green and glossy as a blade of aloe. On the coffee table in front of him, she set down another earthen cup with an assortment of tea sachets. He rifled through them, trying to make sense of the unfamiliar names.

"Might I trouble you for cream and sugar? Never mind," he said after she returned a blank but potent stare. After making a selection, he watched the water turn amber tinged with red. The tea was sweeter than he expected but with bitterness lurking in its folds. But it went cold long before he could finish talking— or, rather, responding to her questions.

"So what happened after the exorcism?"

"I didn't dream about the swamp anymore. By then the scratching had stopped, but the fights in the swamp and the fear I felt at night were still pretty bad. But then, like I said, I had the other hallucination."

Her questions had been very unpredictable and had made his story zigzag as though she were an animal trainer jerking him about on a leash. He was beginning to weary of the seemingly patternless inquisition. Already she had ignored his questions about treatment. He would have to press her.

"So, what is the road forward? Dr. Holland said bipolar symptoms come and go."

"If you wanted to feel better, why did you throw away the medication?"

"Defiance, I guess. He had said many of his patients start off in denial."

"Yes, that's true. Before I got into transpersonal psychology, I did treat a few bipolar patients."

He edged himself forward in his seat and took a sip of cold tea.

"It can't come back. I can't go through what I went through again." He looked at his watch. The session would be over soon, and for his money, he was no closer to getting a meaningful answer.

"Why did you disbelieve Isaac's account of what happened with Saj? Why did you believe that your account—the story under the mango tree—was real?"

Seth shook his head in confusion. "When I came back here, I guess I accepted that I was still in denial about what had happened—with the two hallucinations."

This time it was she who shook her head.

"Because the eternal soul within you knew they were real, that's why. Same with the scratches. You suppressed this knowledge for the sake of survival while you were in Freetown, but the eternal soul within you knows you could not have caused those scratches."

Seth raised a finger to his face and found his face moist with sweat. He sat back in his seat. She looked down, as though giving him some privacy.

"I'm from a culture that believes in the supernatural, in witchcraft," he began. "And I've heard of miracles happening in the deliverance churches. I hear crazy things happen, but in my case—"

"Modern psychiatry believes that any experience that is paranormal or mystical falls in the realm of pathology. For which the solution is drugs. With some exceptions—like Jung who gave psychology a road map for the collective unconscious—this deep, primordial world of universal symbols and states that people tap into is far beyond the realm of what they could have directly experienced. Even religion, even the practices more inclined to believe in the day-to-day supernatural, stigmatize it—maybe calling it not 'pathology,' but 'evil,' a sign of affliction or possession by evil spirits."

He took this in. "But after the exorcism, things were much better."

"There are real mental pathologies out there that can be treated by psychiatry, just as there are possession states that perhaps respond to these ministrations. And these things can overlap. Maybe something in you responded to the pastor. But, by and large, what happened to you, what all this suffering is about, is far different."

He did not have to say anything, only wait for her to speak, sensing that nothing would be the same after.

~

FROM HIS TINY balcony, he looked out at children shouting and propelling themselves on tricycles in the shared space between apartment blocks. He threw back a sip of spiced rum and rattled the ice cubes absently.

Spiritual emergency. That was what she had called it. A process as ancient as the shamanic journey and *kundalini* awakenings, as recent as the nightmare of apocalyptic revelation that had gripped Mother Teresa. There were "sufferers" like him all over the country, the world, she said, not aware that their agony was caused by a soul expanding faster than their ego could cope.

"But something in me feels broken forever."

"Something in you is broken. The birth process 'breaks' the woman's body. A caterpillar practically digests itself within its cocoon in order to become a reimagined being. Likewise, there is a repetition compulsion in your life of not being seen—by your mother, by the educational system—and eventually by yourself. You had even shunned your inner self, assumed the mask forced upon you that had to be broken. The universe—or God, if you prefer—can cause this violence, this terrifying entry into the paranormal—to get your attention and make this breaking happen. Your soul has to learn the true essence of what it is."

He tried the words again like a new pair of shoes. Spiritual emergency. The children's shrieks grew louder, their happiness like kites riding the breeze. Like physical growth, spiritual maturation could take years, she said—but if he did the work, it would get better and better.

The work?

The work you started in Freetown—not of overcoming *The Thing*, but of becoming a better person. That's what all this is about.

~ FIFTY ~

AT THE BACK of the house, the yard sloped down to meet a thickening of trees—what was left of the forest after the developers took over the land. The leaves fell around him, hungry for death. On the ground they quivered in shifting layers, so treacherous in their depth that Seth had almost twisted his ankle in a depression.

The air called attention to itself, bearing smells both of want and of promise.

He found pleasure in raking the leaves. The long-toothed rake cleaved to his hand in obedience, faithful to its one purpose. Together they made mountains. Joanna had protested until she understood how much he enjoyed the task. He had come early for the quiet. She and Stella would be home soon.

He heard the car in the driveway and then the sounds in the house. Stella came out first to chat with him, until her mother called her in to get changed.

When Joanna came out, she had on a pair of Crocs and a soft flannel zip-up blazer.

"I'm glad I came back in time for fall," he said.

She smiled, nudging leaves with her toe. "I'm sorry that I never got to see Sierra Leone again. Sam and I always talked of going back . . ."

The rays of the falling sun were in her face, and she narrowed her eyes to mere slits.

He thought back to how when he was in Freetown, her frank questioning about whether he really needed the medication had saved him. Then he felt a rush not only of gratitude but of a yearning that caught in his throat like a strangled cry.

"I can see that you love Stella," she said, smiling up at him.

"I do. I love her not because she's part of Sam but because she's Stella. I just want you to know that."

The wind blew, and the leaves on the ground stirred, and a few more spiraled down to the earth from the knuckled branches of the trees. It would be dark soon. Joanna shivered and rubbed her hands together.

All around them he felt a murmur of bartering and ceding, of conquest and replenishment, as the wind washed over the branches, whispering change to their bending forms. A sensation of sharpened knowing came upon him all of a sudden, like when a waterlogged ear opens and sound comes roaring in.

"Joanna."

She raised her eyebrows.

"What would have happened if Sam had never come to visit me that time in college? Do you think we would have ended up together?"

His boldness didn't surprise him; it felt as though it had been there all along.

She said nothing, then sat down on the ground, pulling him down with her. They sat cross-legged like children on the carpet of leaves. The day was extinguishing itself with urgency. There was a marking of shadows on her face from the branches of the tree.

She looked at him and opened her mouth as though to speak, and then closed it again, anguish lining her face. She tried again. "It's hard to remember anything the way it was before Sam. It's like having a child, wanted or not. Once they're there, you can't imagine life without them."

The light was almost gone; her eyes were wide and open, shielded no more. He could imagine her now, hair in a ponytail, opening the physics textbook with margins marked in her neat hand, her eyes holding his, her voice sibilant as water as she said to him, "You always explain it to me so clearly." He had been such an idiot.

They sat under the dying light listening to the fall. Then he got to his feet and held out his hands to help her up. Standing, they held each other so tightly that they could feel each other shudder in the fomenting cold for the savagery with which seasons change. When they pulled away, they found Stella watching them through the glass doors of the kitchen.

~ FIFTY-ONE ~

THERE MUST HAVE been an accident farther down the freeway. Seth hadn't seen police cars or ambulances, but he couldn't think of any other explanation for why traffic would be constipated on a weekend in this area so far away from the center of the city.

He kept switching radio stations, restless. So many commercials. Unbeatable deals on Ford trucks. Solicitations for donations to a children's hospital. So many strains of activity and searching and purpose crossing on one mediator of sound.

At last his exit came up. Relieved to be out of traffic, he pulled onto the ramp, the joy of release traveling through his body to his foot as the borrowed flatbed truck parted the wind. He questioned once again why he was going to the trouble of buying a piece of furniture that he could do without, but some things did not lend themselves to clear answers.

Before Stella was born, Sam had bought a beautiful ornate rocking chair made of blond wood with hearts cut into it, and also leaves, flowers—things that might once have garlanded the tree from which the chair was hewn. He must have had a vision of Joanna rocking peacefully, cradling their newborn, the picture of domestic bliss. But according to Sam, Joanna had never cared for it. It seemed, in fact, they had gotten into a fight over it. Why, Seth could not understand, nor had he cared to ask.

Hold on to it for me, will you?

This is not the kind of furniture you put in a bachelor's pad, Seth.

Yes, yes, I know, but what is it going to do to you? Just throw a blanket over it and call it a day.

But Gaia had liked rocking in it, and then he'd tried it too and found it helped calm some of the restlessness he increasingly felt within him. Like so many other things, he had given it away when he left for Sierra Leone, even though something tore at him as he watched it being carried away. He could still see Sam's hands gripping the armrests as he carried it into Seth's place that day.

The rocking chair in this ad was much simpler with straight lines, broad slats, and a dark finish—overall, a much more contemporary look. It had caught his eye right away.

The noise of the tires on the gravel driveway announced his arrival. He stepped out of the truck. An oval figure presented itself at the screen door. When it came through, the door closed behind it with a labored creaking and then a loud *thwack*.

The round man waddled to him and shook his hand. He was older with ripe-banana liver spots and wisps of translucent white hair. His egg-like form was clothed in a faded plaid shirt with suspenders that held up an equally faded pair of jeans. Shirt and pants met around an expanse somewhere above his navel.

"Hi, I'm Seth. I called about the rocking chair.

"Nice to meet you, young man. What did you say your name was?"

"Seth."

"I detect a bit of an accent. Where might you be from?"

"Sierra Leone."

"Say who?"

"It's a country in West Africa."

"Ah. I met a young guy, young like yourself, from Africa too. It must have been, let's see, three years ago? My wife was still alive then. Friendly fellow. We had him over for dinner. He went to one of the universities here; studied engineering, I think. Any chance you may have come across him in this city?"

"What was his name?"

"His name? When you get to be my age, you're lucky if you can remember *your* name when you get up in the morning, *heh heh.*"

Seth followed him into what was a living area in crisis. The ivy-patterned wallpaper, white wicker furniture, frilled seat cushions, and sundry feminine knickknacks staring out of a cabinet had been assaulted by an invasion of greasy car parts sitting on sheets of plastic tarp, stacks of old yellowing newspapers, and several cardboard boxes of varying sizes lying among strips of filmy white foam sheeting and packing peanuts. Something new had been welcomed into the space.

Even in the clutter, Seth immediately spotted the rocking chair. It was oddly plain, masculine, and unwelcome in the room.

The man gestured toward it. "This one was my wife's. It was her favorite piece of furniture. She would sit in it and rock. Sometimes she would shell peas in it, read, drink coffee while swearing out loud in the middle of summer because of the heat. Heck, she spent so much time in that chair, it's a wonder it ain't broke."

"Are you sure you want to sell it?"

"I'm moving to a smaller place, and my daughter says all this stuff has to go. It will help me move on, she says. You just enjoy it, that's all."

Seth handed over $30 and picked up the chair. But the man made no motion to let him out. Instead, he stood there looking at Seth with a strange hunger as he absently tucked the money into his breast pocket with a jerky hand.

"Would you like to see my telescope?"

"Your telescope?"

"It's out on the deck."

"Sure." Seth put down the chair, wondering what bewildering turn this day was taking. Outside the sky had gained a textured darkness. On the deck a large telescope glinted in the faery moonlight.

"It cost me $2,350. My wife, she was against it. Had I known how little time she had, I wouldn't have bought it."

"Would that have made much difference?"

"It would have to her."

The man ran a quivering hand along the shaft. Moments flowed on as the man removed his hand and simply stood there, his hands dangling at his side.

"May I look into it?" Seth inquired at last.

"I haven't used it yet."

Sure enough, Seth noticed the black cap was still on the end of it.

"Do you think I should send it back?"

"Why would you do that?"

"I need the money."

"Why don't you look through it first and then decide?"

"Because I'm afraid once I do, I won't be able to give it up."

With a move of boldness, Seth removed the black cap from the telescope.

"Go on."

The man looked at Seth, uneasy, but stepped slowly in front of the lens and put his eye to it.

When he removed his face, he turned to Seth. "I never wanted to look at the stars alone."

~

THE NIGHT CLOSED in upon him like a secret. Within a few minutes, he knew he must have taken a wrong turn somewhere in leaving the old man's place. He glanced down at the directions, trying to remember the way he had come. It was a county with old neighborhoods scattered within the woods. Here and there were parcels of land, tree kingdoms that modern developers were only now beginning to seize. Many of the roads in old areas like this carried the same name even if they branched off at 90-degree angles. It was easy to get lost in a place like this.

He let the envelope with the directions drop and decided to find his way out by instinct, realizing there was a good chance he could end up far from where he wanted to be. A road appeared with a name he remembered from the directions. He took it and then a turn that also looked familiar. But shortly after, he spied the old man's house to the left. It seemed he had gone round in a circle and borne down on the house from the opposite direction. He slowed and looked at the house, a faint light visible through the window.

Seth too had seen the stars, the jealous stars unleashing their light from their prisons of want. If the stars could not quite control a destiny, their longing to be seen was powerful enough that they could bind the human heart and sear it with a force that could be extinguished only through inexplicable wanderings.

He passed houses with land, so much that their driveways were roads in themselves and their lawns stretched out like pastures. He passed naked trees, branches like gnarled hands hoping to clutch at the moon. And still the roads branched and met, joined and receded. It seemed they could do this endlessly, like those Lego blocks he had glimpsed that day at the Matenge River, cleaving themselves together from rubble.

Perhaps he would call Isaac and tell him he would not return, for the camp was like a first and only love. He would find a job. He would travel to far countries with ancient caves and mountains crevassed with healing streams and come back wiser, stronger. Or perhaps he would indeed return to Freetown and walk into Aunty Sia's house and watch surprise light up their faces. In the clearest terms, he would ask Joanna to have him, for with a certainty he would never have had before *The Thing*, he knew she loved him. Like a conjoined twin seeking separation at the risk of death, he had torn himself away from the personhood of his brother. Even if grafting himself into his brother's family was a betrayal of that freedom, he did not worry that he would lose himself once again.

Into his mind they all came now: Ettie smiling behind her curled fingers, Sam playfully putting an elbow around Seth's neck. There were Isaac and Lucky, his mother and father, all far now and yet so real he could almost hear them breathing next to him. He thought of their world and of his and of a third world where one did not have to choose only one place to be, where it was possible to claim new selves. He would do it all again one day, and again and again, for there was life, as strong and as fast as the Matenge River that day, moving through him.

He felt once more, in a way he had not for a long time, *The Thing* taking hold of him. It possessed him, lifted him, and promised to carry him wherever he wished to go. Now he knew its names. It was the enemy that had pursued him into the deepest part of himself. It was the magma of his desire, the yearning that had pulled out his heart like a pit, drawn him toward that flame that slowly renewed. It was the burial and benediction in the lonely waters of the swamp.

His foot pressed the accelerator, and he rolled the windows down. The air rushed in, greeting his face. Loganville Road. He knew where he was now. Going faster and faster, he passed the trees standing like ancient sentries ushering him into the land. The roar of the wind told him all he needed to know. Anything could be made.

FIFTY-TWO

SAM LEFT BEFORE the snow, before the roads grew treacherous with ice. Danger gathered, no matter how bright and twinkling the snow lay upon the land. He had not needed to go out. Joanna had raised her eyebrows and then lowered them as she exhaled deeply. Stella had food. She had diapers. She had cabinets of things she did not need. But he had felt the air in the house was too dry for her. He wanted to get a humidifier for her room.

He would run to Home Depot, and perhaps on his way back, he would get scented wood chips for the fire to make Joanna happy. The traditional wood-burning fireplace was one of the few things about the house that both he and Joanna liked.

The house itself was mainly a concession to her. She had fallen in love with its cedar paneling, the rustic shingles on its chimney, its triangular and octagonal windows. And though, even then, he had felt his love for her waning, he had wanted to please her. If he were honest, though, it was not mere goodwill or love that motivated him to please, but atonement. For he had ridiculed her dreams, bullied her into having the child that was his air (and how could he not have been justified in fighting ruthlessly for something so necessary to his life? And how could she have understood where this desire came from when her childhood had been so different?). When she wept at night, he turned on the TV to drown out the sound.

He had heard the bell intoning the hour of atonement. When he arranged for a cedar treatment to preserve the old home's weathering siding, he thought of his guilt, Joanna's power. When they got the first estimate for what it would cost to replace the sagging deck, he gritted his teeth and said nothing to her afterward by way of blame. He had learned long ago that guilt was like a growing seed nestled in the flesh of an ample fruit.

Even now, and more than anybody would ever suspect, he thought of the Matenge River. Seth had been so small then. He remembered the compact fleshiness of his brother's hand in his, the delicate sculpting of his shoulders, the lines like parentheses around his smooth knees. The memory had only grown stronger with the years. Because the sky had been so gray, so impenetrable, hanging low over them, it seemed as though they were the only two in the world, like gods presiding over that living river that was so fast, so transformed that it appeared impossible that Creation itself had might for anything other than this one river that had always existed and would never run dry.

"You must get it, or else Mummy will whip you."

Seth had looked at the slipper caught within the tangle of branches that must have been torn from some tree in the violence of the storm and fallen into the river. Then he looked up at Sam with forlorn, dark eyes, beads of water glistening like crystal on his upturned lashes.

"How?"

"Wade in and get onto that big stone there, then from it to the boulder. From the boulder you can reach the slipper."

He watched as Seth waded, unsteady, through the water flowing almost up to his middle, climbed onto the first rock, and then, as though unsure, dizzy, or perhaps merely surprised at having made that first step, he turned back to look at Sam. Sam felt his hands tighten on the steering wheel as he remembered that look. It was as familiar to him as his own face in the mirror. He had grown scared then, uneasy, but his voice did not betray it.

"Go on, then, you're almost there."

And Seth had made that last great jump, his short legs splayed for a mere second, suspended between water and heaven. He landed on the rock and put his palms down to steady himself. The rock was flat, ancient and untroubled. In the coming millennia, it would remember Seth's feet as the mere stroke of an eyelash.

Seth eased himself on his backside onto the edge of the rock, close to the first spindles of the branch. Leaning over, he reached, but the slipper was just out of reach. He held one of the inner limbs of the branch to steady himself while he stretched out more of his upper body. He fell into the tangle of the branch, which began to move, the water rocking it. He cried out, a shriek that shattered the gray sky.

Sam and Seth had waded out to that large rock many a time in the river's calmer days. Sam entered the water now to do so again, but as he did, fear nearly paralyzed him as he realized how different a mood the river was in now. He put both arms out for balance, felt the water tug and swirl around him. His toes curled around the gravel in the riverbed, and so he persevered until he reached Seth.

Seth clung to his neck when he reached him. Sam realized he did not have enough strength to both hold his brother and fight the current, though it would only take about eight steps to get back to the bank. He pulled at the branch, which, already dislodged, rolled in the direction he pulled it, its stub gaining purchase on the river floor. He put it in front of them as a barrier against the downward pull of the current. Seth was sobbing, frightened by Sam's silence and mighty struggle. But he too grabbed one of the inner limbs of the branch to steady himself. With one hand, Sam pulled himself and Seth along the length of the branch, and thus, with great labor, they made it to the bank.

From the path cut through the bush, Evelyn appeared. Seth was still sobbing in the circle of Sam's arms. Sam explained that

Seth had slipped and fallen in and that he had pulled him out. The trapped slipper had long since become dislodged and been dragged away by the current. She grabbed the other slipper on the bank and began to beat them both with it, and Seth wailed all the louder. Later, she crowed to others about what a hero Sam was, and neither brother said anything.

If he had known how that day would mark him forever, he would have clutched his brother even more tightly right then and asked for forgiveness. Because even if they were too young to understand the full bitterness of that moment, its contagion would never be contained. He and Seth had never spoken of it, and certainly they loved each other. But he knew the memory remained, noxious and breathing. He could smell it. It was in Seth's hostility toward him that was more than sibling rivalry. It was in Sam's zealous, bewildered bullying of his younger brother, as unfathomable to him as his treatment of Joanna.

The last time he and Seth had spoken, he had sensed a restlessness in Seth as he talked of maybe taking one summer to travel, backpack in South America.

"Are you crazy? Have you heard of Africans backpacking in South America? Can you imagine what Mum and Dad will say?"

But even as he said those words, he knew Seth would explode one day. He himself had imploded quietly long ago.

Brother, I am with you. I know how you feel. He reached his hand into his pocket and closed it around his cellphone. Seth's speed dial number was 3. He would call merely to hear his voice, to talk of the upcoming storm and probe for something new to mercilessly tease him about.

Feeling overheated, he glanced over at the switch to roll down his window and, while pressing it, saw out of the corner of his eye something large and red bearing down on him as he crossed the intersection. As he looked closer, he saw it was a truck whose driver looked increasingly terrified as he approached Sam. Sam found that the soul can stretch and laugh and grieve in a mere second. Before it was over, he found himself descending into that deep well of knowing to find out that Seth had forgiven him long ago.

The air coming in through the window was so clean, purified of strife, and the sky so outrageously blue that he felt as though he had just been born. He had never seen the world look so beautiful.

~ ACKNOWLEDGMENTS ~

THE CREATION OF a novel-length story is a story in itself; for the many characters who have played important parts, I thank you. In particular, I would like to thank:

My late mother, Dalisay Cheney-Coker, for her unconditional love and support of my dreams, and my father, Syl Cheney-Coker, for showing me that being a writer was possible and for providing feedback on early drafts.

My English professors, Dr. Mary Pettice, Dr. John Kearney, and Dr. Philip Billings, at Lebanon Valley College, for validating my writing abilities and instilling in me writing discipline and literary discernment.

Vanessa Marinkov, my exuberantly supportive host mom from my international student days, who patiently read and edited the first bad drafts—and yet somehow didn't give up on seeing my book in print someday.

Christina Chan, one of my earliest supervisors who, even in a context that had nothing to do with creative writing, instilled in me editorial disciplines that have served me to this day.

My second mother, Janet McCaskey, for believing in my writing, providing the psychological support I needed to write, and making her house always available as a "writing cabin" for critical writing sprints.

My husband, Jay Black, who, in addition to being my number one reader and editor, has given that rare combination of invaluable critique, enthusiastic praise, and ongoing encouragement that have kept me going through many periods of self-doubt and fatigue.

My sons, Asher and Zayn Black, for their curiosity and pride in their mother's writing career.

My friends, who never questioned and always encouraged my writing path, even if it meant I was not always fully present in their lives.

Dr. Marianne Celano for sharing her professional knowledge on bipolar disorder, and Lorrell Fryshe for sharing her professional knowledge on spiritual emergency.

The Atlanta Writers Conference and the indefatigable George Weinstein, without whose labors I would never have met my publisher. They do so much to bring the publishing world to Atlanta.

My manuscript editor, Tory Hunter, for going above the call of duty by giving not only a superbly insightful critique, but the moral support and practical advice every insecure writer needs.

My publisher, William Burleson, for being what every writer dreams of: a reader who loves your writing.

~ ABOUT THE AUTHOR ~

MALAIKA CHENEY-COKER was born in Nigeria where she spent her earliest years, along with time spent in the Philippines with her maternal relatives. She spent the remainder of her childhood in Sierra Leone. After immigrating to the United States, she earned a bachelor of arts degree in English and French from Lebanon Valley College and a master's degree in international affairs and development from Clark Atlanta University. She then pursued two careers—in writing and in international development—with the latter taking her on world travels, and she later moved into social justice work in the United States and abroad. She is the founder and principal of the organizational creativity and social impact-focused consulting firm Ignited Word LLC. She lives in Atlanta with her husband and two sons.

www.ingramcontent.com/pod-product-compliance
Lightning Source LLC
Chambersburg PA
CBHW022107310726
48972CB00007B/1920